CW00802915

Mafia Surrogate

BWWM Dark Mafia Romance

Boston Irish Mafia Romance
Book 3

Jamila Jasper

Edited by
Haley O.

www.jamilajasperromance.com

ISBN: 9798397662314

Thank you to my Patreon subscribers for your support with this book.

✾ Created with Vellum

Boston Irish Mafia Romance Series

Mafia Playmate

Mafia Property

Mafia Surrogate

Mafia Possession

Mafia Stalker

Click here for the complete collection:

www.jamilajasperromance.com/catalog

Description

Rian craves the new younger housekeeper's touch.
She's young. Beautiful. Innocent... and black.

Observing her turns into something more dangerous.
Rian can't help himself. This isn't just love -- it's obsession.

She fears the mysterious stranger stalking her at night.

He can't reveal the truth.

He's the masked man watching her every move.
He's the one who climbed through her bedroom window.
He's the father of the child she's now carrying...

Book #3 in the five book interracial romance series. If you enjoy black woman/white man dark mafia romance stories, you will enjoy this story following the Boston Irish mafia -- the Murray family.

This BWWM romance series is a perfect blend of suspense and high-heat black woman/Irish man love, perfect for fans of the Pagonis, Doukas or Vicari mafia families in Jamila Jasper's book universe.

Thank you to all my patrons for your support with this story.
www.patreon.com/jamilajasper

Thank you to my most supportive readers:

Gwendolyn, King Turtle 22, Jessica Lawrence, Nic, JustChill,
Dashauna, Atira, TheeLastHokage, Yvonne K., Chrissy, Janelle, Rian,
LaRonda, Deanna, Dlawson382, Jasmine, Haley, Belinda, Sercee,
Yvonne, Jadelock, Farah, Tamiya, Quin, J.Payton, Geek Girl, Ashley,
Rubi, Pilar, Sandra, June, Anni, Shannet, Joneesa, GlitzyHydra,
Amanda, Barbara, Brianna, Jamica, Lyons, Mary Ann, Marketia,
SarahD, LoverofHawaiiHearts, Cortney, Yolanda, Monagirl, Dianna,
Mary, Amna, Nysta, Fayola, Ty, Shyra, Andi-Mariee, Keisha, Jennett,
Fredericka, Candece, Lydia, Sabrina, JM, Jackie, Mo, Ashaunte, Tolu,
Lori, Dionne, ZLB, Nicol, Elbert, Jesi, Brenda, Desiree, LaShan,
Only1ToniD, Debbie, Tiffanie, Shawnte, Lisema, Christine, Trinity,
Monica, Juliette, Letetia, Margaret, Dash, Maxine, Sheron, Javonda,
Pearl, Kiana, Shyan, Jacklyn, Amy, Julia, Colleen, Natasha, Yvonne,
Brittany, June, Ashleigh, Nene, Nene, Deborah, Nikki, DeShaunda,
Latoya, Shelite, Arlene, Judith, Mary, Shanida, Rachel,Damzel,
Ahnjala, Kenya, Momo, BJ, Akeshia, Melissa, Tiffany, Sherbear, Nini,
Curtresa, Regina, Ashley, Mia, Sydney, Sharon, Charlotte, Assiatu,
Regina, Romanda, Catherine, Gaynor, BF, Tasha, Henri, Sara, skkent,
Rosalyn, Danielle, Deborah, Kirsten, Ana, Taylor, Charlene Louanna,

Michelle, Tamika, Lauren, RoHyde, Natasha, Shekynah, Cassie, Dreama, Nick, Gennifer, Rayna, Jaleda, Anton, Kimvodkna, Jatonn, Anoushka, Audrey, Valeria, Courtney, Donna, Jenetha, Ayana, Kristy, FreyaJo, Grace, Kisha, Stephanie E., Amber, Denice, Marty, LaKisha, Latoya, Natasha, Monifa, Alisa, Daveena, Desiree, Gerry, Kimberly, Stephanie M., Tarah, Yolanda, Kristy, Gary, Janet, Kathy, Phyllis, Susan

Thank you to my Patrons *for allowing me to use your names to name some supporting characters after you!*

I offer this fun little option for patrons who are at the $10+ tiers behind the scenes.

Thank you also to everyone who helped name the other characters in this book. ♥

Content Awareness

Read this passage if you require content warnings for sensitive material. I do not give detailed content warnings that will spoil the plot, but be aware of this note.

This is a mafia romance story with dark themes including potentially triggering content of **all** varieties, violence, frank discussions and language surrounding bedroom scenes and race.

All characters in this story are 18+

Sensitive readers, be cautioned about some of the detailed romantic material in this dark but *extremely hot romance novel.*

1

Rian

Freedom. *It feels fucking good.*

It would feel a lot better if I could be done with Aiden for the day and alone with my daughter for once. I missed her like hell, and our reunion since I got out of prison has been more anguish than I could have ever imagined. My daughter has been through worse than I have and I need to know that she's going to be okay.

While I was behind bars, my half-brother kidnapped my daughter, held her captive, and brutalized her in ways I can't even imagine while I had my ass locked up behind bars. My brother, Aiden, stand-in leader of the Boston Irish Mob, pulled every string he could to get me out, but I still had a year for manslaughter. Every day behind bars was fucking agony. Add to that agony the news about my daughter.

Tegan's gone. I'll remember hearing those words and the powerlessness I felt in that situation for the rest of my life. I wanted to help my daughter, but I couldn't. I'd done dirty work for my family, but I couldn't protect my daughter. That nearly broke me.

I had to find out that some motherfucker kidnapped my

1

kid on a revenge quest while I was doing push ups and fighting over ramen noodles. I wanted to get out. I thought about paying some motherfuckers to help me escape, but Callum called the night I nearly did it and I backed down. I waited every painful fucking day to get here – to the minute I get to see Tegan Murray again – and she's scowling.

Aiden stands next to my daughter with his hand on her shoulder. She's looking at him like he's her father figure. He's standing where I should be and I want to sink into the ground. But you grow up and you have to face the shit you've done – including all the bad shit like leaving your daughter behind because you couldn't stay on the right side of the law.

My stomach hurts when I see how much older she looks. Seeing my daughter for the first time is painful. Pure pain. She's taller, but her hair is shorter, which I didn't expect. She lost her childhood blonde completely. Her hair is completely brown now, like mine.

Holy fuck, I feel guilty. I missed so much more time than I should have. I know I have to say something and be her dad but… it just hurts. I should get used to the pain, but I can't. It tears at me. The pain of knowing how much I missed has forced me to hurt more people than I probably should have. I just want her to smile, even if I know I can't force it.

"Tegan," I say her name as loudly as I can, but it's barely louder than a whisper.

Nine hours ago, I emptied two magazines into a room full of Italian men and killed twenty-five people. Four of them were women, which is forbidden in our family. I didn't give a fuck. As far as I was concerned, these people were responsible for what happened to my daughter. She's safe now. *She's here.*

"Hi dad," she says, her voice all sarcastic and grown-up, like she's already tired of me. She sounds like a fucking teenager. My heart drops. Where's the bouncing little girl? Where's her smile?

My throat tightens and I fight back tears. I love her so much it hurts.

"I missed you," I tell her.

I've thought about this moment a hundred fucking times, but I get here in front of my daughter and I can't say shit. The words don't come out of my mouth and I feel stupid as fuck, the way I always did in high school.

"Whatever," Tegan says. Her voice cuts at me. I bristle immediately.

"Not whatever. I'm your fucking father. I can't stand that we've been apart."

Tegan glances up at her Uncle Aiden for support. He rubs her shoulder slowly to calm her down. I fight the urge to deck my brother in the fucking face. It's pure envy on my part. I want the bond she has with him. I wanted to be totally selfish about my bond with my daughter, but my family fucked it up. My father effed it up. He made me the fall guy on purpose. He's been making me the fall guy Tegan's entire fucking life, and I'm done with that shit.

I'm just glad he's nearly dead. Awake, but nearly dead. We'll have time to sort our shit out before he starts messing with us again. Once he's sure he'll survive, Padraig Murray will be back on the prowl. I'm sure of that much, at least.

"It'll be a matter of time before you're in jail again," Tegan says stiffly, mumbling an apology when Aiden loudly clears his throat.

I don't respond to her harshness. I guess I fucking deserve it, but it surprises the hell outta me because she's my kid and the only thing I want in the fucking world is for my princess to love the hell outta me the way I love the hell outta her.

"Not this time. I'm here for good. I'm here to make up for what I missed."

Tegan stares at me with round eyes that make me nervous. She has my eyes. I knew she was mine the second I saw her, even if I knew her mother messed around on me a couple times. I was never in love with her, and never thought she would get pregnant, so I didn't mind her messing around. I got pissed about the kid though. She wanted to "get rid of it", but I told her I would blow her shit up if she tried to mess with my daughter.

She never wanted Tegan, but I always did. She's mine, through and through. You can't mistake my daughter for anyone else's and I love that about her as much as I love everything else.

I wish I could get the time back, but I just can't.

AIDEN DRIVES me and Tegan to the place Darragh sorted out for me. He stuck to my specifications despite his bitching. I like a very specific type of home and I refuse to compromise. For my type of business and lifestyle, I need an older home well suited to my temperament. I like dark corners, libraries stuffed with books, velvet, the color black, dark leather, robust shades of red, and Victorian mansions.

My bedroom is down the hall from Tegan's. Her bedroom has everything she needs and the theme she wants — *Harry Potter*. I read those books when I was locked up and I enjoyed them too. I tried to bond with Tegan and help her pick everything out, but she wants nothing to do with me. It's like I'm fucking foreign to her.

Evie and Valentina, Aiden's girl, want me to give it time

but she's my kid. Shouldn't this shit be easy as fuck? She knows I would do anything for her. Fuck, now that I'm outta prison, I'm proving to my daughter that I love her and I'm there for her.

I'll always find a way out of trouble and back into her life. Once Aiden clears up the shit with the Italians, I'll be the father Tegan needs.

I'll make up for lost time if she'll just give me a chance. Maybe some dick heads are too fucked up to deserve second chances.

Tegan rushes to her bedroom and I head straight to the kitchen to ensure Darragh followed *all* my instructions. Aiden lets Tegan bound upstairs alone and hovers around me like a mountain lion, which means my brother must have something important on his mind. I pretend I don't notice the shift in his stance or the way he fixates on me obnoxiously as I open my liquor cabinet.

Darragh. He might hate my guts, but I can count on him for whiskey. The brand new bottle of Glenfiddich calls to me. I hurriedly twist it open and swig as much as I can handle. I haven't had a proper drink since prison. Hooch made me sick to my stomach, but I had to drink it to survive the bullshit behind bars. This is delicious. Sharp. I love the way it burns down my throat.

Merciful Aiden allows me to enjoy a few swigs before he interrupts me.

"I want payment for what you're making me cover up," he says. "It's going to cost me a fuck ton of money and we'll have to pay three more lawyers to deal with the evidence and the BPD bullshit."

"What kind of payment?"

Aiden and I can talk straight with each other. It's what I like about him. He doesn't pretend that he thinks I'm some great fucking guy, but he accepts me and treats me with the respect I deserve as long as I don't fuck with him. He's not as easily ruffled as Darragh.

"Dad woke up. We're all fucked up over it. I just think about Tegan and what she went through..."

He trails off and I try to be a little less harsh. Jail and prison fuck you up to the point where it kills any softness that might exist in your heart. You learn not to trust anyone and you get in those bad fucking habits that don't serve you on the outside. I trust Aiden, but I'm still wary of him. I haven't been out long enough for this shit to be normal to me.

But Tegan. She's the one person on this earth who can make me get my shit together. If it weren't for dad, I would have never left her. It's my fault this shit happened to her, and if that's what Aiden's implying... I can't hold it against him.

"I know it's my fault. I know she won't forgive me..."

I throw back more whiskey. Enough to make Aiden raise an eyebrow and then quickly lower it once he realizes I notice his flash of judgment.

"That's not what I meant," Aiden says. "I didn't explain how dad reacted during Tegan's... *ordeal.* I didn't want you fucked up in prison any more than you already were."

"My child was missing. I killed someone."

My voice is flat as I admit that to Aiden. He nods, but he doesn't seem surprised, which means that he already knows. I don't know which of the guys inside told him, but it's at least proof that Aiden has been a competent boss in my absence. Although, there are other signs of his competence.

"I know," Aiden says. "I didn't want you doing anything worse. I didn't like how dad reacted. Like Tegan wasn't family. I know you screwed around but... she's just a little girl."

"Is this related to your request for payment?" I don't want to discuss my pain with Aiden. What matters is that I'm out of prison and I can start putting this shit behind us. Dad might be awake, but he's far from healthy and probably more fixated on his survival than fucking with us. *He's weak.*

"Yes," Aiden says. "And you understand people better than any of us. In that fucked up head of yours, you understand power, control and people. What motivates them. Their hidden desires. So you already know what I want to ask."

I *did* suspect what Aiden would ask. Anyone in his position would make the same calculation that I made when I heard the news about dad being in a coma. He's weak. This is the best time for the next leader of the mob to strike. If it's not Aiden, it'll be someone else and whoever comes for our father's spot might not want to leave any challengers alive. By any calculation, even if dad didn't have it out for me, or Tegan, or anyone with a different skin color, this would be the most humane time to do it.

"You want me to kill our father and risk more jail time away from Tegan."

"Don't fuck with me, Rian," Aiden snarls. He's more subdued than he used to be. I've been gone a long time, so it's reasonable to assume that life has changed Aiden as much as it has changed me.

"Okay."

"What the fuck does that mean?" Aiden barks impatiently.

"It's not my job to question your orders. Dad's weak. If you don't kill him, someone else will. You make the incident in Little Italy go away and I'll handle this."

"I don't know who has the tougher job," Aiden grunts.

"What was the final body count?" I ask him, more out of curiosity than concern.

Aiden's voice flattens. "Twenty-eight. It'll take time and a fuck ton of money, but I can make this go away."

"Do we have to worry about the press?"

"No."

"Good," I tell him. "I don't want anything getting in the way of business once I'm settled in."

Aiden's scowl intensifies. I offer him some whiskey, which calms him temporarily.

"You will keep your ass out of business until you handle this shit. Four days. That's all the time you have to finish this shit."

That isn't exactly the most generous timeline, but I owe Aiden my loyalty. Not just for getting my ass out of trouble this time, but for the way he took care of my daughter when I was gone. Aiden has done more for me than anybody. But he's asking a lot and he wants it done quick.

"Will you be ready when I do it?" I ask him. "Because I can't be reckless this time. I have to be careful."

Any hesitation with regards to his issued orders makes Aiden uncomfortable. He scowls at me, like a simple question signifies reluctance on my part. He's wrong. I share no compunctions about doing the job I have to do. Aiden's my boss now. He's been my boss since dad entered the coma.

"Yes, asshole," Aiden says. "I'll be ready. Now... let's discuss more pleasant matters like your reunion with Tegan. You need to get her a cat and a nanny."

IT'S AN ORDER, not a request. I've never questioned my family's structure, so I nod, despite my internal bristling at the thought of having two additional creatures wandering around my new house. I prefer to be alone. After jail, after prison... all I want is quiet.

"I will never know peace, will I?" I grumble.

"Tegan's almost a teenager. Your days of peace are behind you, motherfucker."

I HATE to admit it but... *Aiden's right.*

TEGAN NEEDS A NANNY. She *really* needs a mother, but she can't have her mother in her life right now. Or ever. A nanny sounds like a good first step.

"A nanny suddenly sounds like a good idea," I mutter.

Aiden chuckles and thumps me on the back. "Perfect. Darragh and Kamari will help you find one."

"Darragh?"

"His new girl has a college degree. She's fancy and she'll find someone perfect for you."

I don't know what Aiden means by that. I don't typically get along with anyone, so the thought of finding someone college educated who could handle me sounds... unrealistic. I give him a skeptical look, but Aiden keeps smiling like an idiot. He smiles too much.

"By perfect, I hope you mean Irish..." I grumble, but Aiden ignores me.

"Worry about Tegan," he says. "I'll worry about the nanny."

2

Heavyn

My new boss never explicitly said he's in the mob, but after our first meeting I rushed into my old Pontiac Grand Am, pulled out my sketchbook and drew my best rendition of all the tattoos he accidentally exposed during our meeting. His brother had tattoos too, and I drew those on another page.

When I looked up Rian Murray's tattoos online... I had to face the truth. A nannying job paying $120,000 a year didn't just fall out of the sky into my lap out of nowhere. These people are dangerous. I had to sign an NDA before even going to the first meeting, which is fine by me. I pull my car up onto the gravel driveway of the old all-black Victorian mansion, right into the spot marked with my name. *Fancy.* The sign reads Heavyn Wagner in a dramatic, swirly script.

The house is enormous. It looks like a mansion inhabited by sexy vampires. Since I'm staying here for an entire year, I'll have to adjust to the house's gloomy appearance. Who loves the color black this much? Before I can get out of my car, a tall man knocks at my window. I yelp with surprise, not just because he seemingly appeared out of nowhere, but also because the man is gigantic.

Fuck. I nearly jumped out of my damn skin, but it's just my new boss knocking on my window. It's not his fault he looks so creepy. Kamari explained that he just got out of prison which is why he has these sea-green eyes that look like they've seen some shit. That doesn't scare me. What scares me is that he even went to prison. I looked that up too. He's a murderer. So I'm teaching a murderer's kid Spanish, English, Math, General Science and American History. Perfect.

Rian opens the car door for me, so I hustle to get my things together and exit the car as gracefully as I can muster, which ends up not being very graceful. Rian catches my forearm before I fall. He jerks his hand away quickly and apologizes once I regain my balance, but the force of his grasp catches my attention. He has *very* firm hands.

"I don't have any hired help for your bags," he says. "I can take them upstairs for you."

He gets stern when I attempt to decline his offer for help. I don't mind making one or two trips upstairs, but Rian insists on helping me. I open my trunk and he gazes at my luggage, baffled.

"It's all bright yellow," he says.

"Yup. Yellow is my favorite color. It's the color of sunshine, sunflowers… everything happy and sunny in life."

Rian scowls and then grunts, which isn't exactly a response, and he grabs the two biggest suitcases like they're weightless. All I have left is my yellow duffel bag and a small purse, so I hold onto those and follow Rian up the stairs to the front door of the mansion.

"Your room has an excellent view," he says. "When

there's a full moon, the light comes straight in through your window and makes it look like it's daylight outside."

That sounds spooky, but considering the aesthetic taste of Rian's home, that's exactly what he likes. I half expect Count Dracula to pop out from behind the front door when Rian opens it. Instead, there's a little girl. Tegan. I met her during the job interview and when she sees me, she screams with delight and rushes me.

Rian waits a few feet off with my suitcases for Tegan to greet me. She jumps up and down squealing with excitement a few times before wrapping her skinny arms around me. I hug her back, trying not to lose my balance. Tegan is the sweetest little girl. I know she's been through something traumatic – Kamari never specified what it was – and the thought of her alone with a grouch like her dad in this big house just breaks my heart.

I'm glad she won't have to be alone anymore. I love kids. I just don't think I'll ever have kids of my own though. After college and grad school, I thought I would already have met 'the one'. I never met him. I met guys I liked, guys I would have given up the world for, but none of them cared too much for me. It's hard to relate to other women and what they get out of relationships. Guys never gave me that 'princess treatment' I've heard so much about. I never went out on dates or had a one-night stand like other girls in college. I was always alone, overlooked and ignored. I was never the type to turn heads entering a room and if I went out with a group of friends, they got all the attention, not me.

You get used to it after a while and it stings less to know that every guy you meet ignores you completely if you aren't his type of pretty. And I'm nobody's kind of pretty except my own.

Chapter 2

I'd rather put my big heart to use caring for a little girl who needs someone instead of wasting my time chasing after guys who ain't worth a damn.

"You're here!" Tegan shrieks again when she pulls away from me. "I can't wait for you to meet Camilla..."

I don't have to ask who Camilla is because she comes strutting into the room with all her white fur and glory.

"Mewww!!" Camilla intones, clearly upset that she's not the absolute center of attention. Tegan rushes over to her and pets her on the head, causing Camilla to pause her strut to rub against Tegan's leg until she giggles. I glance over at Rian and watch him suppress a smirk.

Why doesn't he smile? This is cute as fuck and apparently he'd prefer to hold my bags near the stairs with a stoic and impatient look on his face.

"I'll bring these up then," he says grouchily. "You can come when you're ready."

He storms off, stomping up the stairs. The man has issues. *Not just issues, girl. He killed people. So don't piss him off.* I focus on Tegan instead of her huffy father.

"So... How have things been with him since I last saw you?"

Tegan rolls her eyes. "He is the *worst*."

"Come on, Tegan. He's your dad. Did he do one good thing?"

"He got me Camilla."

"See, that was nice of him."

Tegan grumbles, "Yeah. I guess. He just *never* talks."

"If you need to talk, I'll be here. Okay? Now... I should probably head upstairs before he comes storming back down. Maybe I can cook dinner for us?"

"I haven't had a home-cooked meal in *days*," Tegan says. "Please, pretty please cook dinner."

I agree to make her favorite food – corned beef and mashed potatoes – and attempt to follow the sound of Rian's footsteps upstairs. The house is fancy as hell, but it's still old, so sound carries everywhere. It would be hard as hell to sneak out of a place like this as a teenager. I wonder if sound travels from the bedrooms around the house, but there's no way of telling during the tour. I creak around for a few more steps and muse that maybe Rian likes his houses all creaky because they're easier to defend.

"I'm in here," Rian calls when he hears my footsteps getting close. He sounds tense and angry. It's like his entire personality has a resting bitch face.

I follow his voice to a large white door that opens into a room painted a deep, navy blue. Most of the walls in the house are black or dark gray so this is festive by Rian's standards. A large, king-sized bed occupies the center of the room and I have my own fireplace with its own poker and real firewood stacked nearby.

Rian stands near my luggage on the other side of the fireplace. I'm gawking so much that I can barely make it past the entryway.

"I thought the blue room would fit your upbeat personality," Rian says, his tone on the word "upbeat" as disdainful as he could muster.

"It's beautiful. Cozy."

My yellow luggage stands out aggressively against the room's dark aesthetic. I have a velvet navy blue armchair with a black end-table near it and an old-fashioned lamp hovering over the chair. The bed is gigantic, looks extremely comfortable and has a thick down comforter with a navy blue velvet duvet that matches the armchair. This place has so many great reading nooks…

Behind Rian, I notice the window he mentioned earlier.

Chapter 2

It's huge.

"Oh my God," I blurt out. "This view is crazy!"

I pass by Rian swiftly, taking a large whiff of whatever expensive cologne he has spritzed on. Everything about that man oozes wealth. It doesn't even feel like I'm in Boston in his house (and Boston is plenty fancy) but some even more luxurious fairy kingdom.

The view outside of the window includes a sweeping hill which leads into a forest with a large pond. Ducks and geese amble slowly near a little park bench seated close to the pond. I can imagine sitting there under the moonlight and just taking in the sheer beauty of the green landscape.

We're so close to the city that having so much natural beauty just outside my window is dreamy and ethereal. I turn around and shudder. Rian is so close to me suddenly and I didn't even hear him move. I turn back to look out the window because catching his gaze still makes me nervous.

He's so close to me that I can feel a gush of warmth on my neck from his breath.

"I knew you would like it," he says. "If at any point you're uncomfortable, you can come to me."

He takes a step back and this time I hear him, so I turn around. Rian stuffs his hands in his pockets and looks at me curiously. I want to say something, but I sense that he'll react negatively if I don't let him keep... analyzing me.

Still, it makes me uncomfortable so I walk towards my luggage and tip it over so I can unpack.

"Well," he says, finally breaking the silence. I can feel his sea-green eyes, still staring at me. "You seem to have a special touch with Tegan."

"I've always been good with kids," I tell him. "Tegan just wants company."

"She has me."

"She just needs to get used to that," I explain to him. "I thought I could make dinner for all of us tonight."

"Dinner tonight? I can't be at dinner tonight," Rian says. "Nor tomorrow. Or the day after. I'm getting the casino off the ground and that means working around the clock."

Is this man crazy? His daughter needs him. He can't go off to work at some seedy casino every night. Are casinos even legal in Boston? I remember my NDA and decide to keep my mouth shut about the casino thing and focus on Tegan.

"You don't have dinner with Tegan every night?"

I might not be a parent, but I had parents and they worked hard as hell. My mom was a librarian and my dad was a plumber, but they had dinner with us kids every night. They were *there* for us. He's hiring me because Tegan went through something traumatic. She needs him there. *Always.*

"That's why I'm hiring a nanny, isn't it?" he says stiffly. "Bond with her."

I try to hide my disgust, but I obviously do a terrible job of it.

"I'll be at dinner from 6:30-8:45 p.m. Do not deviate from this timeline in any capacity. I expect Tegan to be ready for dinner, bathed for the night and dressed in appropriate clothing."

"Yes, sir."

I probably fail at hiding my sarcasm, but I don't care. Rian has an odd reaction, though. He licks his lips. I don't even think he's conscious of it, but his brows pinch together when I say those words and his tongue pops out of his mouth, smoothing over his dark pink lips. I don't drop my gaze this time. Kamari warned me I would have to be tough to deal with my boss's personality and I want *all* the money promised to me.

Chapter 2

"Don't screw up," he says rudely before storming out of the room.

I HAVE SERIOUSLY NEVER MET a man with a worse attitude than Rian.

3

Rian

I never asked for a nanny. I don't need help looking after my daughter. Take the fall for your family and this is how they fucking treat you – like less than dirt. My daughters fingers are tangled with the womans, and my stomach lurches. They look over at me and Tegan's face falls once she sees me. *She hates me.*

It fucking kills me that my daughter can't even look me in the eye, that she can't see how much it hurt me to be away from her. I didn't sleep for nights. I nearly caught another charge. I killed a guy. I got in a fight and killed him and the only reason they didn't catch me up on those charges was because Cousin Liam took the blame. He's a lifer and dad instructed me to take his offer, so that's what I did.

The new nanny looks up at me with a smile that makes me deeply uncomfortable. She made Tegan's favorite for dinner, causing my daughter to fall even more in love with the woman she's known for a handful of hours when she can barely look me in the eye without curling her lip in disgust.

My own fucking daughter hates my guts and I gotta pretend like it doesn't kill me. Tegan's mother was right, I'm too selfish to have a kid. For the fuck up parent, I'm doing better than her, though. At least I'm here. I got here as soon as the boss let me see her after I got out of prison. When Tegan's older, she'll understand my loyalty to this family.

When I was gone, Aiden did what he had to, rescuing my daughter and killing the sicko who kidnapped her and had her locked up. Valentina helped her get on her feet emotionally. Evie looked after her and Evie's kids shared their books, toys and clothes with my daughter when she needed them most. *One day, she'll understand.* She'll either understand, or she'll die hating me.

I must be scowling too deeply because Heavyn pricks my finger aggressively with her fork. Corned beef and mashed potatoes. It's good, but it's too fucking rich. I still can't eat *normal* food. It's fucked up, but after prison, eating anything at all makes me sick to my stomach. Now drinking. I can handle drinking.

I swirl whiskey around my glass a little and then taste about half of it in one gulp. I fucking missed drinking.

"Tegan, do you want to tell your dad what we're making for dessert?" Heavyn asks my daughter, who clearly doesn't want to fucking talk to me. Heavyn obeyed my instructions. Tegan's clean with brushed hair and wearing a pair of khaki trousers and a red Ralph Lauren cable knit sweater. She's even wearing pearls. Since they've done so well, I don't want this to turn into another fight. If my daughter wants to ignore me, that's her choice.

"If she doesn't want to talk to me, she doesn't have to," I say awkwardly, but clearly this is the wrong thing to say. Tegan slams her fork down and glares at me like I'm a monster.

"I told you he doesn't care about me," she says. "He only cares about drinking and brooding in his stupid study."

Fuck. There it is. My daughter is my life. When she questions my loyalty to her, Tegan fires up this pure rage in me that I can barely express. She's just a kid. I get that. But I hate that she questions how much I love her when I would die for her. I've already killed for her. I would have done worse if Aiden hadn't gone above his duties and killed her kidnapper himself.

She is my family. My blood. I don't care about my father's fucking beliefs or the ink I etched into my own skin. Time shifts and changes everything. Kids change everything.

"I care about you," I say to her, my voice tightening with irritation. "You must never question that I care about you."

The new nanny gives me a scowl. How the fuck am I in the wrong here? It's not like this parenting shit comes with a manual, you know. I never knew Lucia was pregnant. If I'd known... things would've been different. I would've been a different person for her. I had to give up a lot for my daughter – more than my brothers will ever understand.

I took vows worse than what they did and I have something more painful than tattoos. My father demanded payment when he found out about my Puerto Rican child born out of wedlock. I have suffered quietly for Tegan since the day she was born and I will never stop fighting for her.

Heavyn's scowl deepens and she gives me a demanding look like she expects me to say something and that it had better be perfect. Her eyes bulge out impatiently and she leans forward expectantly, her yellow dress pressing her breasts together. It's the wrong time to notice but... I'm a guy.

What the fuck was my brother thinking putting a woman like that within arms reach of a felon? *I haven't had sex in over a year. I never did the sick things other men did in prison. I'm more backed up than I want to admit.*

Chapter 3

"I care about you," I say more calmly. "So I want to hear what you're making for dessert."

It's hollow to her. Tegan glares at me like she hates me, like she doesn't even know me and she doesn't fucking want to.

"It's pumpkin pie, you annoying asshole," Tegan says fiercely. The way she says asshole reminds me of Aiden, who is the person I probably have to blame for her colorful vocabulary.

This time, Heavyn jumps in. Tegan half-heartedly apologizes. I say nothing, but continue forcing the corned beef down my throat. If I speak, it'll only turn into another fight.

I lost her, I think. My daughter will never bond to me again. She'll never love me and it hurts like fuck to admit that I just... screwed up. They don't fucking tell you that there are no second chances with kids. You either get it right, or your kid hates you forever. That fucking sucks.

After she's done eating, Tegan runs upstairs to her bedroom to continue listening to her *Harry Potter & The Goblet Of Fire* audiobook. She's in slightly better spirits than earlier, most likely because of Heavyn's kitchen entertainment.

Heavyn stays downstairs in the kitchen with me while I drink, even if I insist that I'll clean up without her help. Prison is fucking filthy and it gives me some relief to bring my own surroundings to order. I've always been a control freak, but I'm too drunk on whiskey to fight Heavyn tonight. I had to drink a lot to get through dinner.

Her lips are tight with disapproval which means she's probably going to lecture me on my parenting like everyone else in my fucking life. I know Aiden only wants her here as a spy or to stop me from hurting my daughter or whatever strange ideas he's taken into his thick fucking head.

"Tegan needs you to take an interest in her, Mr. Murray."

"She should never doubt my love for her. I fought every day in that cell to get back here."

"She's been through a traumatic event," Heavyn says. "It'll take time. She needs to learn to trust that you're gonna be there for her."

"What the hell is stopping her from doing that?" I growl. "I'm here, aren't I?"

After a day with my daughter, I'd expect her to lose some of her irritatingly peppy and optimistic energy. This appears not to be the case. Her black hair is unnaturally straight, but growing out of her head naturally, not a wig or anything, and it falls to the middle of Heavyn's waist, right where it gets really small before her ass balloons out.

She has a stripper's ass. I can't let that stripper's ass distract me from the difficult night I have planned, or from parenting my daughter.

"I *do* take an interest in her," I snap impatiently at Heavyn, continuing my angry rant despite Heavyn's conspicuous silence. "She's my daughter and I know how to raise her."

If she's frustrated with me, Heavyn does an excellent job hiding it. She holds herself straight and speaks all fancy and educated. It's a little annoying and a little hot. I try not to think about the hot part. Couldn't my stupid brother have picked an older nanny?

"I'm not saying you don't know how to raise her," Heavyn says calmly. "But she's been through a lot. She needs someone *gentle*."

I raise a single brow and examine Heavyn carefully. How much did Darragh and his wife tell her about this job before she accepted it? I can provide for my daughter, I can be a strong person for her, but I'm no stuffed animal.

I grunt and pour myself another glass of whiskey. I finish

the bottle, which annoys me a bit, since I could use a hell of a lot more liquor to make it through the day.

"I'm the furthest thing from gentle."

Heavyn scowls. "She's your daughter. I don't care how tough you think you are, she doesn't need this kind of toxic masculinity in her life. That includes binge drinking."

I'm not binge drinking, I'm catching up on all the drinks I missed in prison and what the hell were those other words?

"Toxic masculinity?"

What the fuck is Heavyn talking about? I've spent the better half of my adult life behind bars. I've seen men kill each other over something as simple as a fucking chess game. I'm a goddamned monk compared to some of the mother-fuckers I've seen. I might have done some dirty shit, but I never beat someone's ass over a chicken sandwich.

Heavyn scoffs, her full lips all pouty and haughty. *Ignore her lips.*

"You are *dripping* in toxic masculinity," she says, making a little huffing sound. "I feel sorry for Tegan."

"Is this how you talked to your last boss?"

She stiffens again, apparently unafraid of my intensifying glare. "My last boss gave a crap about his daughter."

Her attitude gets under my skin, but there's nothing I can do about it. She might have her instructions to stand up to me, but I have instructions from Aiden not to fuck with her, not to mess around with her, and to keep the nanny happy. Happy nanny, happy Aiden. Happy Aiden, I don't go to jail for murdering upwards of twenty people. It's a deal I can work with to avoid wasting more of my time talking to fucking lawyers.

"I give a crap about my daughter," I tell her, lowering my voice to a threatening tone which Heavyn heartily ignores.

"Then act like it," she says. "Take some initiative. You're

breaking Tegan's heart. So I'm here to protect her and look after her."

Heavyn couldn't possibly understand the sacrifices I've made for my daughter. Her insinuation that I don't care for Tegan fills me with nothing but cold rage. I can feel the flicker of blackness within my heart that I try to suppress growing in Heavyn's direction. *Suppress it.*

I respond to her coldly, "I don't have time for a lecture about my parenting. I have business to attend to. Make sure Tegan gets her homework done and has dessert. I don't want to come home to another tantrum."

Her eyes flicker with a mixture of outrage and indignation at my coldness. I can't let it get to me. I am the cold bastard she thinks I am. I'm worse than that – I screwed up my kid by spending most of her life behind bars, I screwed up with her mother by exposing her to my fucked up family, and I screwed up by disobeying my father, and then Aiden.

At least Aiden was merciful. Unlike dad, he doesn't enjoy causing pain. But he's not unwilling to inflict it. I have the mark of my disobedience on my left shoulder – a small brand in the shape of a clover with a small 'M' in the center.

"Never forget where your loyalties lie," Aiden had said as he pressed the hot brand into my flesh himself.

He hasn't rid us of all the old punishments yet, but at least he didn't kill me, which he could have since I put bullets in more than twenty people in the old Italian neighborhood.

"You should have given them the choice to run," Aiden had said. "They weren't all guilty."

I did something more important than giving some bum ass Italians a choice about how they fucking die. I cleaned up. I did the dirty work that Aiden couldn't do and left him the self-righteous one. That's my job – the dirty work. Violence comes easily to me. Like Darragh, I enjoy it. Unlike Darragh, I don't suppress my urges with boxing matches and cultured blood sports.

I prefer the real thing. I prefer to smell the adrenaline on my prey.

HEAVYN STORMS off muttering under her breath as she stomps up the staircase to check on my daughter. Tegan just needs to adjust to her new environment and treating her like a victim won't help her as much as everyone else thinks. She needs to live a normal life. She needs to forget everything that happened to her in captivity.

How fucking ironic that I'm the only one who understands captivity, but I can't reach her. I just...

I WASN'T MEANT to be a father. I love Tegan, but I shouldn't be her only parent. She deserves more than a killer. Her nanny thinks I can will myself into being a better man, but I can't do that. I'm not a good person.

I'm a murderer, a criminal, a low-life Irish mafia thug. Nothing can change who I am at my core – a villain.

4

Heavyn

Three Days Later

I'm so grateful Rian's gone again tonight. It's one of my first nights alone with Tegan. She's been slow to warm up the past few nights while Rian has been at work. I enjoy the nannying part of the job best because I don't have to pester Tegan about school work.

Since we're just staying home alone together, we can relax and I don't have to have my "teacher brain" on. I can tell Tegan's nervous about being in the house "alone" even if I'll be there with her. She gets nervous every night her dad leaves us alone and I don't blame her. I don't get why her dad bought a house straight out of an old vampire novel. It's beautiful, and I love all the old fixtures, but it's a bit doom and gloom for a girl, especially a sensitive kid like Tegan.

She doesn't want to let her father go as he leaves. Even if they fight, she still recognizes that he's a source of protection for her and support. At night, she gets scared and doesn't seem to care about her total disappointment of Rian.

She just wants someone who can make the monsters go

away and while Tegan loves and respects me, I am incredibly short and non-threatening, unlike her 6'5" father Rian.

I watch as she hugs him goodbye, accepting the fact that Rian will probably never talk to me again as long as it's absolutely necessary because I criticized his parenting a few days ago. I wasn't trying to be a dick about it, but I'd had enough of Rian's attitude towards Tegan. Someone has to stand up to him and she won't. She's afraid of him.

I can't believe he doesn't see that. I don't know how much she knows about his lifestyle, but Tegan isn't stupid and she's terrified of her father. He needs to be more sensitive to that if he wants a genuine relationship with his daughter. The crazy part is I think some part of him wants that more than the world, but he has so many walls up, nobody can break through.

I don't know if it was prison or something else that turned him into a beast, but I can't stand when he turns that on Tegan. I can handle it, but she's just a little girl. I'm getting paid and she's stuck with him forever.

After Rian leaves, we watch her latest favorite movie, *Encanto*, and she reads herself to sleep in her room upstairs. It's crazy that Rian doesn't see the similarities between them. I had a whole night of activities ready to go, but she just wants to curl up in bed with a well-worn copy of *Twilight* and Camilla. The white cat sits near Tegan's head, staring at her as she reads.

When I check up on them thirty minutes later, they're both asleep, so I turn the lights off, and make sure I turn on the house's alarm system per Rian's instructions. The house might be a little creepy, but it does feel like a fortress with the alarm system and the lights outside that turn on with any movement.

We're far away from the property line too, so there's very

little reason for anyone to come close to the house. I don't know where Rian is tonight, but he promises that if anyone trips the alarm, he'll be there within fifteen minutes, which is enough time for me to grab Tegan and hide in the attic panic room. (He was *not* joking about the panic room like I initially believed.)

I'm safe. I don't have too many doubts despite Rian's paranoid proclamations. This is the nicest part of Boston. Who the hell is shooting up Brookline? Nobody. The only way people my age can even afford to live in this neighborhood is if they have three or more roommates. Rian has a *mansion* out here. This is pure luxury – and so is my bedroom.

Once I settle Tegan in, I wander upstairs to indulge in the luxuriousness of my Victorian mansion suite. Aiden must have made sure that Rian went *all out* on decorating my bedroom. I love that the walls are navy blue, even if it's a dark color because at least it's a color instead of beige or white.

I have a king-sized bed for the first time in my life, which I've come to appreciate with each passing day here. My favorite detail about the room is the giant painting of sunflowers on the wall Rian had delivered after my first day here. They're my favorite flower, but I don't know how he found out or if he even knows. The painting just showed up. Maybe Aiden or Rian asked Kamari about my favorite flower, but she never brought it up, so I don't know what to make of it. (She's my friend from college who got me this job.)

I lock my bedroom door and turn on the baby monitor in case anything happens downstairs that needs my attention. When Tegan can't sleep, she normally gets herself snacks in the kitchen or watches TV in her bedroom, so I doubt I'll hear from her.

I slide into bed with a steamy romance novel and turn on

the light, diving into the story about a very erotic vampire and a female main character who almost seems too naive for her own good. Tegan wants me to read *Twilight*, but the description of this book called it *Twilight* for grown ups which sounds more like it's my speed.

I love unwinding with books that I wouldn't get caught dead reading in public. It's not that I'm ashamed, it's just that the relationship between me and my books is private. The book gets a little smutty which sends a thrill straight between my thighs. Obviously in this living situation, I can't have a man, but that doesn't matter to me since there's no one I've even entertained.

Not everyone can get lucky like Kamari. Her bae is fine as hell – 6'5" with long blond hair. Now, I don't usually find blond men fine. They're too pale and with the yellow hair, it's just shiny and a lil' too much. But Kamari's man, Darragh. He's a snack.

It's hard to imagine him and Rian are brothers. Rian's more like the main character of my vampire novel than his brother. He has dark brown hair, for one thing, and Rian's eyes are a greener shade of blue. Rian has way more muscle on his frame than Darragh, too. He's *huge*. And grouchier. With more of a beard...

A strange gush warms between my thighs as I think about Rian's beard. I have no business thinking about that beard or gushing. I focus on the main character of my novel, *Nikolai*. Now *he's* sexy and he's nothing like Rian because Nikolai is a brooding, dark and utterly dreamy... vampire. Rian's nothing like that.

After reading two very steamy chapters, I close my eyes and set my book on the nightstand. It's time for me and my imagination of Nikolai from the book to have some alone time. I've never had more than my own fantasies and romance novels to fill my imagination before bed, so it comes naturally to picture Nikolai, the sexy dark-haired vampire in all his ethereal glory.

My hands snake between my thighs as I picture Nikolai's patient hands touching my hips and then spreading me open. He presses his lips to my neck and bites me in my fantasy. My fingers slip into my underwear and I slowly touch myself to arousal as I picture a sexy vampire about to put it down on me. But as the vampire pulls away in my fantasy, his face transforms. He's no longer Nikolai from the book... but Rian.

I bite my lip and try to push thoughts of my boss out of my head. It doesn't work. I imagine his lips on mine, roughly spreading mine open as he pushes his tongue into his mouth. He just seems like the type of guy who has this calm exterior but would kiss you with the fiercest passion. Before my fantasies can get any further, I cum hard. Just touching my clit gets me off if the fantasy is *really* good or I guess in this case really bad and fucked up. *What's wrong with me?*

I slip out of bed and quickly wash my hands and change into fresh underwear before climbing back into bed. Feeling so much more relaxed, I fall asleep effortlessly and I don't wake up until an icy chill blows in through my window. My *locked* window.

I FREEZE in place after the realization has hit me. Instinctively, I know something's wrong. The bedroom is too cold. I'm lying on my stomach with my head turned away from the window, and I don't want to draw attention to myself by turning to look. When I climbed beneath the sheets after touching myself, I was warm and toasty, but it's freezing in here, which can only mean someone opened the window I locked before going to bed.

Chapter 4

Which means someone is in this room. If there's an intruder, I probably only have a few seconds to react. My phone is on the nightstand. It would only take a few seconds to call Rian, but there's no way to reach for my phone without attracting attention. I'm screwed unless whoever broke in here doesn't know I'm in bed.

My heart pounds as I hear footsteps moving around my bedroom. *Fuck.* There really is an intruder. I'm so terrified that I can't move.

Okay, Heavyn. Just jump outta the bed. Your best bet is trying to escape and grabbing Tegan on the way out.

It's crazy, but as I hear the footsteps and a few seconds later, the heavy breathing, I worry more about Tegan than myself. That poor baby can't handle any more mess in her life. Before I can launch myself towards the door, fueled only by adrenaline, a knee presses into the bed and a very heavy man climbs on top of me as I lie on my stomach. *Holy crap.*

He's huge. I don't have time to react. I can't even scream because he wraps a firm, large hand over my mouth and pushes his hips into my ass, settling all of his weight into me. He must be nearly 300 lbs of pure muscle. I know it's muscle, because I can feel his stomach pressing into my back and ass.

I try screaming into his hand, even if I know he's holding me too tightly. Struggling physically is out of the question because of his weight.

"Good evening, Heavyn," a smooth, almost familiar voice whispers into my ear. The tickle sends a shiver straight through me. Terror. I feel my bladder about to let go, but I will myself to stay in control.

"I know I'm doing something pretty fucked up right now, but I'm not gonna hurt you, okay? I'm not gonna hurt you, but I'm not gonna let you leave this room until we're done."

Done with what? I still can't place his voice and it really bothers me. Maybe if I could see his face, or if I had some other clue aside from his weight like the size of his hands. A lot of men have gigantic hands, but this one could cover my entire face and suffocate me. I can barely breathe with his large index finger right beneath my nose.

I know I'll scream if he lets go of me.

"If you scream," he murmurs. "You're gonna wake Tegan. You *really* don't want to wake Tegan with me in the house, do you? So I'm gonna let you go and you're gonna stay quiet. "

Tegan. *How the fuck does he know about Tegan?* Him mentioning Tegan terrifies the crap out of me. She's my responsibility and I don't want a dangerous psycho to snatch her in the middle of the night.

I try to slow my breathing down so I don't yell when he lets go of me. His body moves with mine as I steady my breathing. He's firm and so fucking big. It hurts to take air into my lungs but for now, even with his weight on top of mine, it's possible.

He shifts his hips and I try to ignore his dick digging into my ass. The giant removes his hand from my mouth and I don't scream. But I try to turn around. Just as I move, he grabs my hair and whips my head right back around. I didn't catch a glimpse of him.

The man shoves my head forward and I grunt in pain.

"Look at me again and I'll cover your ass in so many welts you won't be able to walk for a week."

I nod with understanding, hoping that he'll release his tightening grasp on my hair. He does and I don't bother turning around to look at him.

"What do you want?" I gasp. It's still hard to breathe with a heavy man on top of me, but the fastest way out of here is finding out what he wants.

Chapter 4

"I need your permission."

"For what?" I gasp. He strokes his fingers through my hair and wraps my hair around his wrist, giving him utter control of me. I've never been in this position of complete submission and my reaction to him completely humiliates me. My cheeks burn with shame which transforms into terror again as I move beneath him and my ass grazes his dick. He's hard. This sicko who climbed through my window in the middle of the night is rock hard.

"To cum inside you," He says simply. I flip out and thrash beneath him, but his grasp on my hair and his threat about what would happen if I scream give the giant utter control over me.

"Stop it," he snaps and I stop, but mostly because all my thrashing intensifies the feeling that he's crushing me. His body completely dominates over mine in every way.

"Good girl," he whispers and that forbidden thrill rushes straight between my thighs again.

Think of a way out, Heavyn.

"I need another baby," he says with a demanding tone that suggests he expects this baby to come from *me*.

"Good for you," I grunt. "I don't see how that's my problem."

But I *do* see how he's going to make it my problem because this intruder has his dick on my ass. It doesn't take a genius to figure out what he wants. *To cum inside me.*

"You're in a very dangerous position," He says, thrusting his hips forward so I can feel just how hard he is. His warm breath tickles my ears to the point where I lose control of my body's response to his warmth. "Working with the racist, Irish mob. Those people would kill their own family for fucking with the wrong kind of people."

He releases his grip on my hair, but only so he can turn

my face to the side and kiss my neck. It's still too dark for me to perceive any of his features except... his lips. The instant his rough lips make contact with my neck, my pussy gushes. A sick twisted guilt forces its way into my stomach as I respond to the kiss, but I can't *ignore* the response.

My previously fresh underwear are officially soaked. I gasp and try to move away from the intruder, but he returns his tight control over me, tightening his grip on my hair and fiercely holding me still.

"If you carry my baby for me, I will protect you," he murmurs. "I will pay you. I will give you whatever you want, but I need your permission."

"You're asking a lot of me for a man who won't let me see his face," I manage to push out despite my body's intense response to the intruder's ministrations. His neck kisses have my pussy gushing and I want to get away from this mind game.

"I won't let you know my name either," he says. "It's safest. I just need a pussy to cum in and a body to hold my child."

"I still get nothing out of this deal."

"Sex," he murmurs, teasing me with warm breath on my ear again. I need a break from the kisses. My neck is soaked and this crazy criminal's oddly smooth voice has me far too relaxed considering the situation.

I don't know why I stopped fighting him and I don't remember when it happened. He strokes my hair gently and continues talking, "I'll give you the sex you crave, Heavyn. Dirty. Kinky. Rough..."

"Sex with a stranger doesn't excite me," I croak out, although apparently the thought of sex with this stranger who broke in through my window awakens my body completely. *He's just too familiar...*

"Sex with a stranger doesn't excite me either," the man says calmly. "Your pussy excites me. Thinking about your pussy excites me. Knocking you up and making you carry my surrogate child excites me."

"Your surrogate?"

His body tenses with frustration. Whoever he is, he's quick to anger. I should be careful, but there's not much I can do in this situation.

"Yes."

"Okay," I grunt, ignoring my traitorous body and forcing myself to listen to the strong, educated woman inhabiting my brain. "What do I have to do to get you to leave?"

His body moves purposefully over mine, baring his intentions before his words. This intruder isn't going anywhere. I can't see him, but I have clues about him even without my eyes. He's tall, I noticed that much. Unusually tall. He also has a light Boston accent, very deep voice, and... he smells familiar too. I'm too focused on surviving to run through a catalog of scents in my head and find his.

"Do this for me," He says. "Be my surrogate. I told you, Heavyn. I won't hurt you. I just want to cum inside you until I get you pregnant. When the baby is born... you'll be free. I know you're stuck here for a year. Make a sweet deal even sweeter."

I grunt and push my back against him roughly.

"What about this deal is sweet for me? I have to have a baby."

"You get my tongue in your pussy as often as possible. You get to feel my big cock inside you until you cum. I will take care of you physically and sexually in every way you need while you live in this castle. You don't have to get me birthday gifts or remember our anniversary, just wait in bed for me to come fuck your brains out whenever you need it."

Our anniversary? Oh, he's crazy. Very crazy. I shudder. He's so muscular that I can tell when I shake and inadvertently move against him. *Damn.* I bite my lower lip and try to stay focused on something other than his weight pressing into me.

"That's not every woman's dream," I say sternly, even if the intruder's disturbing plan for our relationship forced a gush of wetness between my thighs. My body's traitorous responses have nothing to do with my logical interpretation of the situation, or my desire to get this man off me. "I want... a relationship."

He responds with a condescending chuckle. "This is better than a relationship, sunshine. This is you, getting great sex every night while you grow a baby for me."

His cock jerks again. This intruder really likes the idea of knocking me up.

"This is crazy," I whisper. "I understand what you want but... if I agree to that... I would be fucking crazy."

It's like I'm talking to him and trying to work out how the hell to get my ass out of this situation at the same time. He has me pinned in a way that completely immobilizes me, and I only just realized how much I need the complete use of my arms and legs in every situation.

I could always take Plan B.

It's like this motherfucker can read my mind. He pushes hair away from the back of my neck and kisses the back of my neck, forcing me to feel his lips again. A shiver travels straight through me. That gush between my legs returns.

"If you take Plan B, I'll know."

I believe him. I don't know who the fuck he is, but clearly, he's watched me for a while. Maybe a few days, maybe since the day I first had an interview here.

"I won't," I lie immediately.

He runs his tongue over my neck possessively and when he finds a spot he likes, he grabs some of my flesh between his teeth and bites hard. I moan and thrust back into him, rubbing my ass against his erection inadvertently.

"You won't," he commands. "Because your pussy will be mine until you give birth to my child."

"I need more from this deal," I say. "I need you to leave me alone when I have my period."

"You won't have to worry about that for long."

"Don't hurt the little girl who lives here," I whisper. "Please..."

His muscles tighten against me. "I would *never* do such a fucking thing. And I would never hurt you, sunshine. That's why you can't know who I am..."

He roughly pulls my pajama pants down over my ass. Terror heightens as I expect a painful first time intrusion between my legs. Instead, he pulls his body away from mine, finally allowing oxygen into my lungs and he runs his tongue furiously over my mound through my underwear.

"Fuck, you're already juicy," he grunts. "Fuck yes..."

5

Rian

Blood rushes past my ears from the thrill. Killing never torments me the way it torments my brothers. Killing gets me high and what I've done tonight requires rewarding my greatest most taboo urge of the past few weeks, since the day I met her.

I did it. I fucking did it. I texted Aiden 'It's done' but then I turned my phone off so I could celebrate my hard work and the shifting sands beneath us.

I understand how my brother works. Darragh's too soft, Callum's too stupid and my brother Odhran is too young. Aiden needs a right-hand – what the Italians call a consigliere – and that will be me. It's all the power that I want and need to keep Tegan safe for the rest of her life. I'll rebuild all the wealth I lost fighting the manslaughter charge so whether I die by gunfire or old age, Tegan will never suffer again.

This is pure fucking bliss – having power just within reach and taking it.

. . .

Chapter 5

I KILLED my father and I celebrated by climbing in through the nanny's window. My heart pumps furiously as I push her into the bed and reach for the knife in my pocket and cut her panties away. I didn't use the knife in the crime. I'm not a sick fuck. He died in his sleep from a drug overdose. I watched. Painless, after a while. The knife I brought for her. *Just for her.*

Heavyn struggles beneath me as I cut her panties away, sweating with panic. I kiss her thigh and toss the knife aside. My dick pushes against my jeans. I'm so hard, I can feel my Jacob's Ladder piercing rubbing against the fabric between us. Six barbells, all of them stuck through my shaft, making my hardness even more impossible to ignore. *I need to cum. Bad.*

"Hey. Don't be afraid."

I know she can't see my face, but she's gotta know it's me. My heart races with the uncertainty of it all. If Heavyn knows it's me, she'll probably recognize the logic what I'm doing and maintain the pretense that this is completely anonymous.

She's here for Tegan. It's not my daughter's fault that Heavyn fills me with insatiable lust. She looks like the pin up girls guys in prison used to draw – sexy pictures of naked black chicks that would sell for over five packets of ramen noodles.

Heavyn is an eight packet girl. Thick. Voluptuous. She's so hot that it messes with my fucking head. My cock wants her, but she won't fucking relax. I bite her thigh more forcefully and she yelps loudly.

"Hold still," I say commandingly. "Didn't I say I wouldn't hurt you?"

My frustration only terrifies her more. I want to be more

gentle with her considering the circumstances, but I need her to accept me tonight. *I fucking need release.*

"You climbed in through my window. We didn't exactly establish a basis of trust."

"Ah. I give you an orgasm, then you trust me. Understood?"

I peel the remainder of her panties away while she struggles by moving her hips. Heavyn's struggling stops when my tongue slides between her lower lips and flicks gently over her clit. *I'll never hurt you. I just want you to feel good. And fuck, your pussy is so soft...*

My tongue moves around her clit in a slow circle. She moans and then emits a guilty squeak. *No, sunshine. Feel this.* I push her thighs open and allow my tongue to explore her entire pussy. Heavyn's pussy smells delicious and transports me to another fucking galaxy. I was already high when I climbed in through her bedroom window, but her scent heightens every sensation. I want to taste every inch of her lower lips.

And suck on them...

Heavyn moans louder as I suck on her lower lips and then return my attention to Heavyn's clit. Her body writhes beneath me, but she stops fighting me and it's easier for me to get my tongue inside her. I roll my tongue around her clit and then outside her lower lips before pushing my tongue back between those lips and swirling it around Heavyn's entrance.

Her hips thrust back against me as I eat her pussy, tenderly lapping at Heavyn's folds until I feel her body tighten and I sense her getting close to an orgasm.

"Cum for me, sunshine," I growl. "Let go..."

She gasps and I feel her pussy pulsing as she releases. I run my tongue along her slit and lap up Heavyn's juices. She tastes even better than she smells and it drives me wild. My fingers grip her thighs possessively and I spread them apart as she gushes into my mouth. Every inch of her trembles with desire.

She whimpers and then her body stops shaking with pleasure.

"Good girl," I murmur, kissing her thigh and then the top of her ass. "That was perfect."

"That was my first..." she croaks out. "Never mind..."

My palm curves around her ass as I grope her soft flesh, stopping when she says first.

"First what?"

"First orgasm. First everything."

My heart pounds and there's an initial surge of guilt as she says it. Her first? This girl has multiple college degrees. She has a body that is so insanely fuckable that it's impossible to imagine that a thousand men haven't tried to get her into bed.

"You came so hard," I murmur.

"I don't know why..." she says, sounding visibly distressed. "I don't... My boss is dangerous..."

She really doesn't know? I thought it was obvious. Maybe she's just pretending. Ah... That makes sense. Why else would she mention her boss? Well, good that she's playing along.

I chuckle. "He's not more dangerous than I am. Now, will you at least let me make you cum again?"

She shudders. "I hate this..."

I kiss her thighs and her outer lips until she whispers, "Yes... Yes, please..."

My tongue presses to her clit again and I eat her pussy until she cums again. Once I get her thighs soaking wet and get her comfortable with moaning and cumming in my mouth, I pull away from her and kiss her thighs.

"I still want you," I murmur. "That's why I'm here. Not because I want to hurt you, but because I want you. Your body."

"I'm a virgin," she says. "This isn't how normal people lose their virginity."

She shudders with pleasure as I kiss down the length of her spine. Her body is so fucking soft and my cock is about to burst with how much I want her.

"But you aren't normal," I murmur. "You're the au pair to a dangerous man and I suspect you took this job because you have a fascination with darkness..."

"You don't know anything about me."

"I know what makes you cum. I know your pussy tastes delicious. I know you're wet as fuck because some part of you is desperate to feel a cock between your legs. I'm not just any cock, sunshine... This one is just for you."

I HAVE six rungs in the Jacob's Ladder piercing along the bottom of my cock. As I stiffen to my full length, my mouth waters with anticipation. I don't know how a virgin will respond to my cock. The rungs in the piercings are solid 24K gold and each ring was punishment for sleeping with a woman of a different race.

I haven't been with a woman since they were forcefully pierced. That includes the time I was locked up; I haven't been with a guy either. Not my thing. I wanted her the second she walked in the door of my mansion. Aiden should've seen how I looked at her. He should have known that if I let myself go, allowed myself to kill again unrepentantly... I would allow myself to succumb to these other dark urges.

"I can't have a stranger's baby..."

42

Chapter 5

I push the hair away from her neck again and shift my body so I'm resting against her again, my hips nestling against hers so my cock digs into her soft, round ass through my jeans.

"I won't be a stranger," I murmur. "And I promise to take care of you. If your boss is ever cruel... ever hurts you... then you'll have me."

"I need more..."

"More?" Her request makes my heart race. Her pushing back against me doesn't bother me at all.

"I need assurances. I need you to tell me a secret. Something that could make me trust you."

My cock thumps against her ass. She'll know one of my greatest secrets soon enough. I never told my brothers what my father did to me. He enjoyed it too. He put every piercing into my cock with my naked body strapped to a chair. Blood rushes past my ears. Secrets...

"I killed my father tonight," I growl. "Now let me fuck you, Heavyn. I need you. I need your pussy and I know you're so fucking wet for me."

I ease out of my pants and underwear and rest my bare cock against her ass. It hurt to get hard for months after the piercings. Keeping them clean was hell. The gold makes my cock heavier and my blood pulses. I want her. I want her so fucking bad.

I don't want her to freeze in fear. I hold her against me and nibble her ear slowly. She melts in my arms. Her soft body leans into mine.

"Why did you do it?"

She shudders as I keep kissing her. I don't want her to run. I don't want this to scare her.

"To protect people I love. To do my duty to my family..."

"That's noble."

"Don't romanticize me," I murmur. "I can be your lover in the bedroom but... that's all we can be. So let me make you cum again... trust me."

"How can I trust a stranger?"

"Because I told you a secret. And I made you cum... and I promised you protection. It sounds like a good deal..."

My cock thumps against her ass again and she wriggles against me, getting me even harder than before. She's fucking perfect and I can't stand waiting any longer. I keep kissing her body and letting her scent intoxicate me.

"Okay," she says, her voice falling to barely above a whisper. "This might be crazy but... okay..."

"No," I respond. "It's not crazy. I'll keep you safe, sunshine. And better than that, I'll keep you wet."

I spread her thighs apart and run my fingers over her wet slit and rub her clit slowly. Heavyn whimpers and spreads her thighs apart slightly.

"You're so fucking wet..." I growl. It's been so long since I've touched a woman like this. I can't wait to touch more of her and to feel my cock sink inside her gorgeous pussy. I know she'll be the best I've ever had. I trust my instincts about women and Heavyn drew me in the second I saw her. It's not just her body... it's how she carries herself.

"Be gentle," she gasps. "Be gentle..."

I could never hurt her intentionally, but she must feel my cock against her ass and sense that my cock could very much hurt her unintentionally.

I want her lips around my cock almost as much as I want to enter her, but doing that to her tonight would totally break her trust. I want her to feel good as long as she's in my house. As long as she's my nanny.

Her thighs spread slightly for me and the head of my cock presses against Heavyn's entrance. She won't feel my piercings yet, but once I'm inside her, they'll rub against the inner walls of Heavyn's pussy. Precum oozes out of the tip of my cock and I rub it against Heavyn's wetness to prepare her for me. She winces.

"No condom," I say to her firmly. "It'll feel good..."

She'll understand why a condom is totally unrealistic once she feels my dick inside her. The wetness gushing out of Heavyn coats her thighs and makes it easy to find her entrance and slip inside. I push the head of my cock inside her and Heavyn moans from just the head of my dick.

The head of my cock is large, the size of a small apple. Heavyn moans as I pierce her. She's so soft, but there's resistance to my cock as I attempt to push inside her. She's a virgin and not just that, there's a thin membrane in the way.

Heavyn whimpers as I push my cock into her another inch. My cock hits Heavyn's hymen, but doesn't break it because she emits a pained yelp. My heart races. I might be a killer, but hurting Heavyn brings me to a dead stop. I can't hear her scream like that. To calm her down, I wrap my arms around her, putting my hand around her mouth to silence her. We can't wake my daughter.

"It'll hurt," I murmur. "But then I'll make you feel good. You won't regret trusting me. You just won't."

She freezes and then I thrust the rest of my dick inside her, breaking past Heavyn's membrane with an urgent push. I feel her bite down on my finger and it hurts like fuck, but I just move my hips forward and get the rest of my dick inside Heavyn, taking her virginity. Claiming her as mine. *You know how possessive you are, Rian. You can't handle relationships...*

I release my grip on her mouth. She gasps loudly and I move my hips slowly, allowing her to adjust to my size. As I move, she moans loudly. The barbells on my dick piercing touch every inch of her inner walls and the slightest movement of my hips delivers a world of pleasure and possibly pain to Heavyn's pussy.

"Does it hurt?" I grunt as I withdraw my hips.

"Your dick… It has… It's…"

Those would be the barbells. Her pussy shudders and tightens around my cock as she grips me like a vice. I've hardly moved and Heavyn responds by cumming hard all over my dick. I push my hips back inside her and I can feel her pussy pulsing and gripping my cock like she's ready to milk the cum out of me.

Her pussy feels so fucking good that I nearly cum right away. I grip her hips and try to move in a steady rhythm, but each time I thrust, Heavyn has another orgasm which grasps my cock so tightly that I can barely hold back.

She enjoys this. Heavyn moves her body against mine, throwing her hips back to meet me after her third orgasm, no longer resisting me but moving her body in a steady rhythm with mine.

"You feel so good," I murmur into her ear and teasing her with my warm breath. "I can't wait to cum inside your tight pussy. You're so fucking tight…"

She gasps with pleasure and I wrap her hair around my wrists, tilting her head back so I can watch her ass bounce against my body as I bury my dick inside her.

Her body does something completely fucked up to me. Any control I might have had vanishes. I lose myself in my lust for Heavyn. Her soft pussy grasps my cock so tightly and the barbell piercings through my dick massage her inner walls with my hips' slightest movement.

Once I take control of Heavyn's body by grasping her hair, I unlock a completely submissive side to her that I didn't expect. She allows me to take her from behind, gripping her hair to control the pace I make love to her. I run my tongue over her neck possessively and this drives her mad again. Heavyn cums hard all over my dick, making it nearly impossible for me to hold back.

"I'm gonna cum," I growl. "I'm gonna knock you up with my baby, sunshine..."

She gasps so softly that it's almost like it's her fucking subconscious talking.

"Yes..." Heavyn whispers. That's all I can take. Hearing her whisper that magic word pushes me over the edge and I erupt. I drag her body closer to me with a wrestler's force as my seed spills from the tip of my cock. The first hot gush pulses between Heavyn's legs and her thighs instinctively squeeze together, milking my cock of every damn drop.

If this doesn't get her pregnant, then I don't know what will. She whimpers and moans with pleasure as I keep my dick inside her and wait for her to stop shuddering from the euphoria of her orgasmic high.

"That felt fucking good, sunshine," I whisper. "Your pussy feels fucking good."

I suck on Heavyn's neck until she moans.

"I can't be a mom," she whispers.

"When was your last period?" I respond coldly. I'm not asking her to be a mother. I have something more efficient in mind. She ends her tenure at my house by giving over her baby. I grow my family, give Tegan a sibling r and... everything works out great. I can't see anything wrong with this plan, nor any potential ways it could go wrong.

"I don't know," she says. "I don't keep track. Believe it or not, every woman doesn't obsess over her period."

"I'll keep track for you," I respond. "In case tonight doesn't work."

"How do you plan to get your baby from me?" She says.

Rian

"In your brilliant scheme, how are you going to sneak into a guarded mansion and steal an entire baby?"

"The same way I got to you," I murmur. "Now don't move. I need to take my dick out of you and I don't want it to hurt…"

6

Heavyn

When I wake up in the morning, my head hurts. My pussy hurts. I tell myself that everything that happened last night, including the intruder leaping out the window of my bedroom, was a fucked up wet dream. With more daylight entering my bedroom window, I can see the stains on the sheets and the sticky residue on my bare thighs. Not a wet dream. Very real.

A psychopath climbed in through my bedroom window and I somehow agreed to become his surrogate while cumming all over his dick. There's a part of me that's numb with shock from this. No woman pictures losing her virginity to an unknown man who knows all the right places to put his tongue when he eats her out.

It freaks me out how easily he got into my bedroom, how effortlessly he dominated me by pushing my weight into the bed with his. My thighs tremble as I remember the size of his cock and hurriedly gather my sheets for the laundry. I'd better wash them before Rian gets up. I don't want him to see this.

What would I even tell him? The story doesn't sound

believable. Rian has airtight security around his mansion, cameras everywhere and intense facial recognition. I wouldn't be surprised if his brother Aiden had his own surveillance. Whoever could get past all of that could make good on their threats to hurt Tegan. It would kill me if something happened to her.

After successfully sneaking my sheets into the laundry without Rian noticing, I take a quick shower and clean myself up before dressing in a professional, but comfortable modest orange maxi dress. "Modest" still means the dress hugs all my curves. I try to cover up, but it's impossible for people not to notice that I have giant boobs and a big butt. I don't cover up out of shame, it's just frustrating that people think I'm "easy" because of my body or judge me as unintelligent because a woman with big boobs couldn't possibly have a brain.

Last night's encounter with the intruder heightens my motivation to cover up. It's not like I think Rian will know, but it's like a private, personal walk of shame. Why did that freaky experience make me orgasm? Will this psycho really get me pregnant? The thought makes my pussy throb and I tell myself that my pussy throbs with worry and not arousal, which would be too messed up for words.

I don't know what I was thinking saying yes to that man. He's definitely going to be back. He promised that and he might be deranged, but he's not a liar. He could hurt Tegan. *I need to think about what to do when he comes back.* I won't be anyone's victim, but I have to be careful. I can't let myself romanticize a masked intruder. It's like this gothic Victorian mansion is getting to my head or something. Creepy.

Once I'm dressed, I head up to Tegan's room. I can hear her blasting her favorite Katy Perry song *Firework* on her bedroom speakers. Rian went all out with her bedroom decor and she has a private space nicer than any place I ever lived before moving in here. When I knock on her door, she yells, "Come in!"

Tegan sounds more upbeat than usual. I push her bedroom door open and feel like I've walked right into my favorite childhood novel.. The childhood nostalgia is too much. Tegan has Ravenclaw themed bedding with navy blue sheets, and a navy and gold duvet cover. She props up several themed stuffed animals against her giant fluffy pillows — Hedwig, a chocolate frog, Dobby, and a few of the other characters. A music box sits on her dresser playing through the song automatically. Tegan told me the music box was a gift from her Uncle Aiden. It's gorgeous, and fit right into Tegan's bedroom theme.

She bounces towards me to give me a big hug as I walk in and then excitedly drags me to her bed where she has her outfit options for the day. Once she gets dressed, I take her downstairs with her homeschool books so we can have breakfast before we get started. I don't notice any signs of Rian, which means he's been gone since last night.

I've spoken to him several times about making an effort to show up for meal times, so as I fry Tegan some strips of bacon, I get myself all worked up with another lecture I need to deliver to Mr. Rian Murray, a man who won't be sharing any father of the year awards any time soon.

As I flip the bacon and prepare my arguments in my head, I hear purposeful footsteps across the wooden floors that can only be Rian's.

Tegan focuses intently on her math problems, eager to get a head start on our worksheets while I cook. She stops once she hears him coming and folds her arms.

"Great. Here comes Mr. Grumpy," Tegan complains.

I wish they could just... *connect.* I expect Rian to look like his typical grouchy self in the morning and complain that I'm not feeding his daughter broccoli or something healthy, but instead, he's… *smiling.*

Or smirking. I don't know if Rian is completely capable of smiling, but something approximating a smile cuts across his devilishly handsome face. He walks straight over to Tegan and hugs her, kissing his daughter on the head.

"Hello, beautiful," Rian says. He holds her close for a second in the most loving embrace I've witnessed from him since I moved in. When he pulls away, even Tegan looks like she's seen a damn ghost.

He glances between us like he doesn't notice the utter shock on our faces.

"What do you say we skip school today and go shopping, huh? Evie called and told me Marc Jacobs has new sweaters in and you need some new ones, Tegan. Heavyn, you're welcome to join us. I'm sure my daughter would welcome a woman's opinion on her wardrobe."

Rian? Skipping school? My mouth looks like a pond koi's for a few seconds too long until I get a hold of myself. I pause a beat, giving Rian a chance to reconsider. He's not the "fun dad" who skips school. He's the guy who nearly blew up on Tegan for getting too many math problems wrong during her multiplication quiz.

Did he hit his head? He doesn't look any different. He's calm, tastefully dressed as usual in a crisp white shirt, black pants, an expensive belt, shiny shoes and cologne that smells too delicious for words. I can smell his aftershave too from across the kitchen.

Tegan sets down her pen and gives her dad a funny look.

"Do you have the flu?"

"When's the last time I've taken you shopping?"

"Uh, never," Tegan says. "That's not your thing."

"Who says it isn't? Spending time with you is my thing, or it's about to become my thing."

Tegan gives him a skeptical look, but deep down, I know she wants to connect with him. She sets down her pen just as her toast pops up. I start getting her a plate ready as Tegan dances excitedly in her chair. That girl is so damn cute.

"Once she eats breakfast, I can get us ready for an outing," I say to Rian, who has already moved over swiftly to the drip coffee I made for him. He pours himself a gigantic mug and scoops way too much cream and sugar into it.

Rian turns to me with a warm smile. "That's not necessary. I can handle getting ready today."

Rian crosses over to me in the kitchen and says so only I can hear, "I like your dress, sunshine."

Sunshine. My heart skips a beat. I glance over my shoulder at him, but he doesn't have a glimmer of recognition on his face. Rian is as smooth and calm as when he entered the kitchen, but that pet name, that very specific pet name. It can't be a coincidence.

My heart races in an outright panic and Rian appears to notice. He puts his hand on my shoulder.

"Everything okay, Heavyn?"

"Yes, sir," I say, regaining my composure. My reaction to him is completely silly. Rian calling me sunshine doesn't mean he's the man who came in through my bedroom window. That would be crazy. Beyond fucking crazy. He's a mobster, but as far as I know, he was in prison for manslaughter, so that doesn't mean he's climbing in through bedroom windows having his way with women.

Rian sits next to his daughter and strikes up a conversation with her about what clothes she wants or needs, and what else she can buy on Newbury Street. I'm stunned that Rian's in such a good mood and making an effort, so I offer to make him breakfast as a reward for good behavior. Positive reinforcement works great with men.

I can't help looking over at him every few minutes though because of that word he let slip. Sunshine. Did he do it on purpose? Does he want me to know it was him? I'm tripping. Rian is... let's just say, he's not my type. He's the type of dark-haired green-eyed guy they use to advertise vodka. Rian's in the mob. He could have easily disguised his voice — I assume they do that in the mob, but I don't know.

With stolen looks, I have to analyze Rian's size and compare him to a memory that felt almost like a dream. By my rough estimation, it's possible for Rian to be the intruder. The man on top of me felt large and muscular and... well... his dick was....

I was a virgin before last night, but I understand the basics of a penis. I suspect the dick between my legs last night had piercings, several fucked up piercings along the length of the shaft with tiny balls on either side of a barbell. There's no mistaking a dick like that with anything else.

But what the hell can I do with that information? I can't stalk my boss to see if he has a pierced dick and it doesn't seem like the type of information that could slip on accident. There's only one person I can think of to contact about this, but she might just think I'm crazy. I text my homegirl who got me this job, Kamari Roberts, a burning question before I get on with my day.

Me: Do we know anyone with a pierced dick?
Kamari: Uhhhh... not that I know of? Odd question.
Me: I'll explain later

Chapter 6

I'M under no obligation to keep this a secret from Kamari as far as any of the strange coercive contracts I made with the intruder might go. The intruder stays on my mind, even when I don't want him to. I don't feel "traumatized". Shaken up is probably the best phrase to describe the strange sensations traveling through me. I had an amazing sexual experience with a monster and agreed to let him get me pregnant.

How could I let something so crazy happen?

AND WHAT IF the person who climbed through my window is my boss? While we're shopping today, I can search for clues. If Rian Murray is the man who came through my window, then there ought to be signs. *Like a pierced dick?* And maybe there were other clues too, if I can force myself to bring the details of last night tonight.

I'll have to watch him closely today, although I don't know what I expect to find. Knowing what I think is Rian's occupation, I bet he can keep a secret.

I'LL JUST HAVE to be smarter than him, and if not him at least smarter than the man who came through my window.

7

Rian

I forgot that I hate shopping. It's not the act of shopping that bothers me. I love clothes and have all my shirts, jackets, and trousers tailored once I buy them. It's the people I hate. After so much time behind bars, I appreciate keeping to myself now more than ever. I was always the most reserved of my brothers, happy to grow up in the shadows where I could do what I wanted without my parents bugging me. My desire to be alone only strengthened after jail and prison. Most of the men behind bars aren't men any more – they're fucking animals and that fucks with your head.

I just want to be alone.

Newbury Street isn't very crowded, but there are still too many people for my taste. Tegan wants to go into Marc Jacobs first, as promised. Heavyn wanders around the store with her while I sit on the soft leather bench for impatient dads near the cash register. I pretend like I'm not paying attention to them, but my attention is always on my daughter when we're out in public together.

She holds hands with Heavyn, the two of them as thick as thieves despite the fact they haven't known each other long.

Chapter 7

Not even Lucia connected to her like this. She never looked at Tegan the way Heavyn looks at her. They wander through the racks of dresses and Tegan chooses a long-sleeved velvet green dress that Heavyn holds up to her with a big smile on her face.

Seeing my daughter smile makes me smile instantly. My face struggles to contort into what ought to have been a natural state. Life behind bars will do that to you. Showing any weakness, including joy, can lead to some asshole deciding you're a mark and fucking your ass up completely. It's hard to get myself out of that survival state. But fuck... last night was good.

Everything that happened last night makes it easy as fuck to keep a smile on my face. I'm finally turning my mess of a life around.

MY FATHER'S DEAD. I fucked the nanny...

LIFE IS FUCKING GOOD.

SPENDING money on my daughter and bringing a smile to her face only makes this euphoria better. Heavyn helps too, although the longer I look at her, the more I struggle to hold myself together. She demonstrated no signs of recognition this morning, nor did she show any signs of fear. Or trauma.

She knows. She has to know.

Heavyn glances over me and I quickly look away, pretending to be immensely interested in the mannequin wearing a white crop top and jeans. *Fuck, she totally caught me looking.* I keep my gaze on my daughter and the nanny until they approach me with a large stack of clothing. I've never seen my daughter smile so widely.

"She wants to try these on," Heavyn says, putting her hand affectionately on Tegan's back. "Want to come over and watch her fashion show?"

I raise a skeptical eyebrow. A fashion show? That's not exactly my sort of thing, but at this point, I'll do everything Tegan wants to make her not hate me. I don't know if I have a realistic goal here, but no father wants his daughter to look at him with contempt the way Tegan looks at me. "Absolutely."

My response doesn't wipe the smile from Tegan's face, which is even more progress than before. She grabs her items from Heavyn and races off towards the dressing room with the two of us walking behind her. Heavyn seems nervous now that we're alone – and close. Very close. I want to gauge her reaction to standing close to me and appreciate her. She looks beautiful today, especially soft. Especially fuckable.

I shift to a more comfortable stance, calming my cock from the instant erection I get whenever I'm near her. My piercings would make getting an erection uncomfortable for a while but now that they've healed, it's nearly impossible to stop myself once I start on thoughts of... arousal.

Heavyn leans against the wall near the dressing room door. Tegan's in the last dressing room at the end of the hall, giving us enough room for a private conversation.

"Did you sleep well?"

I'm a bastard.

"Perfectly," Heavyn says. "Yourself? You must have been out pretty late since you almost missed breakfast."

She's lying. Obviously. I asked her not to tell her boss about me, and I'm her boss. Still, I don't expect her to be so *strong* about what happened. Right now, she has my sperm inside her. My seed. And she seems fine... Not hurt. Not broken.

You're a fuck up, Rian.

"I slept perfectly, myself. Business was tiring."

"I can imagine," Heavyn says, although she doesn't have much of a clue what my business entails, so I don't know what she means.

"You didn't pick any clothes out?"

"I'd rather save the money you're giving me, Mr. Murray. It's a great opportunity to do what I love the most and stack my paper."

"I invited you," I say to her, still smiling. "I have every intention of paying for you to enjoy yourself. Consider your budget unlimited. Get yourself something nice."

Heavyn balks. "I couldn't accept that, Mr. Murray. This is a *designer* store."

"And you clearly have an eye for style," I respond. Heavyn bites her lower lip and my cock surges painfully in my trousers again.

Her lips are full, fluffy and look insanely suckable. Unlike my brothers, I've never bothered to curtail my tastes for women. I paid for my bullshit and calmed the fuck down after that, but now, my problem is out of the way. *I can have her. I can do whatever the fuck I want.*

"Thank you," Heavyn says. "That's very kind of you to say."

"You sound surprised."

And I sound defensive, but I hope Heavyn doesn't notice.

"With all due respect, Mr. Murray," she says as formally as possible. "You haven't shown much kindness to me, and you haven't been warm with Tegan. She's a special little girl who deserves more than a grouchy, tempestuous father who storms around all day brooding to himself and issuing sharp commands."

Heavyn's comfort with criticizing my parenting bothers the fuck out of me, and she knows it. My dour expression returns and I imagine getting revenge on her later, but her expression matches mine, like she's readying for a fight.

"See?" she says. "There's that fierce look again. You terrify her."

That word hits me like a punch from Darragh. My best efforts to disguise my feelings won't work when Heavyn touches a nerve as raw as that one. My forearms and shoulder muscles tense as the muscles in my face tighten into a blank slate.

"It's not my intention to terrify my daughter, but to teach her the skills she needs to survive in the world."

Heavyn folds her arms and rolls her eyes. "See, if you would just talk to her, you would know that she already has those skills. She can survive just fine without you breathing down her neck. She needs someone to love her. She needs someone she can go to after she's had a bad day and–

Tegan interrupts us by emerging from the dressing room and sprinting to the end of the hall so we can see her. She's smiling gleefully and spinning around in the velvet dress. It's modest enough that I don't have to pitch a fit. Some of the other clothes in here are definitely not age appropriate for a girl going on twelve years old. But this is... gorgeous. My daughter reminds me of my sister Evie on prom night with her giant eyes and that long brown hair.

Heavyn's right. If I want my daughter to love me, I gotta do better.

"You look beautiful sweetheart," I say to her, and I fucking mean it. I don't mean to be a corny fuck, but all that time behind bars, I imagined what it would be like to see

Tegan again and to watch her smile. That damn dress brings a smile to her face that nothing else could and just seeing her smile like that, like for once she only gives a fuck about kid things, makes me tear the fuck up.

I wipe my tears away quickly on my sleeve. Tegan's still admiring her dress.

"Thanks, dad. Can I really get it?"

Heavyn takes the tag from the back and reads the price out loud to me. $395.

"Sure," I say to my daughter. "Why don't you try on some more, sweetheart?"

Tegan shrieks with excitement and sprints back to her dressing room to try on the rest of her haul. Heavyn grins.

"She is so cute," Heavyn says. "I always wanted to have kids of my own someday..."

I suppress my guilty instincts and stick my hands in my pockets. Be normal. Act normal.

"Perhaps you'll meet the right gentleman after your time with us ends," I say to her. "And then you'll get your chance."

Heavyn nods. "My mom always used to say that the Lord works in mysterious ways."

"I can't disagree," I mutter. "What about you, though? Do I have to beg you to buy something here?"

"I don't think they have anything plus-sized," Heavyn mutters awkwardly. "And anyway, I don't own any clothes that cost $395. I'd just mess it up."

I chuckle, not even realizing how comfortable I've become next to her without her doing much of anything but showing kindness to my daughter.

"You? Absolutely not. You're a very graceful woman and I know if you owned something from the great Marc Jacobs, you would take excellent care of it."

"I don't *need* anything," Heavyn says, glancing around the

store, her eyes lingering on a large teal leather handbag that nobody needs, but of course, the majority of women want. I grew up with sisters, so despite being a grouchy fuck, I understand women and I watch her eyes move around the store. Desire. Guilt. It's all wrapped up together in her head.

"What about that handbag?" I say, pointing to it. "That would be lovely with all your yellow clothing."

Heavyn purses her lips and raises her eyebrows. "How did you know I was looking at that earlier?"

She looks so sexy in what she's wearing that it's difficult to contain myself. I would do anything to see her put on half the clothes that are in here. It's not like there's anything slutty, just cute clothes that would suit Heavyn's figure. I'll start her on the handbag first.

"Sixth sense," I respond with a wink that makes Heavyn stammer nervously.

"I couldn't. It's *way* more than $395."

"I'm your boss. I'm commanding you to get the handbag."

"Is that part of my job?"

"Yes, sunshine. It is."

"What did you just call me?" Heavyn asks, now tense and sharp with me. I run my tongue over my lower lips smoothly. I called her that last night. And now, I'm pushing her, teasing her with the name, as if I want her to know it's me.

"Nothing," I say with a smile, lying through my fucking teeth. "Are you gonna get the bag?"

"You called me sunshine," she says, pushing me.

"Did I? I expect it's a common term of endearment."

She gives me a suspicious look and then walks over to the rack to grab it. She breathes a notable sigh of relief once she takes it off. I gesture for Heavyn to hand it to me and examine it.

"Great quality," I say, running my fingers over the leather

before looking at her. "You deserve it for how much life you've brought to my daughter. I can't put a price on that."

Heavyn looks like she's either about to gush or maybe ask me to put the bag back again. I don't find out because Tegan comes out with another dress. This one is a white, collared tennis-themed shirt-dress, which is again, age appropriate. I nod in approval and Tegan dashes in to try on more of her clothes.

"I'll hold the handbag. You get a dress. One dress. Something you can wear everyday."

"Mr. Murray—"

For a woman who has no problem telling me off, she struggles to be even slightly less than formal with me.

"Call me Rian," I interrupt. "It would go a long way with Tegan if I didn't have you on such a tight leash. She's smitten."

"Rian..." she says, clearly uncomfortable with using my first name (discomfort she'll have to adjust to), "I can't expect you to get me a $400 dress and a $550 handbag. That's insane."

"No, sunshine," I respond. "I'm the crazy one. Don't make me ask twice. Get both."

She gives me a look like she wants to say something, but when I give her a stern "you'd better not disobey me" look, she makes a frustrated huff and scurries off. The quiet and reserved nature that she calls "terrifying" comes in handy when I need it to. She walks over to a bright pink dress. Her love of color fascinates me. She's like a honeybee drawn to flowers and as she flits from dress to dress, I wonder how the fuck I'm going to keep myself under tight control around her when I've already lost it.

. . .

My PHONE BUZZES with a text from Aiden.

> **Aiden:** News hit. Mom's devastated. 9 p.m. meeting at her place. Bring booze. Funeral next week.

I GIVE Aiden points for efficiency. Darragh texts me next.

> **Darragh:** Good work.

THEN CALLUM.

> **Callum:** What beer u want for 2night??

MY SISTERS DON'T BOTHER TEXTING me and I don't need a conversation with Odhran. We're too similar and neither of us need to converse. And as for my sisters... I have a tense relationship with Evie, where I'm not allowed near any of her children, and Orla talks too much, so I'm the one who has a problem with her. If she could learn to shut up for more than sixty seconds at a time, I wouldn't mind her quirky ways. I do appreciate that she can so easily get under Aiden's skin, but aside from that... the woman needs yoga.

Aiden, Darragh and even Callum might be celebrating tonight, but I can't say the shifting power doesn't mean the rise of a potentially larger threat — something bigger than any of us can anticipate. And we'll have to perform too. Grief. I might've felt grief before Tegan's captivity, but mercy has been the furthest thing from my mind for far too long now.

I committed myself to vengeance and happily got it. Tonight, we drive the nail into the coffin.

8

Heavyn

Rian and Tegan both leave for tonight. Apparently, they got some bad news. Tegan's grandfather died. She didn't have much of a public reaction to the news, but if she's anything like her father, she keeps things bottled up. Their absence tonight means I'm alone in the mansion. Rian has security cameras and all that, plus my room and window will definitely be triple-checked, but I'm freaking out about the intruder.

See, since the last time, I knew I'd be left home alone again or home with just Tegan, which meant I'd need to be ready for the next time the intruder tried it. For all I know, I might already be pregnant, which would be devastating, I guess. But I could handle that. There were ways to handle that – some more ethical than others in my opinion.

I *had* technically agreed to be a stranger's surrogate. Wasn't there some blame on my end? Ugh. My mind can't get any damn rest. Rian's presence made me all fluttery and nervous, but his absence made it worse. I couldn't stop thinking about the cold expression on his face when he told Tegan that her grandfather died.

Chapter 8

It was like I could see the part of him suppressing all emotions – trying to be strong for her. He told me that he would see me later, which didn't make much sense, since I would be fast asleep after they came back. (I've never been one for staying up late, it would have negatively affected my grades throughout college.)

But Rian had been weird all day. I put away the handbag he bought me, carefully unwrapping it and smelling it before storing it in the cloth bag and box it came with. I also carefully hung the dress he bought. He'd been so sweet and almost… flirtatious.

That wasn't the only suspicious thing. He'd called me *sunshine* three different times. And he wasn't mocking me. See, if he'd been mocking me, I wouldn't have been suspicious. That would have been a grouchy, very Rian thing to do, mock me. But this… was a term of endearment.

Still, I had to be ready just in case the intruder wasn't Rian. It seems like the death of a patriarch in a family as big as his (and most likely with mob ties) would require planning for a big funeral and maybe even division of assets – that type of thing. I'm not an expert, but I couldn't imagine Rian and his daughter returning soon.

My plan proceeds as if the intruder could return at any time. I'm wearing my typical night time uniform – pajama pants, underwear (duh) and an oversized hoodie that concealed my body completely and engulfed me entirely in warmth.

If he is Rian, I'll find out tonight. For one of the first nights of my life, I don't need coffee to stay alert or awake, certainly not the way I needed it in grad school. I stuff my bed with pillows and clothes in roughly the shape of my body, comparing it to a picture I'd taken of myself under the covers with my cellphone by resting it on my dresser across from the bed and setting a timer. Yes, I put a lot of effort into this plan and yes, it got me out of breath and involved a lot of running back and forth.

I need to be accurate so that I can fool an intruder smart enough to break past Rian Murray's defenses. Once I stage myself in bed, I just need to wait in the walk-in closet, just behind the curtain, with my weapon of choice. I have access to the entire house, which I'm sure has guns somewhere, but a firearm seems incredibly risky.

The intruder had come in with a knife last time, so a gun would have given me an advantage that couldn't be beat. My ass has no idea how to use one from a life of growing up in Boston and for a brief spell, New York City. My mom would have popped me in the mouth if I even thought about going near guns.

After searching Rian's house, I find the perfect weapon. I gleefully remove one of the heaviest golf clubs in his study. He doesn't bother locking the study – although he locks the closet safe inside it – so it's nothing for me to go in there and grab the putter. I take a few practice swings in the giant foyer and then hurry back to my bedroom, shutting off all the lights, and climbing into the closet to wait.

Rian and Tegan have only been gone twenty minutes. If someone wanted to strike, now would probably be the best time, as the other occupants of the house were unlikely to return. At least I can count on hearing Rian and Tegan when they arrive. So if I could make it until then without the intruder bursting in, I would count that as a victory too.

It's not like I'm thrilled about having to assault someone. While hiding in the closet with the golf club, I research more about blunt force trauma on my phone. I don't want to kill the intruder, just knock him unconscious, so I have to be careful. According to the articles, I need to hit the intruder's jaw or the back of the neck, or maybe even on the top of his head, which might work if I didn't suspect the man of being well over six feet tall. *Like Rian.*

My throat tightens at the thought of him again. Tall. Powerful enough to be the villain who climbed through my window. *Sunshine.* But he had a different voice.. It just couldn't be Rian. *It couldn't.*

I lose track of time after an hour or so passes. I have my phone face down and silent on the floor of the closet so that I don't reveal my hiding place. The first sound I hear outside of the house's normally creepy ass creaking isn't Rian's car. It's my window. My window creaks open, despite the fact that I triple checked the locks.

Once I hear the noise, panic takes over. But my determination slowly surges and takes over my fear as I hear footsteps, slow footsteps inching towards my bed. I peer through the curtain and watch a giant man moving towards my fake body lying in bed. My throat tightens. Holy fuck, he's huge. The man in my bedroom looks too big for me to knock out. Too big for anything. No wonder my pussy still hurts from his dick.

Motherfucker.

I can hear myself breathing and I sound so loud that I convince myself the man in my room must hear me. But he doesn't. I still can't see his face and then he turns his back to me, approaching my blankets and pillows gathered on the bed. It's now or never. I have to move quickly and strike accurately, before his psychopathic instincts kick in.

I don't know a damn thing about this man. *He could kill me.* If I think too long about that, I'll never act, so I just go for it. I jump out of the closet and swing the golf club with as much force as I can muster. I grunt as I hit him in the back of the head. The man doesn't double over immediately, but it's clear that I've stunned him.

Hitting him again is risky, but he's so large and terrifying in the dark that I make the quick calculation that *not* hitting him would be significantly worse, so I should take another swing. He grunts as I hit him again, but this time, I've done the job.

I'VE KNOCKED HIM UNCONSCIOUS. He doubles over, facedown on my bed. Silent. I'm covered in sweat and my heart races because I technically don't know if I killed him or not. He could be pretending to be knocked out so he can reach out and grab my forearm like in the movies. And then what? He'll know what I tried to do and exact revenge on me.

He won't be kind.

With shaking hands, I move closer to the giant body slumped over on my bed. I touch his back gently and push him. He doesn't groan or anything, so he's definitely out. And he doesn't grab my hand, which brings me some relief. I hurry away from him to my bedroom door and lock it before turning on my lights.

WHO THE HELL just climbed through my bedroom window?

9

Rian

I know I fucked up when I *wake up*. I shouldn't have to *wake up* because I didn't go the fuck to sleep. I came to see her. Tegan wanted to have a sleepover with her cousins and with everything going on and her mood today, I just wanted to make her happy, so I let her go back to Evie's house. Evie shared my surprise that Tegan wanted to go back there, but she wore one of the new dresses I got her and maybe that put her in the mood to socialize.

I don't know.

Fuck, my head hurts. I jerk my arm forward, but it doesn't move. It just flies right back and slams into a wooden headboard. I'm tied up. What the fuck? My throat tightens. I can't stand this. I can't stand the loss of control. I jerk my other arm and that doesn't work either.

Now I'm awake. My eyes snap open and there she is, boiling with rage at the foot of her bed. *Heavyn.*

She stops pacing once I open my eyes and her fierce gaze meets mine. I don't take my eyes off her. I have no control over any part of my body due to Heavyn's shockingly secure

71

knots. She used a mixture of black thongs, brassieres and t-shirts shredded into strips to secure me to the bed. *Christ, she used her damn thongs to tie me up.*

She doesn't take her eyes off me. There's no sense in saying anything. She didn't just catch me – she knocked the shit out of me. The back of my head throbs.

"Rian..." she whispers, turning her ferocious gaze on me. "You have a daughter."

She's breathing heavily and pacing with a bloody golf club in her hand. That explains the slightly damp sensation at the back of my head. She looks fucking hot holding that thing, though she clearly isn't comfortable with it or the blood.

"I promised I wouldn't hurt you," I say quietly after a few more moments of silence where Heavyn only breathes and paces, eyeing me like I'm dangerous.

"You had sex with me!"

I did a little more than "have sex" with her. I gave her an emotional experience. I filled her with my cum. I promised her I would protect her and give her everything that women want. I asked for nothing in return from her, not even lips around my cock. Not her heart. But I'm not concerned. My head might hurt and sure, she might beat the fuck out of me, but Heavyn loves my daughter too much to leave her fatherless.

I can get out of this.

"Yes. We had sex."

"No!" Heavyn hisses. "You know this is wrong, Rian. I could be pregnant. You climbed in through my window under false pretenses and you... What is wrong with you?"

I could spend the rest of the night answering that question. Where the fuck would I even begin? My life started in the shadow of my brothers, Aiden and Darragh. For the first five years, Evie and Orla essentially kept me as their pet until one day during dress-up I melted down completely and beheaded several of Evie's precious Barbie dolls. After that, I tagged along with Aiden and Darragh, realizing that the quieter I was, the less they noticed me, the more likely they were to want me around.

The silence made it easier for me to read people. I could manipulate my brothers and sisters easily and pit them against each other without them realizing I'd pulled the strings. Only one person noticed my talents – and my deviance. *Padraig Murray.* He taught me how to kill methodically, starting with the chipmunks in the backyard. He'd give me $10 for every chipmunk I killed.

Mom nearly left him when she found out he'd started paying me $75 for larger animals he wanted me to kill in the neighborhood – mostly pets belonging to people he thought wronged him. I always did as I was told, even when it made me sick.

I became the quiet son who embraced violence the most, who my father could trust to carry out any orders he gave quietly and without complaint. The older I got, the more I understood that he broke me. My father destroyed my ability to feel so that I could be the perfect killer.

And it worked.

UNTIL TEGAN.

AND NOW... Heavyn slams the golf club on the bed frame.

"Answer me!" she says. "Don't just stare with your creepy fucking eyes."

"I don't know what's wrong," I answer calmly, smiling a

little to show her that none of this truly scares me. "I wanted a baby."

Heavyn looks like she's about to sputter with rage. "You climbed in through my bedroom window because–

I interrupt her, "I wanted a baby."

I blurt it out without thinking but once I say the words, I wonder if I've gone too far. Fuck, I shouldn't push her when I've clearly done enough to hurt her already. Heavyn's already emotionally volatile and messing with her head will only make that even more fucking impossible to deal with. *It doesn't matter if I mean it, she'll see it as cold manipulation. I should have been more careful. I should have known she would suspect me.*

I don't continue or bother explaining myself further because I'm venturing into dangerous territory. Her nostrils flare impatiently. I've never been great with women. Unlike men, women find silence utterly disturbing to their spirits. Women either think I'm mysterious and become obsessed with interrogating the banal details of my existence in the most invasive manner, or they find my coldness intolerable.

Tegan's mother... she thought sex could change me. She thought giving me a baby could change me and don't get me wrong, Tegan changed me, but not in the way Lucia thought she would.

"You know what?" Heavyn responds to my silence. "I don't give a crap what you want, because I make the rules now. Yeah..."

She doesn't sound entirely confident, but she has a tight enough grip on the golf club still that she doesn't need confidence, just a decent swing.

"Why didn't you kill me?" I ask her calmly. "Instead of rules, wouldn't it be simpler to end my life? You claim I violated you–

"I never claimed that," she throws back defensively. "I'm *not* a victim."

"I never said that either. A victim wouldn't have moaned like you did. A victim wouldn't have cum as hard as you did all over my lips..."

Heavyn fumbles the golf club and nearly drops it. I bite my lower lip as I watch her, struggling to contain a chuckle. Heavyn's clumsiness betrays the slightest weakness in an otherwise capable and confident woman.

"Don't throw that in my face. I didn't know what was happening... I..."

Now I interrupt her with more confidence. "You knew instinctively that I wouldn't hurt you. A part of you recognized my scent, my disguised voice, how my weight felt against yours. I required discretion, but I didn't mean for it to hurt you."

"Discretion?" Heavyn squeaks incredulously. "That's how you interpret sneaking into my bed in the middle of the night?"

"There's no need for you to endure the public shame of sleeping with your boss."

Heavyn's indignant face nearly pushes me to rethink my strategy. I have to be careful with her. She's as sharp as I am, maybe even sharper. I never once thought she'd find a weapon in my house that I couldn't easily disarm from her.

"How noble of you," she responds sarcastically. Even when she's angry, she's beautiful. I've never been capable of hiding my tastes in women. I've always blatantly stared with hungry eyes at the women I want, marking them with my gaze first before pursuit. With age, I've tempered my lustful gaze directed towards ample dark brown breasts or thick asses. If I had a shred of morality, I would have demanded that Aiden ship Heavyn somewhere else.

But I didn't. I wanted her in my mansion from the second I laid eyes on her.

I look at her seriously. She doesn't seem afraid, which means that I'm not entirely off about her feelings. I wasn't wrong about her. A hidden part of Heavyn enjoys what I enjoy. Great sex. Sex that's so fucking passionate that it aches. Sex that makes you feel guilty as fuck for wanting it. For enjoying it.

It's almost like I get off on the guilt and the anticipation of having her, especially knowing that I shouldn't have her.

"My life is very dangerous," I say to her. "Do you know what happened to the last woman I was with?"

"Wouldn't that be Tegan's mother?" she asks. Heavyn, for all her outrage with me, has one feature that she can't deny. Curiosity. She's a teacher and fascinated by knowledge and learning of all kinds. When she brushes up against something different, even if it might be fucking dangerous, she shows no fear as long as she can satisfy her drive to peel back layers of secrets.

I nod, piquing her curiosity with my silent response.

"It doesn't matter," she says. "Because maybe I would have never... if I knew..."

She must have known. I gave her plenty of chances to recognize me. I let my voice slip. I called her sunshine. I made her cum... I got in through the window when Aiden walked her through my intense home security himself. No one else but me could have climbed in.

"My father didn't kill Tegan's mother, but he had three guys beat the shit out of her, including my brother-in-law."

I've never told anyone what happened to Tegan's mother, especially not my brothers. Aiden can't handle information like that without losing his collective shit and I've never had that kind of relationship with Darragh. Callum has his own

Chapter 9

problems and Odhran was barely outta fucking diapers when this shit all went down.

Heavyn drops the golf club finally. I relax, despite the knots still cutting into my wrists. She'll get to those in due time. Once Heavyn understands everything, she'll untie me and then...

I'LL GET what I came for tonight.

10

Heavyn

I should probably worry about Rian firing me since I have him tied to my bed. I took his shirt off before I tied him up in case I needed to torture him, but I'm not so sure that was such a good idea. He seems more powerful now without it and he finally gets me to stop dead and release my weapon.

My boss, Rian, just told me that his father had his ex-girlfriend beaten by three men. I drop the golf club – not entirely on purpose. I tried leaning it against something, but then it fell. I stare at Rian, ignoring the fallen club on the ground. Slowly, without taking my eyes off him, I pick it up again.

I shouldn't want to know more, but I do. I guess this makes sense. Rian's wealth obviously came from somewhere and while I don't know the specifics of his mob activity, I'm pretty sure it's shady and might even involve more serious crimes than laundering money – which is pretty serious. He has so much money that his house reeks of it. The Victorian might be old, but it's gigantic and filled with expensive art and vintage furniture that's ornate and handmade. It's tasteful.

Chapter 10

I tried to piece it together before. I assumed he was in the mob and his avoidance of the subject and the specifics of his 'business' made that easy to accept. All I had were assumptions about what Rian's life was about.

Drug dealing, shady bookkeeping and maybe a little money laundering. That's what the mob is about, right? I don't know if I can accept what else he might be up to. Like murder.

My heart pounds. I never bothered asking what happened to Tegan's mother. Rian's previous relationships weren't exactly at the top of my agenda when I accepted the job of looking after his daughter. I found it strange that Tegan never mentioned her mother and seemed unbothered by her absence, but Tegan *is* a strange little girl. She's been through hell, so when she doesn't mention her mom, I assume it's related to her troubled past.

"What do you mean he had her beaten?"

Rian stares so hard that it seems like he hasn't blinked since he woke up. I know that can't be possible. His gaze unnerves me and looking into his eyes always makes me feel weird as fuck.

"My brother Callum went to her house and got Tegan from the babysitter at gunpoint," Rian says calmly. "My father didn't give him an explanation, just told him what to do. Nobody was supposed to know I had a kid but... Well, Callum got Tegan. Her ma calls, flipping her shit at me but I didn't have a clue what the fuck was going on."

"Why not?"

I want to know if they were still together after what happened to Tegan's mother, if they tried to save their relationship despite his family. I want to know if there's a love story there – if there's still love between them. I can't imagine Rian being in love with anyone. I know he's capable of love, despite his fixation with hiding his emotions. I wish he wouldn't hide them from Tegan because that little girl deserves to know how her dad looks at her.

"Prison."

"Oh."

I inadvertently lick my lips as I finally make eye contact with Rian. I don't want him getting in my head. I already dropped the golf club, which puts me in dangerous territory, especially if I take my hands off of it again. If I didn't have Rian's gigantic body tied securely to the bed, I'd worry more.

Examining his bare chest quickly, I detect signs of prison time that I hadn't noticed before. Or maybe he didn't get those scars in prison. I feel a strange chill looking at Rian's chest. He's clearly spent all his time in prison working out. He's super muscular and he looks less lean and more like a bulky hunk of sexy muscle without his shirt on. I felt his body when he climbed in through my window, but I never *saw* him.

Underneath his clean-cut appearance and fancy clothes, Rian's body is apparently saturated in ink. He covers up completely in white button downs and fitted trousers, but with bared skin, I witness every dirty detail of Rian's body. Scars. Lots of scars intermingled with the ink.

Nearly all his tattoos are Celtic with various swirls, knots and Gaelic phrases that I recognize, but don't understand. Then on his chest, inside a tattooed Claddagh is a name – *Tegan*. Right under his heart.

The last thing I need to do right now is romanticize Rian. *Focus, Heavyn.* Unlike me, large spates of silence don't bother Rian. He runs his tongue slowly over his lips and continues.

"Tegan's mother was home alone. I told her to get the fuck out of there but she wouldn't listen and she wanted her daughter. I ran out of minutes and didn't find out what happened until three weeks later. Aiden came to tell me."

It's hard to keep up with my intentions for tying him up with this revelation.

"What did they do with Tegan?" I ask, utterly failing to hide my shaky voice and just how much Rian's story affects me. My mouth is dry and my tongue feels super heavy in my mouth. What the hell have I gotten myself into? The NDA is starting to make more sense now.

"They kept her," Rian says. "And then I got out of prison and my father punished me. I saved Tegan and her mother but... I paid dearly."

"What do you mean you paid dearly? I ask, trying not to sound annoying and frantic, but failing miserably again.

"Unzip my pants."

I glance at Rian's crotch. There's a noticeable bulge, but I can't tell if it's due to Rian's arousal or just the natural state of his dick.

"I-I can't do that."

What happened before with Rian happened while I had my face plastered to a pillow. I could tell myself that technically I wasn't the one having sex with my boss. If I just unzip Rian's pants... Well, I think it's pretty clear what would come from that.

Rian smirks and his confidence bothers me. How the hell can he stay so confident when I hit him in the head and tied him up?

"Trust me, Heavyn. I'm tied up, I can't hurt you. But I also can't unzip my pants on my own. Knots," he says, glancing up towards the headboard.

Yeah, Rian. I know I tied you up. I sigh and recognize that I might be making a mistake, but I move closer to Rian's pants.

"We're not having sex."

"No," he says. "You're not even unzipping my pants."

Cocky bastard. I swallow and work up the courage to touch my boss's trousers. As I move closer, I notice more about him. Scars. Burn marks. His body looks like it has been through hell.

Rian doesn't make any sudden movements, so I undo his belt. He shifts his hips slightly and I try not to flinch or show any residual signs of fear. He can't hurt me and he seems so calm that I doubt he will. He bites on his lower lip as I reach for his zipper. When I have his trousers unzipped, the bulge looks even bigger than it did before. Is he aroused?

Just underwear and a bulge all coiled up like a python. I stared at it nervously, as if Rian's dick could jump.

"You'll have to take my boxers off too," he says calmly in a gentle, soothing voice that makes me want to obey him without question. Rian's silky voice is... irresistible. He's a natural leader and he's my boss, so I'm already biased completely towards following his orders.

But I don't know why the hell he's doing this.

"What's the point of this, Rian?"

"Do as I say, Heavyn. I've fucked up, so I have to tell you the truth. Isn't that what you want?"

That smooth, syrupy, fucking manipulative voice drives me wild. I slide Rian's pants and boxers over his hips and ass, grazing his butt with my hands on the way down. Rian's ass is way more muscular than I expected. When he climbed into my bed, I never touched his body. I felt his weight, his musculature, and Rian's soft lips against my neck, but I never touched him or looked at the parts of a man that I'd always been most curious about.

Grazing his ass causes an uncomfortable throbbing

between my legs. His thick thighs and bare hairy legs are so masculine and then there's... holy fuck. My stomach lurches as I face the irrefutable proof that Rian is...

I grab the side of the bed and try not to let the surprise knock me over. Rian's semi-hard cock has several barbell piercings along the length of the shaft on the underside of his dick. He looks almost alien with the piercings. The strange shape of his cock inside me and the weird rubbing makes more sense. My core pulses again.

I can barely believe I fit that gigantic member between my legs. And as for the piercings. Rian's dick holds my gaze. I can't even fathom how someone would pierce their dick. *Or why...*

He felt good between my legs but I can't imagine a guy putting their genitals through such an immensely painful process just to make a woman cum harder.

I can't find the right words, so I stammer out the same word. "It's... It's..."

"My punishment," Rian finishes with his eerie calm, like recounting this traumatic incident doesn't affect him. He's always so impossibly icy. Except when... Well, except when he's making love but with Rian's dick out in the open, I don't even want to risk thinking about it. We can't have sex again. *Ever.*

"Your father did this to you?"

"Yes," Rian says, running his tongue over his lower lips. "He tied me up in the basement of one of his mansions and took my cock out. He gave me the first one at the base of my shaft to save my daughter's life. It hurt like fuck, but it was either that or... he was gonna kill her."

"Your father wanted to kill his own granddaughter?"

Blood rushes past my ears. This is too much. Too painful.

Is that what happened to Tegan? Did her grandfather hurt her?

"It's not that he wanted to. You don't officially join the Murray *mob* family without taking certain vows and pledging to keep our family white and Irish. Tegan's mom is Puerto Rican."

I have the confirmation I wanted. He's in the mob. But I can't even react to the news since it comes with worse news. It almost sounds like Rian's justifying the most terrible thing I've ever heard and it feels even more inappropriate that his dick is out, bare, and covered in piercings. I can even see tattoos on his thighs that I never knew he had — a knife on one thigh and a pistol with flowers on the other thigh.

"How can you justify that?" I whisper. The barbell at the base of Rian's shaft is the thickest and was probably the most painful. How can he justify this being payment for the great crime of race-mixing? Rian doesn't answer me, but he keeps talking.

"He gave me the next two for Tegan's mother. One as punishment for fucking her in the first place and the second to keep her alive."

"This is terrible."

Rian swallows slowly and his chest heaves. What a deliciously muscular chest. It's not my fault he's almost naked, with just a part of the lower half of his body covered and that Rian looks the way he does. His looks are the kind to make your morals slip your mind.

But there are still three piercings and I know I won't be able to sleep until I know the truth about this complicated, evil man who climbed in through my bedroom window and might be the father of my child.

"No," Rian says. "It's why I wanted to be careful with you. I just wasn't careful enough."

Chapter 10

What the hell does he mean by that? I want to ask him, but his dick completely distracts me from the question. His cock jerks slightly, growing stiff from his movement, the cool air, or maybe something else. I bite my lip and struggle to look away from Rian's growing dick. Feeling him inside me gave me one impression of his size, but the longer I stare at it grow, the more I wonder how the fuck I fit that thing inside me.

"What do you mean, careful with me?"

"Secrecy," he says in that sexy deep voice that I'm trying so hard not to find sexy. "I want to keep you a secret to keep you safe. I screwed up."

"That's how you think you screwed up?"

Rian gives me a frustrating boyish smirk. I can feel the heat rising to my cheeks. He thinks this was being careful? No way. This was the furthest thing from careful and now it feels like we're both in trouble.

"What am I going to do with you?" I ask him. "Should I like... quit? I mean... I can't send you to jail..."

He's right, I can't keep him tied to the bed forever. But how the hell should I have known that the man climbing through my window was my boss? I couldn't have known the cock belonged to Rian.

"You could," he says. "But that wouldn't benefit either of us. You wouldn't get money and my daughter would be sent to live with my relatives. I trust Aiden, but I don't want that."

"Then *why* did you do this?" I hiss at him, trying not to yell. Screaming at Rian won't work. He's too emotionally cool for screaming to work on him. I have to deal with Rian using other tactics.

"You shouldn't have been so quick to discover my identity," he says, like this is my fault. "I considered all this when I

85

planned to give Tegan a sibling. I would have taken care of you just like I promised."

"Did you hit your head before going to jail?"

Rian smirks. "I'm sure I must have. I've also been shot, stabbed, and burned on the top of my thigh. I still maintain complete control of my mental state. Aiden has already screened you for any potential problems. I've observed you for several hours and… you're great with Tegan."

"So you planned to get me pregnant?"

"If we're lucky, you're already pregnant."

Blood rushes past my ears. I can't allow Rian's sexy to distract from his crazy. He stares at me with such intensity that I know he senses my every emotion. Rian having that power makes me fear him more. In theory. Right now, I'm more angry and betrayed than terrified. I still have the upper hand.

"That's not funny," I tell him. "You can't just climb in through windows and get people pregnant."

"I know," he says. "But you're not just people, Heavyn. And since you so cleverly uncovered my plans to expand my family, perhaps we should just strike up a deal."

His cock jerks distractingly. Rian might be able to hide some of what's going on in his mind, but he can't hide all of it.

"What kind of deal could possibly make me look you in the eye again?"

Rian smirks. "You looked me in the eye all day, Heavyn, hiding that an intruder broke into my house and possibly threatened the safety of my family. When you want to keep a secret, you can."

I don't move. I want more than a deal, but I don't know exactly what I want either. My only plan was to capture the intruder. Maybe if he had been some random person, this would be a different conversation. I would have reacted differently.

But I know Rian is in the mob and that he's fucked up. He didn't hurt me. He pushed my limits. He held me down and took what he wanted from me. But he was gentle. And… he made me feel like I was cared for. The surrogacy stuff…

I don't know why I went for that. It was like having that man on top of me saying such filthy things to me turned my brain off and activated this really deep desire to just have a baby. I didn't care that the guy doing it was crazy or that he'd threatened to take the kid. Like hell he would.

My body wanted a baby when Rian was on top of me. Logic wanted something else, but I couldn't deny how utterly he'd melted me when he teased and touched me. My thighs throb. Rian…

It's Rian and that makes it worse, doesn't it?

"My deal," Rian continues. "We continue trying for a baby and continue our relationship as I previously hoped. In front of Tegan, our relationship will be strictly professional. When I need you… *I'll come.*"

His voice deepens ominously. He means that he'll come through my window. What the hell is wrong with me? Hearing that makes my pussy throb again and sends a guilty flush of excitement through me. Rian might be able to read the emotions on my face, but he can't feel the sensations running through me, so he can't exactly know the effect on me.

"This is crazy."

"Which part? The part where we both get to have great sex?"

"No," I snap. "Obviously the baby part. Do you realize how serious that is?"

Rian chuckles. "I have a daughter. So, yes. I care about her too. She's lonely, Heavyn. You won't just be doing this for me."

"Can't you find some girl on Tinder or whatever?"

Why me? Why did Rian choose me? Would he have chosen any nanny who happened to be in this bedroom? Is this just some weird fucked up mind game that I stumbled into? My heart pounds nervously, but of course, Rian is infuriatingly calm.

He smiles and this time, it's not a cocky ass smirk. Something genuine.

"You really think I could replace *you* with some girl on Tinder? My brother actually found a woman who could put up with me. That isn't easy. Now can you untie me?"

"I never agreed to the deal," I say quickly, stopping Rian's attempt to weave his feelings with some form of manipulation.

"Then agree to it," he says.

"I have my own terms," I say firmly. "And I know doing this makes me fucking crazy, so I *really* don't need anyone finding out about this."

"Done," he says instantly.

"Okay," I reply. "So you do that. I still get paid. And when I have your kid…"

"We will worry about that when you have the kid," he says. "Tegan needs a companion. How we… arrange that will be a question for the future."

I glance at the tight knots holding Rian back.

"Promise you won't flip out."

"I just want you to untie me," he says.

HE'S STILL MOSTLY naked in bed and his dick has lost some of its stiffness. I shiver as I glance at the barbells, examining the part of the skin that healed around the metal. *Burned.* That explains some of the skin on the top of Rian's thigh. Some of his tattoos are interrupted by healed stitches from what looks like stitched up knife slashes. *He's been through hell and he has the scars to show it.*

I can't even identify all the scars on Rian's body. He's still the most muscular man I've ever laid eyes on, but the man has the most marked up naked body that I've ever seen. It's even worse than I originally thought. It's like he's spent every minute of his life fighting. I feel nervous when things get quiet for too long between us. My instincts tell me it's unwise to give Rian too much time to plot.

"I'll untie you if you promise me something else," I say to him. My heart races. I don't know if this will push him over the edge. But I have to ask. If we're going to have a baby together or whatever the hell this arrangement is, I have to try to get something that I want and genuinely care about.

"What do you want, sunshine?" he says. *His voice. I knew that voice. I just suppressed it and denied that I knew it was Rian.*

My stomach flips.

"I know you made an effort today, but I want you to do more for Tegan. Bond with her emotionally. Be there for her. If you want to give her a sibling, I want to trust that you will be a good father to both of them."

"I can do far more for Tegan untied."

Yes, Rian. You want me to untie you. I get it. I scowl at him instead of snapping at him, which is very tempting.

"Promise," I hiss at his manipulative ass.

"I will make an effort," he says. "And if you think I'm an unsuitable father... then you will keep our child."

He sounds so confident. But so far, emotional closeness hasn't been Rian's strong point. He couldn't even be himself when he came through my window. Despite his fierce gaze, he's holding something back, afraid of something too. He's not as fearless as he looks. Rian has vulnerabilities and this is the first time I realize it.

"Okay," I tell him. "I'll untie you."

11

Rian

I absolutely hated the loss of control that came with being bound. I spread my legs and swing them over the side of the bed. Heavyn flinches as my feet land flat on the ground. She glances down at them, her eyes passing over my bare cock first.

"You're too good at knots," I respond with a scowl. It's the first time I've taken my eyes off her and I hate it. After our conversation, I feel closer to her and better about my decision. But until I know that I have successfully impregnated Heavyn, I won't be able to get her off my mind.

I won't be able to stand the distraction. My cock is already out, so swinging the situation to my favor shouldn't be too difficult from this point. She's already stared at it. And I still have three more piercings that I haven't told her about.

"I had to keep a 6'5" man contained. I did what I had to do," Heavyn says sassily, moving around me like a tentative predator.

My eyes rove over Heavyn again.

"We should probably add more terms to our arrangement."

"I agree," she says seriously. "You need to be contained."

"No," I tell her. "But you might need to be. Tied up. Spanked."

"Is that necessary for surrogacy?"

"It's necessary for us to have good sex. Our first night was... risky. But better than I thought it would be."

"Wow. I'm glad I lived up to your standards," she shoots back.

Heavyn misinterprets everything that I say.

"That's not what I meant," I respond calmly, like I do to all Heavyn's emotional disruptions. "I thought... your body might not respond to... everything. But you were wet. Extremely fucking wet."

"Rian..."

"It feels good to hear you say my name," I interrupt. "But I would feel a lot better with your mouth around my cock."

"Rian!" Heavyn says, edging closer to me so she can tell me off, but doing exactly what I want her to do.

"Do you only think about sex?" she accuses as she gets close enough to slap me.

"Only when you're in the room, which trust me, is very inconvenient for me."

"You are ridiculous."

Before she knows what hits her, I reach my arm out and grab hers. When you're tall, people forget how long your limbs are and often underestimate how far away they need to be to avoid your grasp. Heavyn makes just that mistake. I grab her forearm and drag her closer to me as she shrieks. I don't mean for her to fall over, but Heavyn clumsily loses her balance and I pull her body on top of mine to stop her from falling.

She screeches and pushes against my chest as we fall backward onto the bed together. She lands between my legs, her thighs rubbing against mine, and my dick instantly gets hard. *Holy fuck.*

Heavyn pushes her way to her feet, and I sit up so she stands between my legs and I sit on the edge of the bed..

"Why did you grab me!? Rian what the fuck."

"I need you to pay attention to me," I say severely. "When I ask you to suck my cock, I expect you to do it."

I didn't ask her before. When I climbed in through her window, I didn't even think about my pleasure. I just wanted to feel her body, cup her gorgeous ass and then enter her. Once I satisfied that urge, my desires bubbled to the surface.

"You can't get your way by pushing me around," Heavyn says. "I have a right to say no to you…"

I scowl at her. "Yes. I understand that. But… I need control in my life, Heavyn."

"You need balance," she says. My eyes flicker to hers. I shouldn't underestimate her intelligence. I already know she's different from other women. It's not just her cute, voluptuous physique or her advanced degrees. She has the special ability to bring the humanity out of me and to bond with my daughter.

She's… *mine.* My nanny. My surrogate. *I'm fucked up and my family knew it when they sent her here. Or maybe dad was the only one who knew how fucking depraved I was.*

"Balance?"

"I'll obey your commands if you respect me," she says.

"And what about my respect?"

"I can't speak to that."

"If I don't get my respect," I announce. "I'll spank you. There, that's settled. Now calm down and get closer. My dick is desperate for you, sunshine."

Sunshine. That nickname suits her perfectly. She loves

yellow. She always smiles. And fuck, she puts a grin on my face once in a while. That's different.

"Rian. We can't just transition to sex right now."

"What else is there to talk about? You look insanely fuckable and my dick aches for you. I ached for you all night. Whenever I leave you in this house... Fuck... Why the fuck did my brother hire you?"

"Because I'm uniquely qualified for the job," she says awkwardly stammering over the words. Heavyn acts like she's never received a compliment or that she doubts the authenticity of the words emerging from my mouth.

"Yes," I respond to her. "That's clear. But I can't stop fantasizing about your lips. So bring them here and then I'll do the same for you. It'll be hard to fall asleep without an orgasm and I'll be taking your little romance novels when I leave."

"I keep those in my suitcase!" she hisses at me. "What is wrong with you?"

I thought we covered that...

WELL, most of that.

"YOU FORGOT ONE ON YOUR NIGHTSTAND," I explain to her. There was no violation of her privacy necessary.

I continue talking to her, "I looked it up and bought it online. That Nikolai... Very inspiring man."

Heavyn scowls.

"I have a right to read romance."

"You won't need Nikolai when you have me to indulge your fantasies. I know you think I'm crude and barbaric, Heavyn... But I want you. My cock wants you..."

"You keep saying that…"

"Because it's true."

I take her hand and gently put it on my dick. She doesn't jerk away from me even if I grabbed her the last time. Heavyn asks me to change my approach, so that's what I do. I run my thumb along the inside of her palm.

"Suck my cock," I murmur. "Let me have the pretty lips I dreamed about all day."

"How the hell did we go from you being tied up to this?" Heavyn says, hesitating from her position in front of my cock. *I can't take it any longer.* I've waited long enough for her and I can't stand it. Tegan isn't here and I have her all to myself. *I need her.*

"Don't ask questions," I murmur. "Just feel how hard you make me…"

"I don't have a choice," she grumbles, as I curve her palm around my dick. Her fingers slide over the barbells piercing my dick, sending impossible jolts of pleasure through me. Heavyn's independent decision making bears some importance to me but I want her to choose me.

I need her to admit she wants this. Or we wouldn't have fit so fucking perfectly the first night I had her. I was sure she knew it was me. *Sure of it.*

"You can walk away," I say, grunting as her thumbs tease one of the six barbells piercing my shaft. "But if you walk away… you lose the money. You lose all the progress you've made with Tegan…"

I loosen my grip on Heavyn's palm, but she never removes her hand from my dick even if she has the power to remove her hand from my cock.

"You can't use your daughter as a bargaining chip to get sex," Heavyn says disapprovingly, her hand wandering aimlessly over the length of my shaft. She's hypnotized by my cock and can't stop looking at it. I gaze at her with fascination. What does she think of it? What does she think of me?

She's the only woman I've been with since my father mutilated my cock. Over time, I've come to appreciate that this was simply the painful price I had to pay for my daughter's safety and the security of our little world.

"You never told me about the other piercings," Heavyn says, her fingers idling over the head of my dick. She wants me to recount my past now?

I'm hard again, but even stiffer than when she first exposed my cock. I'm not a robot. A beautiful, plus-sized woman has her hands touching my dick. Her scent, her hair and Heavyn's touch fire up my arousal and destroy my self-control.

"Now?" I respond, my hand twitching with desire to engulf hers again. Heavyn's palm never leaves my cock. My dick jerks to touch more of her soft palm. She doesn't even have to grip me for intense pleasure to shoot up my staff.

"Yes," she says. "Because if I do this... I don't want secrets between us, Rian. You're asking me to give up my womb for nine months. You're asking me to trust you with something so intimate..."

"Do you want children of your own then?" I ask her. I never thought to ask. I assumed... Fuck, I don't know what I assumed. She's old enough to have children and she doesn't have them. Heavyn's face contorts but then the expression quickly disappears. She hides from me as much as she accuses me of hiding from her.

"It's not my choice," she says again with a clipped voice.

"I see. Whose is it, then?"

Her hand idly strokes my cock and I'll do anything to keep our conversation going as long as Heavyn doesn't stop touching me. I'll even answer her burning questions about the piercings on my cock. But I'll get to that part...

"Men," Heavyn says sourly.

"You can't just get pregnant by yourself," she murmurs to herself, implying that she wants children, but it's not her fault that she hasn't had any because there haven't been any suitable men around.

"You couldn't find a man who wanted to get you pregnant?" I answer, my voice dripping with skepticism. "You must have had *some* man interested in you. A boyfriend. A suitor. Something like that..."

I'm curious about the men I might have to kill. Heavyn purses her lips and gives me a very unfriendly look.

"I didn't have *suitors*," Heavyn answers, wrinkling her nose with disgust. "Despite what men think, not every woman has to chase away hundreds of guys. Some women are simply overlooked."

"I see. Heavyn?"

"Yes?" More frustration.

"You look ravishing. You always have. I wondered if my brother was playing a joke on me by hiring you."

"Thank you. But I'm not a joke."

"No," I answer. "But he must've known that I wouldn't... overlook you."

She bites her lower lip nervously. "The piercings, Rian."

There are three more piercings left. Three more torturous moments that Heavyn wants me to bring to life.

"Put your mouth around the one you want to know about and I'll tell you."

"That is an *extremely* transparent trick."

"I'll give you the truth," I tell her. "But I'm too hard to think. I need... *relief.*"

When I stare at her, she gets fussy and awkward. For a

woman so outwardly tough, open expressions of sexuality appear to make her deeply uncomfortable. She runs her thumb over the head of my cock, unaware of the effect the small brushing motion would have on me. I groan with pleasure, "Fuck…"

Heavyn raises an eyebrow.

"You're that pent up?" She says with curiosity rather than the revulsion I expect.

"Yes," I grunt. "But I'll tell you what you want to know. On your knees, sunshine. Get on your knees."

12

Heavyn

My knees hit the rug in front of my bed with a quiet thud. My chubby thighs stick together and the damp pool between my legs sends shame coursing through me. What the hell is wrong with me? Did Rian break me the first time he was with me by coming in through my window and getting me addicted to whatever twisted dynamic is happening between us?

I had him tied to the bed. I don't have a fucking clue how I ended up on my knees between Rian's spread legs with his pierced dick in my hands.

"I need your lips," he groans, tilting his head back and letting that crop of brown hair fall away from his neck. His body is an erotic spread of masculinity and up close, I can see some of the scars are bullet wounds. He's been shot twice in the thigh. There's a stab wound in his lower abdomen. New details about him emerge the closer I look at him.

His cock pulses with desire in my hands. I've never done this before, which Rian has to know, and he doesn't seem any more impatient than usual, but he is staring. I close my eyes and move my head forward as the warm member throbs again in my grasp.

Rian groans as I wrap my lips around his dick and lower them slowly until I quickly stop against the first barbell piercing on Rian's cock. The soft head of his cock dampens instantly in my mouth and small warm droplets of fluid escape onto my tongue.

"Put your lips over it," he encourages. "Your mouth feels so fucking good."

I slowly put my mouth over the metal. It moves to the side through Rian's skin and my stomach flips. He shifts his hips a little and makes a low, "Mmmm", noise.

"That's the last one. I had to do that one on my own. Hurt like fuck. I had to prove my loyalty and prove that I was obedient. Because it's closer to the head of my cock, I fainted. But I proved my loyalty. Now wrap your lips around me tighter…"

My hands tighten around the base and then I listen to Rian, tightening my lips around him. How can that feel good? I don't understand, but Rian makes more pleasurable sounds. I can't believe this doesn't hurt him.

"Mmm," he groans. "Now move your lips down."

Getting the head of Rian's dick in my mouth was easy at first, but the task of taking more of him quickly becomes difficult. He's so big.

I'm already struggling to breathe through my nose and Rian is *extremely* well-endowed, so I have so much more to go with him. I breathe slowly and move my lips down a little more, struggling to widen my lips around his dick. He won't have to ask me to tighten my grasp on his dick now because the girth of Rian's cock stretches my lips so wide.

I move another inch and then a little further and my lip stops against the next barbell piercing. Rian groans with pleasure and then does something that surprises me. He strokes my hair. Tingling spreads through me from my scalp as Rian touches me. He's gentle. Really gentle. And that surprises the crap out of me.

I easily move my lower lip over Rian's second barbell without him asking. He wraps my hair around his hand and holds me still with my lips suctioned around the first two inches of his cock.

"I wish I didn't have to tell you about this one," he murmurs. "But you want to know, so you can't react."

I want to talk back, but I have my lips around Rian's dick, which he knows perfectly well since he's keeping my head there with an increasingly firm palm.

"I killed someone I shouldn't have," Rian says, his voice dropping to an icy tone. He sounds detached and cold. A shiver runs through me. My tongue flattens against the base of his shaft, causing Rian to shift his hips again. His two barbell piercings shift in my mouth, which keeps getting increasingly wetter.

From this position, he smells so fucking good, which I hate. I have to just breathe through this. I'm nervous because it's my first time, but so far, it's just nerve-wracking, and it doesn't feel bad. Rian's dick feels good and touching him with my mouth feels so... taboo. I guess the taboo feeling might also come from Rian being my boss. And dangerous. And so strangely unpredictable.

"I killed a woman," Rian says. "Several woman, technically. But I don't regret it."

I want to move my mouth, but I can see now why Rian held onto my hair. *Asshole.*

"You wanted the truth," he says. "Don't try to run away from it. Take me deeper princess. I want to feel my cock touching the back of your throat. Your mouth is fucking perfect."

I've never heard him talk so much.

"Deeper," Rian commands when I hesitate. I slowly lower my lips and feel tightening in the back of my throat as I try to push my head down further on Rian's dick. His shaft is at its largest in the middle and the third barbell is the thickest. I can't imagine how he pierced his shaft with something that thick. I have to take a deep breath in before I move my lips over the third piercing, but my mouth is already completely full of Rian's cock.

He's so fucking big. I gaze up at Rian from my position on my knees with half his dick in my mouth, waiting for him to say something or do something.

When I look up, he's staring at me. I don't know if he's been staring at me the entire time, or if he's only looking because he can feel my eyes on him. Rian smiles and I feel a flutter of pleasure in my chest. Making him feel good arouses me. That's new. Different.

My pussy throbs again with an ache for Rian that I can't really deny anymore. He touches the base of my chin and tilts my head up with his cock in my mouth. I have to squeeze his dick tightly so it doesn't pop out of my mouth. The barbells move through Rian's skin again.

"This one was pure fucking pain," he says while looking into my eyes. "Even more pain than I've given you. This one broke me. I can't get aroused without control. Without... intensity. And I'm sorry if I hurt you. This piercing my father ordered done to me over time, forcing me to stretch my dick to fit a thick metal bar through it. He killed the man who did it when he was done."

Rian grips my hair again, holding me still.

"Your mouth feels so good," he continues. "It makes me

forget how much these all hurt. You're the first woman to ever feel my new cock, sunshine... You're very fucking special. But I can't cum in your mouth tonight. I need your pussy."

And with that, Rian removes my lips from his dick. I gasp for breath and with some relief. I didn't think I could take all of Rian's dick in my mouth. I sit back on my heels, my eyes never leaving Rian's face. He smiles again. Because Rian's smiles are so rare, earning one from him feels like a treat, like I'm the only one who sees this softness in him.

He keeps touching the base of my chin. "That was excellent," he says. "When I'm ready to cum in your mouth, I will. But not tonight."

Rian drags me to my feet and then pulls me against him. He kisses me. On the lips. I'm shocked, but immediately melt against his mouth because I lose control of my body's responses to Rian. He's a damn good kisser. His lips are ridiculously soft and are fuller than I expected. He grabs my cheeks and pulls me closer more possessively. His fingers clutch my cheeks desperately and he doesn't loosen his grip until his tongue moves into my mouth.

He continues kissing me more possessively until my lips feel sore and my pussy is completely soaked.

Rian stands up and I take a step back away from the bed. I don't know what he's planning on next, but I don't feel scared. I just don't understand.

"Why do I feel like this?" I whisper. "Why do you feel... good?"

He takes my hand and presses it to his bare chest. If there was any space left between us, it's gone. Rian's dick pokes forward against my clothes. My leggings aren't thick enough to block the intense sensations of his cock rubbing against me.

Rian smirks again, but he doesn't answer me. He swoops forward and scoops me up. He lifts me like it's effortless. I know he's big, but I never pictured myself getting picked up and swirled around like the petite girls in the movies. I always thought I was too big for that, but Rian doesn't even grunt as he picks me up and we tumble towards his bed.

I land on my back and grunt loudly as Rian's weight presses into me. Memories of our first night together flood back into my head. I gasp and Rian's lips press against my neck. My hands press against his chest instinctively as I attempt to force him off me. If he notices me pushing him, Rian doesn't act like it. He sticks his tongue out and runs it along my neck before finding a spot to suck on so hard that he forces me to moan.

He shifts his body just enough that his weight on me feels more comfortable. I can appreciate his broad muscles, his firm stomach and his dick pressed hard against my thighs.

"Rian..." I whimper weakly, still pushing him.

"I'm sorry," he grunts. "I'm not leaving you tonight until you cum..."

He lifts my sweatshirt and kisses all over my stomach. I flinch and try to wriggle away but Rian easily pins my hands over my head, pressing me into the bed and running his tongue from the base of my bra over the curve of my stomach to the top of my mound.

He tugs at the waistband of my underwear with his teeth, holding my hips firmly as he slowly tugs my underwear and leggings down over my thighs. I wriggle as the fabric slides over my legs, making me shiver.

I whimper and push my toes against Rian's body which does nothing to move him. He drags my underwear off with his teeth and as I attempt to push his head away from my pussy, Rian sticks out a tongue that seems impossibly long.

Chapter 12

He slides it between my lower lips and I moan loudly as he wraps his tongue around my clit and sucks on me like an ice pop.

I moan and drop my hands away from his hair. Rian's tongue feels too good and I'm so fucking tired of fighting. I had him tied up. I had everything under control.

THAT WAS ALL AN ILLUSION, clearly.

RIAN SPREADS my thighs and teases my clit by swirling his tongue in slow circles. My body heaves with desire and I want to stop myself from moaning loudly, but I can't. Rian eases my thighs wider and runs his tongue over the length of my pussy, kissing all over my lower lips and then pushing his tongue against my entrance.

He can taste me and taste how wet I am, which still makes me nervous. My hot boss has his tongue in my pussy and it feels... *good*.

"You taste delicious," he grunts before massaging my clit again with his tongue until I can't hold back an orgasm anymore. When I cum, I feel a gush of juices coming out of my pussy. Rian licks my juices up from all over my thighs and then grunts with desire as he sucks the juices off my outer lips.

I moan again as Rian's tongue makes me cum without him even touching my clit. When I cum again, he grunts and pushes an index finger against my entrance. I shudder and moan, which Rian interprets as approval. My heart races as I remember the first time he touched me and how good it felt.

Rian pins me down again with his free hand and then thrusts his index finger inside me. I cry out as Rian's finger enters me deeply. He swirls it around like he's mapping my pussy with his finger and getting to know it. Just when I think I can't stand the pleasure of his finger inside me, he adds another one and I cum instantly.

I'm sensitive. *So fucking sensitive.* He pumps his fingers inside me, massaging my walls and focusing on the spots of my pussy that are the most sensitive. Rian makes me cum again with two fingers and then removes them, pushing his fingers into his mouth.

"Mm," he grunts. "You taste fucking good."

He kisses my pussy again and then moves his hips to mine while re-aligning his his to mineAs he kisses me, I taste something weird and salty. Maybe a little sweet. My throat tightens. It feels weird to taste myself, but Rian doesn't seem embarrassed by it.

"Like how you taste?" he murmurs.

There's a part of me still shy about staring my boss in the eye and talking to him about this stuff. It's so personal and intimate. And how will he react to all of this in the morning?

"Don't be shy," he says. "Tell me."

"Yes," I stammer, because beneath Rian's gaze, I feel powerless to do anything but agree. "I taste good."

"I want to feel you, sunshine," he murmurs, pinning me down harder to the bed. "I know how wet you get when I hold you down and fuck you hard. But if you want me to stop… all you have to do is ask.""

I shudder as Rian spreads my legs open and caresses the flesh on my thighs. He's so strong that he can move me effortlessly in a way I don't think most men would be able to do. My heart flutters as he eases his fingers towards my clit again. Rian's fingers feel rough at first but when he starts moving them, his touch feels gentle and arousing. I move my hips to meet his hands, losing myself in Rian's touch.

I close my eyes but when I do, he stops touching me and demands, "Look at me, Heavyn. I want you looking into my eyes as you cum."

Despite the pressure building between my thighs, I force my eyes open. Rian hovers over me powerfully and resumes stroking my clit as he presses the head of his dick against my entrance.

"You took my cock before," he murmurs. "But it might still hurt. I'll go slow."

My heart races as he removes his fingers from my clit, leaving me both desperate for orgasm and terrified about what his dick might feel like a second time. I remember losing my virginity with pain. There was pleasure too, but it's hard to forget the initial pain that goes along with your first time.

Rian kisses me tenderly, in a way that didn't feel contractual. I shouldn't let his behavior confuse things. The pleasurable feelings from sex are just a bonus. All he wants from me is a baby. And to relieve whatever pent up energy he built up behind bars.

He doesn't seem to mind that I close my eyes when we kiss, but he forces me to open them as he presses the head of his cock against my entrance and slides inside me up to the first barbell. He groans with pleasure as he stretches me wide around his dick.

"You are so tight," he gasps. "Holy fuck, it's incredible..."

Rian presses his weight into his forearm as he hovers over me and then he moves his hips forward to push the first barbell inside me. It's a slightly different sensation from the first time he climbed in the window, but still familiar. Still slightly painful. I emit an unwilling moan, which turns Rian's skin bright red.

I hate that I have no choice but to notice every small

detail about him from the sea-green color of his eyes to how his skin flushes and how his brown hair sticks to his pale neck. He has a scar there too, but no tattoos. I can't tell if the scar is from a gunshot wound or a knife — I'm no expert — but it looks healed, so it's probably old.

When he catches me staring at him, examining his body as he slowly slides another inch inside me, Rian closes his eyes and kisses me again. He craves my vulnerability but when it's his turn, he shuts his eyes. He pulls away. It's not fair.

I've given him so much, and yet I'm still giving even more.. He stole my virginity and he's going to give me my first child.

I won't let Rian run away. I tilt my head away from the kiss and gasp, "Look at me. I want to..."

He keeps his eyes shut and cruelly thrusts his hips forward so that several of his piercings massage my inner walls as he enters me. There's too much euphoria for me to focus on anything but his dick entering me. I squeeze my eyes shut and cry out. Rian presses his lips to my neck and then... he bites me. He keeps my hands pinned to the bed so I can't fight back. I have to yield to Rian's cruel pleasures.

I moan as he pushes deeper inside me. His bite hurts at first, but the possessiveness of it gets me so hot. Pain pulses through my body from more of Rian's piercings entering me. It's not just that he has six barbell piercings rippling through his shaft. Rian has a large and thick member that would be difficult to fit inside me on its own.

He stretches me completely and everything about him is so large that it forces me to submit to Rian without protest. He eases up on biting my neck and kisses me softly instead. Rian grunts as he buries the rest of his dick inside me and I cry out loudly.

"There you go, sunshine," he growls. "Feel my big cock inside you. I love how tight you are. I love your soft stomach and your thick thighs... You get me so fucking hard..."

I don't know if he wants me to respond to his dirty talk. His dick fills me so much and the pleasure is so intense that forming words is out of the question. I moan and buck my hips to meet him. *I don't know why I want him. This is completely messed up, but I can't deny that I'm attracted to him.*

"I love having you trapped beneath me," he murmurs. "Knowing that you're all mine..."

He withdraws his hips and thrusts into me slowly, smirking with delight at the mixture of pleasure and pain across my face as he fills me with his dick again..

"I love how you moan when I fuck you slowly," Rian says. His voice is like butter and it's sexy enough to make me cum hard.

"You are so fucking pretty when you take my dick," he says. I bite my lower lip as I try to slow down. It shouldn't be this easy for him to make me cum. Does it make sense that I saved myself for all these years only to get completely turned on by the most depraved fantasies of my mafia boss?

"Look at me," Rian commands, sensing me getting distant. He demands closeness on his terms and his terms only. He frustrates me, but he's also so fucking beautiful that I stare at him instinctively the second he commands it.

He thrusts into me as we gaze into each other's eyes. It's so intimate that I can't hold back for long. I cum hard on Rian's dick, my pussy getting tighter and convulsing as I finish around his dick.

He feels so fucking good. Once I finish, Rian kisses my neck and moves his hips between my legs, making love to me slowly. He takes his pleasure from me with my hands pinned above my head. I cum twice before Rian gets close to finishing. His cock gets stiff between my legs.

"I want a baby," he grunts. "Fuck, I want a baby."

His face reddens and his dick swells between my legs.

"I wanna give you a fucking baby," he growls as he cums. Rian edges his hips forward so he buries all of his dick in me and a hot jet of his seed spills out of his dick. He releases my hands once he finishes and grabs my cheeks to kiss me. His dick keeps pumping cum between my legs as we kiss.

Rian holds me and kisses me for a long time before rolling off of me. My chest does a little thump of guilt and confused expectations. I don't want him to run off. We just had sex and hormones are raging through me. I want to cuddle. To kiss him. But I don't have any right to ask for that from Rian. He's my boss and the contract we made doesn't include relationship stuff.

He rolls off of me and onto the bed next to me, but he doesn't leave. He lies on his back with his brow furrowed.

"I'm not that much older than you," he says, seemingly out of nowhere. "Under other circumstances... well... Fuck, I don't know."

He looks over at me expectantly, although he never formed a complete sentence. He just gazed at me with wide, creepy sea-green eyes.

"What does that mean?"

I don't want to let him off the hook. He's already been secretive and mysterious enough. And he wanted me to have his baby.

"It means," he says. "I'm staying here tonight and tomorrow we return to our professional relationship. I'll send you a text when I'm coming back or... maybe I'll surprise you."

"Your idea of a surprise scares the crap out of me."

Rian grins again. I've never seen him smile this much in such a short space of time. It's crazy how handsome he looks when he smiles. Rian reaches over and touches my cheek.

"It also gets you wet. That makes it easier to get my cock in you."

"Send a text."

"I'll send a pregnancy test too," he says. "We shouldn't have to try too many more times. When did you last have your period?"

"Do I have to answer that?"

"Yes," Rian says. "I need to know that this is working."

"I haven't. But don't expect me to update you on my period. You're still my boss when the sun comes up."

Rian raises an eyebrow. "Do you make the rules now?"

"I have to make some of them," I say sternly. My heart flutters nervously. I don't know how Rian will react to my defiance. He's made it clear that control is the most important thing to him.

"We'll see," Rian says. "I'll leave to get Tegan in the morning. Come closer. It'll help you get pregnant if you bask in my hormones."

"That sounds disgusting."

"I read about it in an article," Rian responds sleepily. "Don't make me ask twice. Women need cuddling after sex, anyway."

"And you don't need it at all, I suppose?" I mutter sarcastically while scooting closer to Rian.

Rian drags me closer to him, ignoring my last sentence and burning his nose in my neck.

"I'm tired," he murmurs. "So sleep with me, Heavyn. Just... sleep."

· · ·

IT's easy to get sleepy in Rian's arms. He's gigantic, warm, and an amazing cuddler. He has a broad chest, perfect for snuggling against and his arms never got tired of holding me against him. His chest moved with steady breaths that made it easy for my eyes to flutter closed.

When I wake up, Rian is gone. I might have thought the entire night was another delusional sexual fantasy if he hadn't left plenty of evidence of his presence. I'd hit him hard enough in the back of the head for him to bleed a little and he'd stained one of my pillows with the blood.

I grimaced at the sight of it, partly guilty for how hard I'd hit him. Yes, he'd snuck in through my window but technically, this is his house. He thought I recognized him the first night. How the hell could he have thought that? The guy is totally fucked up.

I don't know why I cum so hard when I'm with him. Rian introduced me to sex and maybe he got in my head with his roughness and raw masculinity. Because it's what I crave. I put my hand on the side of the bed where he was and my stomach flips. I can't get any ideas about him. Just because he's good in bed doesn't mean I need to take him seriously.

He's just doing this to sweeten the pot to our little deal and I'm doing this because... well... It's not like I have anything else going on in my sex life. I don't have a boyfriend and I've never had one. I've never even been asked out on a date. I've never been special enough for anyone to have a crush on. The closest I came to dating someone was a guy in college trying to get close to me so he could get to my best friend — who had a boyfriend at the time.

Rian is probably the only chance I'll ever have to get laid. What do I care if he's using me? I roll over away from the spot where he slept and try to get Rian out of my head for the time being. When I get up and put my clothes on, I find

Chapter 12

more evidence of Rian's presence. He stood the golf club up against my dresser and left a note.

He wrote in cursive on a piece of paper:

I'll see you downstairs bright and early for breakfast with Tegan.

This afternoon, I'll take her to the park so you can get the pregnancy test from the medicine cabinet downstairs and find out.

I'll be in touch soon.

−R

P.S. Rip this up and throw this out. Kids are nosy.

I ROLL MY EYES. If I were Rian, I wouldn't have even risked a note. But I do what he asks, ripping it up and throwing it out before panicking over what to wear to breakfast. I've faced him before with a big secret, but this time, it's different.

Keeping a secret from Tegan will be different. Can we really get away with it? Should we even try to get away with it?

I shake thoughts of "coming clean" with anyone out of my head. Rian doesn't want to "come clean" about me. He wants to use me as his surrogate due to convenience and then send me on my way. I can't be foolish enough to romanticize him.

Heavyn

13

Rian

Heavyn and I spend five weeks living together pretending we don't have more than a professional connection. It hurts, but I have to play it cool. It's not all bad because I feel like for the first time, I'm making progress with Tegan. Heavyn does her job perfectly and my daughter has fallen in love with her nanny entirely.

My daughter and I spend time together now without fighting. Heavyn helps with that a lot. She understands Tegan in ways that I don't. When I watch how she acts with my daughter, I learn how to be gentler. I've never met anyone as gentle as Heavyn before and it hurts not to be close to her. Not to touch her.

But I have to wait. When she finally texts me, her words hit me hard. I never expected to care this much, but I do. I instantly know I've made the right choice once I see her message.

I'm pregnant.

. . .

SHE WAITED until I left for work to text me. Judging by the time, she must have just let Tegan outside for a break. It's amazing how much Tegan has come out of her shell the past five weeks. Watching my daughter heal little by little with Heavyn's help gives me hope that I didn't screw up completely with my kid.

I just need to stay out of jail. My fingers hover over the keypad. It's big news. A text message doesn't seem like enough to celebrate it. But I have to say something to her. *Fuck, Rian. You're crazy.*

But I'll have what I want. Heavyn's a good girl. I could tell the second she walked in through the front door of my house for her job interview, the first time I saw her with Tegan and when I first made love to her. Women have a harder time finding a good man than men do finding a good woman.

She'll be a good mother. And... we'll have plenty of fun together while she's pregnant.

I'm never going back to jail. I can't.

I'll see you after Tegan goes to bed tonight.
11 p.m.

SHE DOESN'T RESPOND to the message — she just does that new thing with the hearts on the message to show that she "likes" it. Whatever the fuck that means.

"Are you done?" Aiden growls at me. He hates when I text on the job, but I get nervous leaving Tegan and Heavyn alone. It's my job to care for both of them and Aiden isn't here to give me good news. I can tell, because he's extra red and cranky.

"Yes," I respond calmly, putting my phone into my pocket. "I had family business to attend to."

Aiden doesn't seem like he believes me. But I continue to act cool. I don't need trouble with my older brother. He's the most hot-headed and difficult to deal with.

"Mom's depressed," he says. "She wants you to visit her."

"I don't want to visit."

"Why not?"

"Well, Aiden. I killed her husband. It's a bit awkward."

"She's your mother," Aiden snarls. "*Our* mother. Christ, you are so fucking stubborn."

He gets up from the leather chair in the corner of my office. The casino I own is open nights, but I work during the day managing the accounts, watching the money and handling the bigger business moves in a very comfortable office that would be a lot more comfortable if Aiden wasn't raging over nothing.

"Don't you think you're overreacting?" I ask him. "She's grieving. Let her cry it out."

"Do you have a soul, Rian?"

I shrug. "Does it fucking matter? I do the shit nobody else wants to do. Let me catch a fucking break. I've got my daughter to worry about. If mom wants to see us so badly, she can leave the house and come down to Brookline."

"You know she hates leaving the house," Aiden says. He's a mama's boy, I swear. If he weren't the boss of the Irish mob, I would consider slapping some sense into him. Instead, I stare, holding back all my emotions. They're useless when dealing with my family.

"So does Tegan," I tell Aiden. "She comes first."

"Fine," Aiden says. "But she keeps asking."

"Did you seriously come all the way down here to tell me I need to visit our mom more?"

Aiden knows I struggle to hold onto the relationships in our family. I come around a couple times a year, which is more than plenty. Nobody misses me much either. I'm too quiet. Too... different. I don't want my mother to pester me about Tegan. I want my daughter and I to heal on our own time.

"No," Aiden says. "Obviously not. We've got a problem. Well. A potential problem."

"I see."

"Darragh got a phone call today from an unknown number with a disguised voice and a recorded message. He's a paranoid fuck, got his girl to record the call and I thought I had to tell you in case... there might be something to it."

I wait patiently for Aiden to continue. He seems hesitant to tell me the contents of the phone call, which surprises me. But I just wait for him to finish.

"Whoever sent it is threatening to exterminate the Irish mob and our families. But... dad received threats all the time. There might be nothing to it."

"You seem too calm about this."

Aiden shrugs. "We should watch our backs, but we won't live in fear. I have Callum working on tracing the caller. It shouldn't be more than a couple days of him working his connections. Can you stay out of trouble until then?"

"I don't know. Can you?"

"Don't get smart, Rian. I worry about you," Aiden says. I sense that he's genuine. Over time, my doubt in Aiden and my family subsides. But he worries too much. I took the burden of our biggest problem – our father.

"We shouldn't worry," I tell Aiden. "I have Tegan on a tight leash and her nanny understands our need for security."

Chapter 13

"How is the nanny working out?" Aiden asks. "I haven't received any complaints which has... startled me."

"I'm not completely out of control and Tegan's a good girl. There hasn't been trouble."

Aiden gives me a smirk that makes me a little uncomfortable. He can't possibly know about what's going on between us and even if he found out – I wouldn't apologize for it. I've been behind bars with very little access to women and I need to be careful about the women I allow into my daughter's life.

Heavyn's safe. Aiden assured me himself that she was the right woman for the job.

"Good," Aiden says. "You might have to give her more information if the threats become more... real."

"We shouldn't worry about receiving threats. We should be making them."

Aiden chuckles. "Haven't you spent enough time in prison?"

"I have. But we have brothers and people loyal to us. I don't mean to overstep my role, Aiden, but I want you to consider what's coming ahead. I've had a lot of time to think... A lot of time."

"I appreciate your insight, Rian. Truly. But right now, we don't need a warrior. Focus on your family. Focus on your daughter. If I need more from you, I'll let you know."

I have to accept my brother's words. I don't like the sound of threats any more than he does, but I believe in our strength.

"Is there anything you need from me right now?"

"Stay out of trouble. Don't kill anyone."

Murder is the last thing on my mind. Heavyn just texted me the best news I've received since I found out about Tegan. I want a bigger family and I want it with her.

"You don't have to worry about that."

Aiden gives me a suspicious look. "There's something different about you."

"Nothing for you to concern yourself with," I tell Aiden. "Call me if you need anything."

He raises an eyebrow, but gives me the benefit of the doubt. After a quick goodbye, Aiden leaves my office and I'm alone with my thoughts. My excitement. I can't wait until 11 p.m.

I have to make tonight special to celebrate. *My sunshine. My surrogate. Mine.*

How will I ever let her go once the year is up?

I already know I can't.

14

Heavyn

Rian is nothing but professional to me when he gets home at 6 p.m. He looks damn good when he walks through the door and I feel like I'm living a fifties housewife fantasy. I even have dinner ready on time (by pure coincidence). He hardly looks at me when he walks through the door, but Tegan explodes off her chair to give her dad a hug.

They've been getting closer, which gave me mixed feelings about the news I told Rian today. I've been wanting to celebrate since I took the pregnancy test that Rian slipped into my room this morning. I'm pregnant. I didn't know how I would react to the news. The three minutes waiting for the stick to change were the hardest of my life.

I wanted to tell Rian before anyone else. I texted him, but now I feel guilty for not texting anyone else. It's like we have a big secret and it's one that could bite me in the ass. How are we going to explain a baby to Tegan when I start showing? *We need to talk.*

I convinced him early on that he could get all the work done for the casino during the day and be home in time for dinner, but we still have several hours of pretending that we have nothing more than a professional connection in front of his daughter.

He rolls his sleeves up once Tegan breaks away from their hug.

"What's for dinner?" Rian asks, giving me a warm smile that I can't read any deeper meaning in. I glance away from him quickly to avoid betraying how weird and fluttery he makes me feel.

"I opened one of the recipe books and made some Tuscan chicken with sun dried tomatoes and pasta."

"That sounds good but... Italian. I don't want Tegan eating too much Italian food."

Tegan rolls her eyes. "What's wrong with Italian food, dad? It's good."

"You're Irish. You should eat Irish food."

Tegan wrinkles her nose. Rian's insistence that we add Irish history alongside American history in her home-schooling program has improved Tegan's knowledge of her culture. Unfortunately, she doesn't seem very impressed.

"Who wants to eat potatoes all the time?" Tegan says.

"We don't just have potatoes," Rian says. "Keep talking like that and I'll send you off to Ireland for the summer."

I glare at him. Maybe don't threaten to send your trauma-tized daughter to a foreign country, Rian. Tegan, luckily, doesn't seem affected by his threats. She's too excited for the Tuscan chicken tonight to care about her dad's typical grumpiness.

"We're having chicken, dad. Heavyn worked *really* hard on it," Tegan says.

"Did she now?" Rian asks. Thanks, Tegan. I try to ignore the fluttering in my chest. I don't answer and just serve dinner to distract everyone. Yes, I put extra effort in but I blame my pregnancy, not my wanting to impress Rian. I don't care if he likes it. I made it because Tegan asked anyway.

"Yes," Tegan says. "It's delicious. I love pasta. I don't care if it's Italian."

"Hm," Rian says. "I'll give it a try."

"You'd better," Tegan says jokingly. Her dad leans over and kisses her cheek. Tegan giggles and gives him another hug. They seem so close. I wonder if Rian is doing the right thing with this surrogacy plan. I never know what to make of my interactions with him.

He's not the type of guy you tell your friends about. I can't imagine my college friends like Kamari understanding that I let my boss climb through my window and get me pregnant. I can't tell anyone about my pregnancy, what happened with Rian, or my new complicated feelings about him.

As I eat, I think about his text message instead of my internal panic. He always seems like he's in control. I never feel like that with him. I guess that's how he likes it. I glance over at Rian as I eat, but he isn't paying any attention to me. I'm his surrogate and his nanny, not his girlfriend or wife. I have to know my place. *I'm getting paid well enough to know my place.*

I don't have to worry about Rian enjoying the food. He has seconds. And then third helpings. Tegan enjoys her helping of chicken and pasta, but saves room for dessert unlike her dad. Rian doesn't eat anything sweet. After dinner, I clean up while Rian and Tegan play ping pong together in the basement. I hear Tegan shrieking with laughter and occasionally Rian's smooth voice travels up from the open door.

They're a family and when I have Rian's baby... where does that leave me? Tegan is a curious kid and we're close. I don't want to lie to her, but I can't exactly explain my relationship with Rian to her. He won't want me around once he has his baby and a better relationship with his daughter anyway. Tegan will start school and I don't know what will happen to me.

I'll go back to my old life, I guess. My old, lonely life. I don't want Rian to know how much I dread leaving here already. It's not like he would care. I'm just a womb for him to use, not someone he really cares about. It's not depressing or anything, just reality.

I should just be happy I got to experience something close to romance once in my life. I really thought all hope was lost. At least I had sex. Good sex.

That makes it all worth it.

As Tegan's bedtime gets closer, Rian strides past me out of the kitchen as he parts from Tegan for the night, walking up to his bedroom with the sleeves of his white button-down rolled up. He doesn't look me in the eye at all. I shouldn't care, but a part of me thinks it would be at least *nice* for him to acknowledge me.

Tegan heads upstairs to her bedroom to get ready for bed while I finish cleaning up in the kitchen. As I walk up stairs to say goodnight to Tegan after finishing my cleaning, I feel my phone buzzing in my pocket. I check my phone and see a text from Rian.

All I could think about during dinner was bending you over and watching you take my cock.

Chapter 14

MY HEART RACES. What is he thinking texting me something like this right now? I reach the landing and knock on Tegan's door before shoving my phone into my pocket a few seconds before she opens her door. She likes me to put her nightlights on for her before bed. It's one of her strange habits from the traumatic experience she had.

My phone buzzes again.

"Is that a boy texting you?" Tegan asks curiously while petting Camilla, who's sitting next to her on the bed. Tegan's fingers disappear into Camilla's white fur as she purrs loudly.

"No way," I lie to her instinctively. "Just... Kamari."

"Oh. My mom is crazy," Tegan says.

"I'm sure she's not crazy," I say to her. I don't know much about Tegan's mother, but judging by what Rian said happened to her, I don't want to judge her too much. It doesn't feel like my place at all.

Tegan gives me a "get real" look that makes her look a bit older than she is.

"Okay. Whatever you say," I tell her. "I'm not gonna argue. I'll just put the lights on and wish you good night."

Tegan gives me a big hug. She's such a sweet girl. I hug her back tightly. I can't believe I'll have to leave in nine to ten months. After my baby's born.

"I love you, Heavyn," she says. "You're my best friend."

My heart nearly breaks into a million pieces. "I love you too, Tegan."

HOW THE HELL am I going to leave her for good? I give Tegan one last kiss on the forehead and then she climbs into bed on her own. She hated going to bed alone before, which wasn't normal for a girl her age. I'm happy that she feels safer. I give Camilla some love before I turn towards the door.

She mews and tilts her head up so I can give her better scratches.

Tegan loves going to bed with her little cuddle buddy. I leave Tegan's door cracked just the way she likes it, and head towards my own bedroom. I have so much time before Rian comes to my bedroom.

On my way there, I check my phone again. That second buzz was another text from Rian.

I expect a response, Heavyn.

I ROLL MY EYES. Rian knows I'm busy right now.

My boss wouldn't approve of sending those types of texts on the job.

ONCE I ENTER MY BEDROOM, I fool myself into thinking that I can put my phone on my nightstand and ignore Rian until he inevitably climbs in through my window or (more recklessly) comes straight through the door.

You're off the clock. Send me something juicy.

Chapter 14

I'M TEMPTED to run downstairs and send Rian a picture of a glass of orange juice. I have until 11 p.m. to get myself in a somewhat mentally stable mindset around him. I can't just fall into bed with him now that we have the big news. We need a plan.

Why did I think he wouldn't get me pregnant? Part of me wanted to indulge Rian's fantasies, telling myself that I wouldn't get pregnant the first time or it would take several months of regular effort. Getting pregnant was apparently extremely easy.

I guess since I'd never had sex before, the risks of pregnancy didn't seem real enough to me. *I'm too naive about guys to be mixed up in this.*

I know he'll text me again if I don't reply quickly, so I delay Rian's lust temporarily.

Like what?

HE DOESN'T TAKE LONG to respond.

Your ass in a thong.

I'VE NEVER SENT a guy pictures like that before and his text sends me into an instant state of panic. I have a thong — one — and it's not that sexy. It's simple and black and my ass swallows it completely. A lump forms in my throat. My phone buzzes again.

Heavyn

. . .

You get my cock so hard.

MY HEAD SWIMS with nerves again. I slip out of bed and into a thong, which I wear beneath the giant hoodie that I like to sleep in. Rian told me to expect him at 11 p.m. He didn't ask me to dress up — until now. I walk into the bedroom's en suite bathroom and examine my butt in the mirror.

I've always felt self-conscious about my ass. It's not that I mind being plus-sized and thick now, it's the bullying I endured as a kid. It's hard to let go of it, even if I try to feel confident. Boys would make it a game to smack my ass as hard as possible. Whoever hurt me the worst considered themselves the winner. Girls made fun of me for being big and ugly and for never wearing the "right" jeans because I couldn't even get my butt in jeans.

I bite down on my lower lip and tilt my butt to find an angle that makes me look like a Kardashian. What a joke. My ass could swallow Kim Kardashian's entire body. But home-girl does know how to pose. I try a couple poses I've seen on Instagram, but I don't look like Kim K. Hell, I don't even look like myself.

You're beautiful.

Chapter 14

SCREW IT. I keep trying my best to get a good angle and I send the picture to Rian without overthinking it. He sends several heart-eye emojis in response. He really is a millennial...

I climb back into bed with my phone on my nightstand, waiting for Rian to say something after the heart-eyes. If he texts me anything else, I don't hear my phone buzz, because I fall asleep. The next sounds I hear are footsteps which I immediately recognize as Rian's.

"Good night, sunshine," he says, announcing himself as he prowls the floor of my bedroom.

I didn't mean to fall asleep. I sit straight up and turn my lamp on. Rian stands at the foot of my bed.

"What are you wearing?" I ask in surprise, taking in every inch of his clothing. He's holding a flat black box with a red ribbon in his left hand.

"Something for you."

He's wearing nothing but black boxer briefs and a black masquerade style mask. He's nearly naked already, making it clear what he just climbed in through the window for. He doesn't want to talk.

"You look..."

Stunning? Fucking hot?

"Good," I finish. It's the best compliment I can manage. He looks too good for me to form complete sentences. Rian promised a special night tonight and judging by his apparel, special means something kinky. The type of kinky you read about in romance novels and think... *no way*.

I can't stop staring at him, but Rian sticks the gift out for me to take it, forcing me to stop staring at his abs and marked up body. I grab hold of the box. It doesn't feel heavy, but I still can't tell exactly what's in it.

"Open it now," Rian commands. "I want you to wear it."

He doesn't remove his mask as he watches me pull the ribbon. Rian. If he wanted to disguise himself, he could do better than a mask. I could never mistake his sea-green eyes for anyone else's. Once I remove the lid on the box, my stomach turns.

I've never worn anything like this in my life. Plus-sized women don't wear lingerie. At least... that's the message I always received growing up. It wasn't just from guys either. The messages came from my mom and my aunties. They were all big growing up, just like me, but that didn't stop them from mocking other women with our body type and making me feel like I wasn't ever going to be *that* girl. The sexy girl.

The girl Rian wants me to be.

"I'm not really a lingerie type of girl," I say, trying to make it sound like a moral stance or something. Rian stares at me.

"Hm," he says. "I think you are. I spent a fair portion of my day tracking down the correct size and fit to ensure this would fit your body perfectly. Try it on."

I gave him a look that I intended to be fierce. He was already pushing my limits by forcing me to face this insecurity. I could accept that he wanted to sleep with me or get me pregnant for his own purposes, but I struggled to believe that Rian wanted to see what I looked like in lingerie.

"I'm fat, Rian."

Rian chuckles. "That's not... bad. But I prefer using sexier words like... thick. Or just sexy."

"You can't possibly want to see me in lingerie."

He leans forward and kisses me. It's soft. Too sensual for our relationship. He's kneeling on the bed now in front of me. I can see his bulge pushing through his boxers. It hits me how badly I want him, but I don't know if I can put myself out there the way Rian wants.

Chapter 14

I don't know if I'm meant to be... sexy.

"You have nothing to be insecure about," Rian says calmly. "I knew what you looked like when I climbed into your bed the first night and since then, I've only wanted more."

Rian doesn't know what it's like to grow up the way I did. I can't imagine anyone looking at this man and thinking he was anything other than drop-dead gorgeous.

"You know, I'm generally a confident person," I say to him, trying to pick myself up. I hate this about myself. My insecurity. I dress well. I like how I look in clothes most of the time. But sharing my body with another person requires crossing a level of insecurity that I'm not sure I'm even prepared to acknowledge. "I just... I'm not that sexual of a person."

Rian snickers. "Agree to disagree."

"I'm not," I protest, my heart racing.

"I want to see you," he says. "Indulge me. Or... I'll have to punish you for being so disobedient."

He grins, which makes him look terrifying in the mask. Maybe that's the point — not to disguise himself but just to make this entire experience darker and kinkier.

"You are not going to punish me."

"Good," he says. "Then get out of bed and put that on."

I step out of bed with the box, not because I originally plan on listening to him, but because I completely intend to throw the box at Rian's head and attempt an escape out the window. Like he can read my mind, Rian steps off the bed between me and the window I would have used to escape.

I can't run away from this. I either choose the lingerie or whatever twisted thing Rian considers to be punishment.

"This is how you want to celebrate?" I ask, giving one last

half-assed attempt to back out of dressing up in lingerie in front of my boss.

"Yes," he says. "I've been waiting to see you all day so I can see you in this outfit and then fuck you in it."

He's staring at me with such earnest eyes. They're the main features of his face I have to focus on, so I stare back at him, which Rian doesn't seem to mind. I take the lingerie out of the box and hand the empty box to Rian who responds with a half smile. I can already tell that he won't budge until he gets what he wants.

Even if he's more talkative in the bedroom, the dark-haired man in front of me is still my grouchy and very demanding boss.

"I'm warning you," I tell him. "I'm not going to model or be the type of girl—

"Quiet, Heavyn," Rian says. He rarely says my name when we're together instead of *sunshine,* so I pay close attention when he says it. "No more insecurities. Ditch the pajamas and show me... everything."

"Everything?"

"One item of clothing at a time. You can drop the sweat-pants first," Rian says. "I want to watch."

The tingling between my thighs intensifies when Rian speaks. He sits on the edge of the bed with his legs spread in a wide stance as he gazes at me expectantly. He wants me to strip for him. I set the lingerie on the edge of the bed next to Rian. He runs his tongue over his lips as I take a few steps away from him and then face my dresser instead of watching my boss stare at me as I strip for him.

I don't want to see his reaction to me. Unfortunately, Rian has other plans.

"Turn around."

"I don't need you seeing everything."

"Wrong. Turn around."

I turn around, not bothering to hide my frustration. Rian just smiles like he's won some type of victory already. I still have my sweats on, so he hasn't won anything.

"What?" I say to him, wrapping my arms over my breasts, suddenly self-conscious about everything and wanting to do what little I could to cover and comfort myself as Rian forces me to do his bidding. My self-consciousness appeared to frustrate the hell out of him.

"No more self-consciousness," Rian says. "No more hiding. What are you afraid of, Heavyn?"

"Nothing."

"You never seemed insecure about your body before," he says. His voice is gentler now. He wants this badly enough to slow down and listen to me. It's strange and makes my heart flutter uncomfortably. This seems like the kind of moment you have with a boyfriend — not with your boss.

Not with a mobster.

"I'm not. It's not about my body completely. It's about how other people react to it. I like myself. I like myself a *lot*. But I understand guys have an idea about how they want their dream girl to look and... it's not like me."

Rian chuckles, which frustrates the crap out of me, because I'm clearly not joking at all.

"What the hell is so funny?" I say to him huffily.

"It's not funny exactly," he says, "Odd, maybe. Because you don't have to look like anyone's dream girl to be fucking hot. Who gives a crap what other guys think, or anyone else for that matter? You're beautiful, sunshine."

My chest does another flip when he calls me sunshine. It's the last shred of confidence I need to take my clothes off in front of my boss in a lit room while he's wearing nothing but a mask and boxers. (He still hasn't explained the mask.)

Once I take the sweatpants off, Rian's body tenses and a tent forms in his pants with a slow, steady growth. I can't face away from him without provoking a negative reaction from Rian, so I hold steady and strip in front of my boss, working hard to shed my nerves about getting naked.

I thought facing Rian would make the process more nerve-wracking, but he nods approvingly once he sees me in my underwear.

"More," he says. Rian's sexy voice could convince anyone to do anything. He just has one of those especially deep voices like James Earl Jones. Rian's voice could melt the panties off a nun.

More of my clothes come off until I stand in front of Rian in just a bra and underwear. Now I'm really nervous. My stomach sticks out, in the front no matter how I stand. I'm not one of those women who can suck in to hide her features. Every part of me is out there and sometimes I feel beautiful but other days, I don't.

I never had a guy want me like this until Rian. He visibly responds to my nudity with pleasure. With his mask, I can't see his cheeks change color, but I can guess. His dick pushes through the fabric of his boxers and his tongue runs over his lips again in his typical unconscious reaction to seeing me in a state of undress.

"You already look good enough to eat," he says. "But before we get to that… lose the bra, sunshine."

15

Rian

Controlling myself tonight will be incredibly difficult. I don't want to unleash my desires and my love for her all at once. I've always struggled to hold myself back and if I push Heavyn too far, I know I can lose her. I can be... *intense.*

Women bond closely when they make love. It's my greatest pleasure to be the one Heavyn bonds to. Her first. Her everything.

She stands in front of me wearing nothing but a bra that could never hope to support her ample breasts and underwear that her gorgeous figure swallows the fabric everywhere it meets her skin. I never want her to doubt herself.

"Take the bra off," I command again. "Hurry."

She undresses quickly and then her hand darts for the lingerie resting on the bed next to me. I don't want her to cover up so quickly.

"Stop," I tell her, changing my mind about hurrying now that I can see her. I push Heavyn's hands away. "I want to appreciate you."

"I'm cold, Rian," she says, covering her exposed breasts

and nipples with folded arms. Her hair hangs in loose waves in front of her and Heavyn's smooth chocolate brown skin instantly gets me hard. Her body is just a bonus.

"I don't care," I reply sternly. "Move your hands so I can see you."

She rolls her eyes, but sensing my stubbornness about tonight, she removes her hands exactly as I ask her to. My cock nearly escapes my boxers as I observe every inch of Heavyn. God, I'm a fucking stereotype. Rich guy fucking the nanny. *I fucking like it.*

I'd rather that stereotype than being a drunk Irish fuck stuck behind bars.

"You're fucking hot, Heavyn. So fucking hot it hurts. Now put the lingerie on. Let me see your sexy ass in something... lace."

She reluctantly reaches for the lingerie. This time, I let her take it. She holds it up and fusses with the fabric until it faces the right way. Heavyn makes a confused face as she holds it up. The entire process is ridiculously fucking sexy. There's something disturbingly arousing in watching a self-conscious and innocent woman turn into a sex goddess by slipping into something dirty that she would never get caught dead wearing on a regular basis.

She slips into the one-piece black lace sculpted shapewear that I chose especially for her because I thought Heavyn would look beautiful and she deserved something luxurious. She makes several different facial expressions as the fabric slips over her smooth brown skin. I love her skin color. I never had my brother's aversion to women of Heavyn's skin color.

The opposite.

I didn't care if guys made fun of me for the type of girls I liked. I didn't care. I was always quiet and kept to myself anyways, so I didn't need the approval of other men. My particular tastes never failed to satisfy me. Heavyn does beyond that.

I love how the clothing pushes her breasts together.

"Come here," I command her. "You look fantastic and now... I want to examine you more closely."

She seems to enjoy how the clothes fit her more as she takes a few steps towards me.

"It's really soft," Heavyn comments, running her hands over the lace and accentuating her hips and stomach. Her softness drives me fucking wild and makes me want to do every thing possible to bury my cock in her. *I want her so fucking badly.*

"You look really soft," I murmur, grabbing her hips once she's within arms' reach and pulling her towards me so I can kiss her breasts through the sexy black lace. Heavyn gasps as my lips touch her breasts.

"Rian..."

"Don't fight it," I murmur. "Feel how sexy you are."

I kiss Heavyn's soft breasts again, enjoying their size and everything about them, and then I whisper, "Feel what your body does to me."

I give her a moment of relief. Heavyn's hand moves obedi-ently to my cock. Her touch makes my cock jerk aggressively in my boxers. She moves her hand away.

"He doesn't bite."

"I know," she says. "But it looks so much bigger than I remember."

"Hm," I murmur. "I'll remind you how big I am later. Come here, let me touch you some more."

I rise from my seat on the bed so I can play with Heavyn's body in that delicious black lingerie. She's soft and I want to grab her everywhere, especially her delicious thick ass. Once I touch Heavyn's butt, my desire to get inside her heightens.

"I want to eat your pussy."

Before she responds, I kiss her on the mouth. It's been fucking painful to avoid her lips for so long, but kissing her feels good. It's like I'm breaking the seal on lust I've kept pent up all day. I want to eat her pussy, kiss her pussy and take her to bed all night. We're going to have a baby now.

This changes shit. This changes *me*.

Heavyn whimpers as I tilt her neck to the side and run my tongue along the length of it. She moans loudly as I kiss her there. While kissing her, I don't stop touching Heavyn's perfect ass. I want to bury my face in that tempting ass…

But not tonight. Tonight is about *her*. I lift Heavyn off the floor and spin her around so she's the one with her back to the bed. She doesn't squeal or show outright terror this time. She clings to my neck like she trusts me to protect her. Her trust in me makes me want her even more. She does things to me I never imagined she could.

It was the news. I'm pregnant. Her announcement made me realize what I selfishly truly wanted. *To own her completely.*

I toss Heavyn onto the bed, unable to take my eyes off her in sexy black lingerie that I bought specifically for tonight. I have no explanation for the mask. I just want to keep her excited, on edge and constantly wondering about what the fuck I'm going to do to her in the bedroom next.

Orgasms are more exciting when you don't have a fucking clue how you're going to have one.

She gasps as I slip my finger past the lingerie and feel how wet she is. Heavyn has all the excitability of someone new to sex. It doesn't take much to get her dripping wet for me, just like the sight of her can get me instantly hard. Despite dreaming about her lips around my cock, I owe her something more special.

With my finger teasing her lower lips, I kiss her thighs and spread them open, showering appreciation all over Heavyn's bare flesh. Her thick thighs jiggle with each kiss and touch. She seems to nervously want to keep her thighs closed, but I hold them open so I can kiss them. All I want to do is put my tongue on her and in her.

Heavyn moans as I massage her clit with my fingers and I can't wait any longer to dive inside her. I rip the lingerie with one swift motion. I don't care if it's expensive at the moment. I just want the primal satisfaction of ripping clothes off my woman. It's our special night.

"Thank you for giving me a baby," I whisper and then I run my tongue over her clit slowly, giving Heavyn the tender pleasure that she deserves right now. I spilled my seed between her legs and now we can celebrate what I've waited patiently to hear. *Good news.*

She moans as my tongue swirls in a slow circle.

"I can't wait to fuck your pregnant pussy again."

Dirty talk gets Heavyn even wetter than before. I love watching her get soaking wet for me, but I don't just want her juices on my tongue. I need her to cum.

"Thank you," I whisper again before eating her pussy like my life depends on it. I lick and suck on Heavyn's lower lips until she pushes her fingers through my hair and struggles not to press my face into her pussy more forcefully. I eat her vigorously until she gets close to cumming.

When I feel Heavyn approaching an intense orgasm, I hold her thighs down and push two fingers inside her as I eat her pussy. With two fingers between her legs, Heavyn completely loses control. She cums so hard that juices squirt out of her pussy all over my hands. Her orgasm is so loud and her body shakes the bed as she experiences her pleasure.

I push my fingers deeper. I love her juicy pussy. Heavyn moans again. Holy fuck, this is hot. I can't wait to fuck her pretty pussy until she cums even harder.

"You... you ripped it," Heavyn whimpers, concern about the lingerie becoming present once she comes down from her orgasm. Even in a flushed and aroused state, she always *cares*.

"I had to eat your pussy," I whisper as I kiss her thighs and spread her juices everywhere. "But I'm not done. I want you to cum at least three more times, sunshine..."

She doesn't hesitate to keep her thighs open after the first time and I lick her honey pot until she cries out and has several more orgasms. Once her thighs are completely soaked and my dick is so hard it feels like it's going to break, I hold Heavyn's hands above her head again and position my body on top of hers.

My baby. My woman. Fuck, this does something primal to me. I've never wanted any woman this badly. I need her.

I kiss Heavyn's neck and massage her pussy more before I ease my boxers off and rest my cock against her soaking entrance. She's so slippery that my shaft slides between her lower lips, adding excitement and anticipation to the moment. I nearly cum before I put my dick in her pussy, but I hold back with complete effort as the barbells in my shaft tease her clit.

Heavyn moans and bucks her hips against my dick. I love feeling her rub herself against my dick and use my shaft to pleasure herself. Watching her moan and squirm with delight beneath me makes me feel like I'm finally getting into her head, getting her addicted to my cock.

"I can't wait to feel how tight and wet you are," I growl into Heavyn's ear as I press the head of my dick against her perfect entrance. Her softness makes me lose all sense of myself. I thrust my entire cock inside Heavyn without thinking about the impact on her tightness. I just have to feel her. I need her. She moans loudly as my body pushes against hers and my cock touches the back walls of her pussy.

Her tightness squeezes the life out of my cock and I catch my breath, desperate not to cum too early. She just feels so fucking good.

"I love knowing you're pregnant," I murmur as I move my hips slowly between Heavyn's soaked thighs. She spreads her legs around me and submits completely to me as I pin her to the bed. Heavyn's scent surrounds me completely and I revel in it as we make love.

"You smell so good…"

She responds with a loud moan and I stop it with my lips. As I kiss her, my hips move slowly between Heavyn's legs. She can't stop herself from cumming as my barbells massage her inner walls. Her body joins perfectly with mine and Heavyn's softness draws out sensitivity in me that I'd long tried to suppress.

I want to feel her hands on me, so I release them from my grip and kiss Heavyn slowly as I tease her pussy with slow strokes and draw her into another state of utter euphoria. Heavyn touches me gently, making it harder to hold back my pleasure. Her hands trace over my scars like she wants to love them. She touches old bullet wounds, stab wounds that healed in prison, stab wounds I *got* in prison. My tattoos.

It's like she's right here with me at this moment, feeling what I feel. That she's more than just a surrogate. That there's a chance this weird fucking thing I did is leading to something.

"You're so hot, baby," I whisper. "I love the way your pussy feels."

My heart swells with emotion as she moans back and touches my face, dragging her hands through the reddish-brown stubble on my face. She likes it. Heavyn's pussy grips my cock tighter as she touches my face and I keep my slow steady pace as I kiss her neck. Every sensation heightens as I plunge my dick between her thighs.

I don't have control anymore. Emotions rush through me as my balls tighten against my body.

"I'm gonna cum," I growl. "Fuck, you feel so good."

My cock jerks as hot fluid erupts into Heavyn's pussy. Cumming inside her fills me with absolute euphoria, a deep sense of happiness that I thought I would never experience again. At one point behind bars, I'd decided to be alone forever. Once I got out, I thought all I had to live for was Tegan. If I could just focus on her and the work I gotta do for the family, everything would be okay.

Our bodies move together slowly as I kiss Heavyn and allow my cock to grow soft inside her after I cum. My emotions have never been more intense than this. I hold her soft body against me and words spill out of me before I can get a hold of myself.

"I love what you've done for my daughter," I say slowly, my heart pounding as my gaze fixes on Heavyn's cinnamon-brown eyes. They look almost black in the dim light, but that doesn't make them any less beautiful.

"And I love... you, Heavyn."

What the fuck did I just say? I don't want her to answer. I kiss her and withdraw from her. Heavyn props herself up on her elbows, clearly stunned. Her full lips open slightly and my cock jerks just from taking notice of her pretty mouth.

She's staring at me expectantly, like there's something else I could punctuate that statement with that would make this better.

Chapter 15

"That's the sex talking, Rian," she says in a completely flat tone. I can't tell if she's trying to convince me, or if she's trying to convince herself.

My heart beats so fast that it feels like blood is rushing past my ears. I maintain control of myself in most tense situations from one-on-one fights to gun battles, but this time, I'm spiraling. I let myself go with her and intense feelings that I didn't think I could have for another person rush out of me. *Fuck.*

That was never part of the plan. I don't know how to explain my emotions, but Heavyn's resistance to them makes it harder for me to express words. I just scowl at her, which I know doesn't help. She stares back at me, still confused.

"Rian... you can't..."

"I know what I said. Maybe it's just the sex talking but it doesn't feel like it. You are... special."

Heavyn scoffs too immediately. "I'm not."

"Bullshit," I growl, leaning forward and taking her lower lip between my teeth. I won't let her scramble away from me or worse, kick me out. I kiss her slowly, but Heavyn pulls away.

"I'm just your surrogate, Rian," she protests. A dark urge to possess her completely rises in my chest. I don't want to let her go and tonight, I won't. I grab the small of Heavyn's back and pull her body close to mine. She's not going anywhere.

"You're mine," I growl. *Not just my surrogate. Mine.*

16

Heavyn

Rian and I make love three more times before he finally exhausts himself from celebrating. I don't want to sound greedy or ungrateful, but I'm new enough to sex that I got exhausted much faster than he did. It's hard to say no to orgasms and it's hard to say no to Rian's body.

But maybe I should have said "no" to his proclamations of love. I didn't respond... I just let him make love to me several times. He said he loved me more than once but... I think it was just the good news overpowering his emotions. Rian really wants a family and he's mistaking his desire to make his daughter happy for... all types of things.

But this isn't love.

It's a bad idea, that's what it is. Once we're done making love, Rian lies next to me on his side, staring at first. I turn to him with a serious expression.

"Why do you look like you plan on falling asleep here?"

He drags my comforter over his naked ass and covers himself up to his shoulders. Rian has a *great* ass. It's big, muscular and very attractive compared to most guys. He gestures for me to come over and cuddle.

"I'm not cuddling, Rian," I answer.

He grins at me and he looks like a little boy when he does it. Rian's smile has never looked so cute before and he's never looked so innocent. The resemblance between him and Tegan seems super strong, which fills me with complicated emotions. Rian's staring doesn't help. I know I should probably get used to the staring from Rian, but his new proclamation of love makes it even more nerve-wracking to look at him.

"Yes, you are," he says. "I don't bite."

"I know that but... what about secrecy? What about Tegan?"

"She's sleeping," he whispers, drawing me close to him and utterly melting my resistance. "We have a few more hours before she wakes up. It's nothing to worry about."

This is too risky but... It's Rian. He's too tempting for me to stand much of a chance against his efforts at persuasion. Rian is physically attractive, we just had more sex than I thought two people could have in one night and... he wants me close.

I haven't let the news of the pregnancy hit me the way it's hit Rian. Maybe it's because I know this baby won't always be mine. Since he made me sign an NDA, he'll probably have a contract drawn up once he has proper confirmation that the baby will make it to full term and I'll have to give up the child he wants me to celebrate.

But cuddling...

Cuddling might not fix everything, but it can definitely fix my heart feeling like it's torn in different directions. I move closer to Rian and he wraps me up like I'm precious, hugging me close. I've never been cuddled like this before and the flood of emotion from having Rian's body pressed against mine is nearly too intense for me to stand it.

I shudder and turn away from him, nuzzling my butt into his crotch. He pulls me closer.

"Perfect, Heavyn," he murmurs. "Now close your eyes. Let me hold you. I think we both need this…"

I can't argue with my need for cuddles. I want to pretend that I'm above such things like needing the body of a strong man to keep me warm at night, but after our night together and all the vulnerability shared between us, fighting the urge to push Rian away is too difficult.

He's caught up in the moment and thinks he loves me. Where's the sense in denying him this when I've already let him cum inside me several times tonight and put his tongue all over his favorite forbidden places. I try to move away when he puts his tongue in my butt but eventually, I just give in to the arousal.

As I press my ass against Rian's crotch, I feel his cock throbbing against my butt, but not coming back to life. He makes a low growl of pleasure in my ears.

"I love how soft you are. Cuddling with you is… Good."

He sounds sleepy, which makes his voice even sexier than it was previously. My pussy throbs and I don't even want to sleep. I want to stay in this moment with Rian as long as I possibly can because even if I can't let myself believe any of this is real, it's the closest I've ever had to real and I want to soak up every part of it while I can.

Some people never find love in their lives, much less have their mafia boss confess his love to them while they're in bed together. I also never thought I would ever lose my virginity, especially in this way. I don't know how I got here, but I nuzzle in the crook of Rian's arm and try to appreciate his scent, the warmth of his body and everything else about Rian Murray.

I doubt I'll ever experience anyone or anything like him again.

WE SHOULD BE ALONE. Safe. Peacefully entangled with each other. So when I hear a loud strangled shriek, I jump straight out of bed. I have no thoughts, just *get up*. I fling my legs over my side of the bed with a blanket covering my completely naked body, and nearly throw up when I see who just walked into my bedroom.

"Daddy!" Tegan shrieks, her voice sounding shrill and confused. "Daddy!"

Rian groans and moves his arm slowly so it's touching my thigh. I quickly smack it away and shove him.

"Rian, wake up."

Tegan finally draws her gaze away from her father and looks at me. She seems confused. Hurt. And I'm naked in bed with her father, frozen in guilt as Rian finally sits up and mutters one useless word.

"Fuck."

The room gets quiet and all I can hear are the sounds of Tegan's heavy breathing and then Rian sighing and trying to form words. After a few seconds of silence, Tegan yells, "God, I fucking hate you, you fucking asshole!"

It's a colorful string of words for a girl her age. She sprints out of the bedroom. Rian climbs out of bed and mutters a series of expletives that explain how well Tegan takes to colorful language. He's naked and his cock smacks against his thighs as he struggles to find sweatpants so he can hurry after his daughter.

This is bad. *Really bad*. Tegan should be asleep. I swore I locked my door. How did she get in here? Panicked thoughts rush into my head. I can make all the excuses I want but at the end of the day, that little girl who trusted me woke up to find me in bed with her dad.

I can hear Tegan racing through the house, tearing across to her bedroom just screaming. Rian chases after her, his powerful footsteps bounding down the hallway.

"Tegan…"

His low voice disappears as he enters her room. I find enough clothing to seem somewhat respectable. Shreds of the lingerie Rian ripped off me lie on the floor right near where Tegan was standing. My stomach lurches with the complete humiliation of it all.

I race down the hallway after Tegan and Rian. Once I leave my bedroom, I can hear their loud fighting clearly.

"You ruin fucking EVERYTHING!" Tegan screams. I hear something shatter in her bedroom. I hope it's not her golden snitch lamp. She loves that thing.

Rian, naturally, handles her screaming in exactly the wrong way. I stop in my tracks in the hallway as I hear him say, "If you don't be quiet right now, I'll put you in my car and take you straight to a goddamn boarding school."

Tegan lets out a fierce wail. A sharp instinct twists in my chest. I have to get to her and hold her and I don't care if I've fucked up or if her dad loves me or if he's being a complete asshole right now. Rian stands in the doorway, his face nearly purple with anger as Tegan continues throwing items across her room.

She's too far away to actually hit her father with any of them, except a Hedwig stuffed animal, which lies at Rian's feet. I push my way into the doorway next to him and ignore his completely indignant look. Tegan hasn't even noticed or acknowledged my presence. She's just as red as her father and she seems twice as angry as he is.

They rile each other up so much and it's mostly Rian's fault. He's the grown up here. Tegan's the kid. It doesn't matter that he spent time behind bars or that he was a kid himself when he had her. He is all she's got in this world and he has to act like it. I step in front of Rian boldly and call her name in a firm but kind voice to get her attention.

She's had tantrums before, but none as bad as this. Her room is completely trashed and she looks more like a caged animal than the sweet little girl I bonded with.

"Tegan."

She looks at me and then her face softens. I expect her to be completely outraged with me, but she just seems sad. I give her a warm look, trying to connect with her, trying to show Tegan without words that she will always be my girl.

I take a step closer to Tegan and that seals it. She runs over to me and wraps her arms around me. Rian makes a gruff, impatient sound in the back of his throat. What the hell was he thinking threatening to send his daughter to boarding school?

Tegan's chest heaves the second her body contacts mine. A big hug brings her emotions out and she cries in such a heart-wrenching way that my guilt surges to an insurmountable level. How dare I do this to her and then try to comfort her. I feel like a horrible person. Tegan sobs and holds onto me.

"Don't go, Heavyn... I don't want him to make you go..." she sobs.

Rian makes another gruff impatient snort. While holding onto his daughter, I give him an especially fierce look over my shoulder. No more huffing like a damn goat. Instead of acting like he's still in prison, he should be more like he is with me when we're alone. Gentle.

Where the fuck is that guy?

"I'm not going anywhere, cutie pie," I tell her. "You're my girl and I won't go."

"Yes, you will," Tegan says. "He makes everyone go away."

Rian suffers through Tegan's comment without making another grumbling sound, which I give him the tiniest amount of credit for. Just when I'm about to lose hope in Rian completely, he sighs and says, "I'm sorry, Tegan."

She ignores him and keeps her face pressed into my shoulder, emitting another sob. I can feel her wet, warm tears soaking into my hoodie.

"I shouldn't have lost my temper," Rian says. "Heavyn... May I speak with my daughter alone?"

His tone is cold and intense, but I don't expect him to act like my lover right now. I nod and reluctantly pull away from Tegan. She gives me a pleading look like she wants me to stay, but I have to leave. It's easy for Rian to blur the lines of our relationship at his convenience, but times like this are why I'm glad I never let myself get too comfortable with him.

They're a family – Rian and Tegan – and I'm not part of it. This surrogacy game is nothing but that – Rian's game.

I don't have a choice but to leave them alone, even if it hurts and reminds me of my place in their home. It's no place at all. I don't know what I was thinking. I don't have a family. I've lost nearly everyone close to me. I only grew up with my mom and grandma. Both of them are gone now. My friends in college all moved on and started families of their own while I'd still never had my first boyfriend.

Or my first kiss. That was Rian too.

I'm too close to attaching myself to him in a way that

makes no sense at all. Rian won't be my boyfriend. He won't be anything or anyone other than the person he's always been. A cold ex-convict that's in the mafia and a tortured past who wants to make his daughter whole again.

I'm only convenient to him.

I love you. My heart hurts when I think about how good it felt to hear him say those words and allow myself to believe in the fantasy that Rian could mean those words. I know how intense sex with him can get. The heat of the moment with Rian Murray has more allure than nearly anything else I've experienced.

But I have to let go. I return to my room for a while and then I perform all my typical duties around the house while Tegan and her father talk in her bedroom. After a very quiet and awkward lunch, they leave the house together with no explanation, so I'm left alone in their house with my own thoughts and right then... they don't feel so good.

I FEEL ALONE. Maybe I should reach out to Kamari but... I don't want to seem weak for needing other people. For craving them. Before she passed, my mom taught me the importance of being a strong black woman. The world doesn't treat us the same as other women, so we have to be tough.

I know she just wanted me to survive the real world, but right now, I just feel even worse for not being strong enough.

17

Rian

Tensions between me and Tegan cool by the time we enter the car. She had a horrible nightmare and missed me badly. When she went into my room, she saw I wasn't there and went to find Heavyn instead. When I finally earned her confession, I felt like an asshole, so I offered her something we haven't done since I got out of prison. Ice cream.

"Why can't Heavyn come?" she asks, slipping into the front seat. We've dealt with Heavyn's side of things, but we haven't dealt with mine yet. I calmed her down and promised that I wouldn't make Heavyn leave, but I still need to address what my daughter saw. *Too fucking much.*

"Because I'm your father and we need to spend time together. Heavyn isn't a part of our family."

Saying that out loud feels wrong. She might not *technically* be a part of our family, but she's part of my family routine. In prison, routine grounds you to your sanity and I've kept many of the same habits on the outside. I do the same things at the same time. I've grown accustomed to seeing her face and now I can't imagine her gone.

Especially now that she's pregnant. What was I thinking when I offered Heavyn surrogacy? I know how possessive I can get, and that possessiveness kicked into overdrive with her. I want her so badly it hurts and even now... I'm only doing this because it's the right thing. It's my job to explain this to Tegan. I hope Heavyn understands.

I don't want to lose her, but I don't want to lose Tegan either. I've already come too close to hurting my daughter.

"Heavyn's *my* family," Tegan protests. "She's like a mom to me."

"Your mother is alive," I remind Tegan who rolls her eyes at me, reminding me so much of her aunt Evie.

"So what?" Tegan says. "She never visits and she doesn't even reply to my messages."

"She's not a bad person, Tegan. Just troubled."

"I don't care," Tegan says. "Heavyn's like a real mom to me. She's never mean, she makes amazing food and she's my best friend. I tell her everything."

"Everything?"

"Uh huh," Tegan says. "She's the best."

"I see."

Tegan gives me a funny look. I pay close attention to the road rather than meeting her gaze. Is this what it feels like when I stare at people? My daughter's eyes are a bit intense and I feel heavily scrutinized to the point where I can barely remember the turn to the ice-cream parlor.

"What *were* you doing in Heavyn's room, daddy? And don't lie."

THERE'S no getting out of this, is there? I have to have *this conversation.* I can't be completely honest. I don't want to tell her about the surrogacy yet, but I'll have to explain that eventually.

"I've been very lonely since prison," I tell her. "I thought Heavyn might be lonely and then she and I... spent the night together."

"Oh," Tegan says. I can't help but glance over at her again. It hurts so much to look at her sometimes and to know that for any reason under the sun, I would die for her. I love her so thoroughly that it aches.

"That's it? Do you want to know more?"

"Are you in love with her?"

That isn't the question I expected and I want to avoid it. My feelings haven't changed since my spontaneous confession to Heavyn, but I can't explain that to my daughter without explaining that Heavyn doesn't feel the same way. It's not fair to her relationship with my daughter for me to put this on her. She's doing her job and if Heavyn doesn't return my feelings, I'll have to live with that.

"I have very deep feelings for her," I say honestly.

Tegan makes an annoyed huffing sound. "Whatever. I mean. She's probably too good for you anyway."

"Thank you, Tegan," I grumble sarcastically. I can feel my temper bristling from her criticism, but it's easier now to bring Heavyn to mind and think about how she would respond instead. She's so much less... tempestuous.

"She's so cool," Tegan continues, gushing excitedly. "But she's a hopeless romantic and you're like... a demon."

"I am your father. I am *not* a demon."

Tegan rolls her eyes. "Then why do you wear black suits all the time and stay up all night?"

"Tegan..."

"Just sayin'," she says sassily.

I grip the steering wheel more tightly. The hardest part

about being a parent is knowing your kid is right about some shit, especially when you want to be right about it too. I can't dismiss Tegan as just being a kid. She's seen some shit out there and like it or not, she's mine. She gets me better than most other people.

She's the best thing that ever happened to me.

"Your demon father wants to know what flavor of ice-cream you're gonna get," I tell her teasingly. "Because I'll be stealing a spoonful."

"You will *not*," Tegan says as I park the car, ready to fling herself out of the seat. "You don't even like ice-cream."

I don't know where my daughter gets these ideas. We laugh and tease each other as we walk from the car to the ice-cream parlor window. Tegan seems a lot calmer once she orders a kid's cup of strawberry cheesecake ice-cream.

I normally wouldn't have anything but I don't want Tegan to eat alone. A good father would give in once in a while, right? I end up having my childhood favorite, mint chocolate chip, and wonder what flavor Heavyn would have ordered if she were with us. She would probably comment on me eating dessert since I never have any.

I send her a quick text message.

I'll be back soon.
Trying to do the right thing for once.

I WANT to remind her that I still mean what I said. *I love you.* Since she didn't respond last night, I think it's best if I keep my feelings to myself. My cards are on the table and I want her, but I can't push Heavyn into loving me. While I might have the sexual talent to coerce her body into responding to me, if making love and connecting to her hasn't won her heart, I can't push it.

I just want her to know I still care. I'm not the utterly cold bastard she thinks I am, though I'm still not certain what exactly she sees in me enough to have even said yes to my proposal in the first place. I assumed the attraction between us was shared.

I see another text message from Darragh, warning me to be careful about something or other, but I can't worry about that right now. When they need me, I'm sure Aiden will call and then I'll have to leave her, my family, and everything I love again. I just want right now to be about my daughter.

As we eat together, Tegan asks me more questions about me and Heavyn that I find uncomfortable to answer. She asks if we're friends, which we are. She asks if I'm going to send Heavyn away soon and I tell her that I won't. Tegan insists that she'll need a nanny forever and she doesn't *ever* want to say goodbye to her.

I make an effort to change the subject instead. This time, I find it easier to hold a conversation with my daughter. I ask her about her current interests – Harry Potter And The Goblet of Fire – and then her friendship with her cousins. Tegan likes her cousins, but I can tell she's lukewarm about Evie, possibly a little intimidated by her.

"You'll make more friends when you start school again," I tell Tegan, hoping that she responds well to the prospect of school.

She frowns. "Yeah. I guess so. I just don't want kids to think I'm weird."

"Why would they think you're weird?"

"Because I got kidnapped. Duh," Tegan says, dipping her spoon into some melted ice-cream. It stuns me that she can be this cavalier about the situation, especially when other minor events have provoked meltdowns in the past. I want to tread carefully around the subject of what happened to her when I was behind bars, especially because I blame myself for not being there to protect her. This should have never happened to my baby girl.

"That's not weird. It's just different. There's nothing wrong with being different."

Tegan gives me a funny smile. "That's not what our family thinks. Even Katie and Patrick say I'm not like them because I'm Puerto Rican."

Katie and Patrick are Evie's kids and they're Irish – 100% Irish because my sister wasn't foolish enough to even try bringing a black guy home. She married into a mob family, like all dutiful Irish mob daughters. I hate comparing Tegan to Evie's kids. It's a totally different fucking situation and I don't want them making her feel left out for her heritage. I can't change the bullshit I've done in the past, but I can be a better person and make sure my daughter doesn't feel like crap because of who she is.

"You are *half* Puerto Rican," I tell her. "And our family thinks a lot of things. You decide for yourself how you want to live, Tegan. It doesn't matter if some kids think you're weird. There are gonna be people who love you for who you are. Always."

Dad only kept Tegan alive because she didn't look *that* different. She has more Irish features than Puerto Rican features. Her mother had Spanish ancestry and Tegan looks more white than not. I hate that her appearance isn't enough to keep her safe.

She gives me a warm, genuine smile. I feel like I've done a good thing for once.

"Thanks, dad," she says.

"Yeah," I mutter. "I love you, Tegan. I don't say that enough, but I mean it."

My daughter replies, "I love you too, dad. I'm sorry for freaking out. I just don't want things to end badly and for Heavyn to leave. She's my best friend."

I shouldn't make her this promise, but I want to believe it myself. I don't want Heavyn to leave either. *I love her.*

"That won't happen, baby girl," I reassure Tegan. "It won't."

18

Heavyn

I expect Rian to fire me when he gets home with Tegan. Instead, he lets us spend the rest of the day together while he works in his home office upstairs. He doesn't even pace while he's up there, so I have no clue if he's on the phone or running through accounts or just staring into space. I just know it's so painfully awkward that we haven't spoken to each other since this morning and I don't think I'll feel okay until we do.

I'm still pregnant with his baby. We can't avoid talking things out with each other just because of what Tegan saw. I don't try to bring up anything that happened earlier once she's home. Tegan has her own plans for me and I just want to do whatever will make her happy. I hated seeing her so upset this morning. It broke my heart to know that I could have played a part in hurting her.

When it's time for Tegan to go to bed, I bring up the awkwardness this morning just to make sure she's okay. Camilla curls up next to Tegan on her very own pillow fast asleep with her stomach exposed. The faint smell of cat treats suggest Tegan may have snuck Camilla a few extra treats.

Tegan starts stroking Camilla's belly idly as I walk in and fuss with my clothes in an effort to smooth away the awkwardness I feel about the situation.

"I'm sorry for this morning," I tell her. "You must be feeling pretty betrayed."

"No," she says calmly, shaking her head. "It's not your fault. Women are always attracted to daddy. He mostly ignores them but... every time he loves someone, he pushes them away."

"Your dad doesn't love me," I tell her. "I'm sorry, Tegan, but you're my girl and I have to be honest with you. What happened between us was between adults and it should have never happened."

Tegan ignores most of what I just said to focus on one part of it.

"Daddy loves you," she says. "I can tell."

Her certainty gives me pause before I remind myself that Tegan is a child and she can get wrapped up in daydreams more easily because of that. I shouldn't let her confuse the matter with Rian. We have a contract, mostly about providing Tegan with another sibling, and fulfilling that requires my body.

It's not real.

"Tegan..."

"Daddy is just really stupid," she explains. "He screws everything up. He's like... the black sheep of the family. No offense. I wish you guys could be together."

"Tegan, sweetie... We just... I'm his employee. It's nothing more than that."

Tegan sighs. "Life just isn't like the movies. If it were like the movies, you guys would be like... together."

"Your dad has a lot on his mind, sweetie. I don't think love is one of those things and that's okay. He's a good guy and he loves the crap out of you. That's what I care about. I'll be here for you and for him as long as you both need me. Okay?"

"I love you, Heavyn."

"I love you too, Tegan."

I kiss her on the forehead goodnight and try not to tear up as I head back to my room. Rian is still in his office and I feel like having a kid bed time tonight. Everything is just too difficult and painful with him. After his text earlier, he hasn't spoken to me, which makes his text even more confusing and cryptic than it already was.

I take a shower and change into flannel buffalo plaid pajamas before climbing into bed. Romance novels feel like they would be too ironic, so I just close my eyes and try to fall asleep. It's one of those emotional days that makes me miss my mom. She never found true love her entire life, though she always dreamed of it. She passed away before she ever found a guy who would love her and take her on dates. My dad was an asshole who used her and abandoned both of us when shit got real.

She never got a chance at love. I don't know if I'm throwing my chance away, or am doing the wrong thing by staying with a guy like Rian who shows all the signs of being bad news. I mean… even his dick looks criminal. His dick…

I fall asleep thinking about Rian's dick. I'll never be able to forget him, will I? His dick will forever be imprinted on me as my first. There will never be another guy like Rian.

I WAKE up after only a few hours. I didn't hear him climb in through the window and he isn't moving, but I can feel his eyes on me and I can tell he's been staring for a while. I move so I'm lying on my back and sure enough, Rian's dark figure stands over me in my bedroom.

"Rian…"

He exhales a loud, heavy breath. Why is he in here just watching me sleep? I can't tell if he's clothed or not until my eyes adjust to the light. He's shirtless but wearing black or very dark colored sweatpants.

"Don't speak," he says.

"We have to."

"No," he says. "Turn around and take your pants off. Panties too."

"Rian…"

"Obey me…"

"What about Tegan?" I hiss at him. Rian needs to take this more seriously. We just put his daughter through hell this morning, so maybe sneaking into my bedroom isn't the best move. And I don't want to be loud and wake her up. My heart pounds. Rian's stubbornness will get us both in worse trouble.

"She's sleeping," he whispers. "I checked. I want your ass."

He's focused… on the completely wrong thing. Rian can't possibly have snuck in here in the middle of the night just because of my ass. We have some serious shit to talk about, including those three words he said to me before we fell asleep last night.

"Rian, are you serious? How long have you been standing there?"

"About an hour," he says calmly. I should be completely creeped out, but Rian's voice sounds so hot that it's difficult to even focus on how fucking crazy his answer is.

"Have you lost your mind? We've hurt Tegan enough."

"Yes," he says, breathing slowly. "We have. But I'm not done with you, Heavyn."

"It doesn't matter. We can't think about ourselves. We'll have a big enough challenge hiding my pregnancy."

"I don't care," Rian says.

"Rian," I snap at him, my heart racing as I try to talk sense in the most stubborn man alive. "Pay attention. This doesn't just affect us. This affects Tegan."

"This won't hurt her," he says. "The fact that I love you does nothing to harm my daughter. I'm sure of it."

He sounds frustratingly stubborn tonight – more than usual. My guard is up. He didn't just come in here to watch me sleep. He said as much.

I want your ass. There aren't too many ways to interpret that.

"We can't..."

"What are you afraid of?" he asks. "Because Tegan understands how I could fall for you. She thinks you're the greatest fucking thing in the world. You're already pregnant, Heavyn. Why not just... let it happen."

Let it happen? Rian is acting like I had any choice in the matter. He's already standing in my bedroom and from the looks of my window, he didn't bother to disguise himself or his intentions this time. He came in straight through my bedroom door boldly.

"I'm not afraid of anything."

"Then you have no feelings for me?"

I don't want to lie to him. All my hesitation and uncertainty still matter to me but I still can't bring myself to lie to Rian's face. Even in the dark, he could probably see straight through me. Rian had an incredible ability to read me and to respond to me – and to get me to respond to him. Tonight especially, I'm vulnerable. Too vulnerable.

"I didn't say that."

"Then why are you fighting this, Heavyn?" he asks.

"Because I don't see a world where the rich guy ends up with the nanny. It just doesn't happen, Rian. Once you have the baby you want, your gooey feelings for me will dry up. My mom raised me to be practical."

He keeps staring at me for a painfully long time. Rian's gaze is so penetrative that it's like he's pinning me in place with it.

"That won't be the case," he says. "And I'm sick of talking. Talking won't prove my point. Take your clothes off."

"We can't avoid talking about serious subjects and jump straight into sex."

"Take your clothes off," Rian says. "Don't make me ask you again."

It's pointless to deny the effect Rian's dominant side has on me, but I'm not like him. I can't just suppress all my emotions and release them into an intense sexual encounter. I can't pretend like what happened today didn't affect me. We betrayed Tegan and we're still lying to her. We can't continue lying and we can't keep changing the rules of engagement between us.

There are too many ways for us to get hurt – mostly me. Rian will most likely get to walk away with everything, including the baby he put in my womb. He's not my man or my boyfriend. How the hell can I trust him to be fair? He's a rich man... a rich and *very* dominant man. He likes to get his way.

I don't want to play his games for the sake of it. Tonight, I'm putting my foot down and it has nothing to do with my feelings for him. My feelings for him are obviously complicated and too foolishly misplaced for me to indulge.

"We can't do this, Rian. I'm serious."

Chapter 18

"10..."

"What?"

"9..."

"Are you counting down?"

Rian's intense stare worries me. His brows darken over his angled face and he's clearly trying to make me feel threatened. I can stand my ground against him or let him break me. I have a choice. Part of me desperately wants to submit to Rian immediately. To make this easy for him. But I care about his daughter. What happens to her heart when he doesn't want me anymore?

It's better for us to fight these feelings and stick to the original plan for each other. I'm a twenty-four year old who never had a boyfriend, never went on a date and always focused on my studies and my degrees. Rian isn't good for me and I'm not good for Rian...

"8..." he says, his voice taut and impatient.

"What are you counting down to?" I ask, swinging my legs over the side of the bed. Rian's tone worries me and I have an easy avenue of escape this time since he's not blocking the door he entered through. I didn't lock my door before bed, which might have been a mistake or maybe fueled by some stupid subconscious desire that Rian would show up in my bedroom to have a proper conversation.

"7..."

I scramble out of bed to give myself a headstart but the second I move towards the door, Rian blocks my way, moving even faster than I can because of his impressive height. He's also in much better shape than I am. But tonight, I don't have to give him what he wants. I don't have to let him in.

"Rian..."

"6... I'm not messing around, Heavyn..."

"I'm not either."

"I'm done counting down," he says, surprising me by reaching out a surprisingly long limb and wrapping his hands around my forearm. I yank my forearm away from Rian but fail to pull free. Instead, I stumble backwards and I need him to use more force to keep me on my feet, which renders me entirely under Rian's control.

I've always been a big girl and *felt* like a big girl but, Rian is so tall and muscular that he makes me feel petite and almost instinctively submissive because of his size. Rian pulls me against him and his hands quickly move from my forearm to my hips. He clutches me at the smallest part of my hips and holds me steady like I'm a spoiled child throwing a tantrum.

"You are done protesting," he says. "You're mine and tonight, your ass will be mine."

"Rian, you can't do whatever you want without thinking of the consequences."

"I've thought of the consequences," Rian says firmly, his grasp on my hips tightening. "In every scenario I've explored, fucking my surrogate in the ass ends well for both of us."

"Rian. Your daughter is asleep down the hall," I hiss.

"Yes," he replies. "So you'll have to be very quiet when you take my cock and all my piercings…"

"Even if I were going to agree to this," I protest, my heart pumping faster. I know how stubborn Rian can get when he sets his mind on things. "It's physically impossible for you to fit your dick and all those piercings in my ass."

Rian's lips curl into a cruel smile. I want to wriggle away from him but he's holding onto me too tightly for me to get any power back from him. I'm stuck in his grasp and utterly under Rian's control. I know how much he enjoys control and he knows how much his control of me makes me cum.

I have to stay strong. I have to be the responsible one.

"I'll be gentle," he murmurs, running his thumb purposefully over my lower lip. "I'll go slow as I put my dick in your ass. But I've been craving you all day. Thinking about leaving you alone here…"

He trails off. Rian hates talking too much. He runs his thumb in a slow circle over both my lips now. I can tell he's thinking dirty thoughts about them and a nervous thrill travels straight between my thighs, making my pussy throb.

"We can't," I protest one more time. I sound so weak.

"Yes we can," he whispers. "It'll be like the first time. I'll hold you down. I'll take what I want. Everything that happens in this bed will be all my fault. I can take that. What I can't take is leaving you here with an unfucked ass."

My throat tightens. Rian's lust for me isn't just evident in the way he touches my lips. His cock is already stiff in his pants, protruding forward eagerly. He's punishing me. I didn't say that I loved him back, so now he wants to thoroughly use me, to prove to himself (and to me) that I can't say "no" to him and that every inch of my body belongs to him. Rian's sexuality is so dark that it scares me, but my body seems to find that fear very arousing.

"You're gonna turn around and bend over the bed," he instructs me slowly. "Take your pajamas off and then your pretty fucking thong and spread your cheeks so I can get a closer look at your ass before I fuck it."

19

Rian

She does exactly as I ask. Heavyn is perfectly made for me physically, and her willingness to trust me and submit even against her better judgment makes me want to love and cherish her more. She senses the dark intentions behind my desires tonight, but I need some confirmation of her feelings for me.

If she won't give me her words, I need something else. How much pain is she willing to tolerate before she admits the truth? The chemistry between us has always been mutual, even that first night. Especially that first night.

I don't respect her any less for what she wants in the bedroom. Fuck, I know I'm the furthest thing from a saint. She wants this. If she didn't, she wouldn't obey me so easily. Heavyn's butt sticks out over the edge of the bed like a perfect gigantic peach.

I nearly cum in my pants before she even rolls the pajama pants off her perfect ass. She has a gigantic butt, especially for her height. Heavyn is all ass and I fucking love it. I've always loved women built like Heavyn with something to grab onto all over. She's beyond thick. She gets me so hard and out of fucking control.

She makes a frustrated grunt as she pulls the pajamas over her round butt and slides it over her thighs. Heavyn's ass swallows her panties completely. No pair of panties would stand a chance against her butt cheeks.

I desperately want to push my tongue between those ass cheeks and taste her but right now I need to exercise patience. I'll only get true satisfaction from Heavyn if I'm patient.

Without further instruction, she slides her panties over her ass, pulling the fabric from between her cheeks as they drop to the ground. Her panties are soaked, which doesn't shock me in the slightest. I fucking knew how much she wanted me to do this. To own her. To prove to her that I cared.

My wicked intentions with Heavyn's ass don't come without hints of tenderness attached. I don't want to hurt her or break her completely. I want to pleasure her and get her hooked completely on my cock. She's beautiful, pregnant, and mine until the end of our surrogacy contract. She's under no obligation to remain with me once she gives birth. Even if we haven't worked out the details, I have my suspicions about what she wants. I want the opposite. If I can change her mind about leaving... I will.

But she'll want her freedom, obviously. I've been caged before and that's exactly what I wanted. I like to think of myself as better than a jailer, but I know I've put Heavyn in an uncomfortable position.

Still... I don't want her to just walk away from me. I want her to change her mind about leaving and about who I am.

I want Heavyn to choose me. I want her to choose to stay

with me forever. *I want her to be mine for as long as we both shall live.*

Her hands hover over her ass cheeks and Heavyn doesn't immediately obey my commands to spread herself open to me. She hates being like this, spread lewdly in front of me. Slowly, I want to chip away at the self-consciousness she feels about her body or her sensuality.

She's fucking beautiful.

"Heavyn…" I say with a warning tone.

"This is embarrassing."

"There's nothing embarrassing about you or your body," I tell her. "Every part of you was perfectly made for me. You're mine and it's going to be hard as fuck for me to let go of you."

She slowly spreads herself for me and I can only say one word.

"Fuck…" I groan. Her pussy lips are soaked completely and fucking gorgeous. My dick presses urgently against my pants as my desperation to get inside her increases. I want to put my tongue inside her and I want to make her cum hard…

"You are so fucking pretty. I love your full pussy lips. I love your thick thighs. You have the perfect fucking body."

She flinches and juices ooze from Heavyn's lower lips. Her pussy is fucking gorgeous. I can't wait to feel her tightness around my dick. She has such a delicious looking set of pussy lips that I nearly forget about my goal for the night.

Her ass. Heavyn has a very tight asshole that looks impossibly small compared to my dick. The thought of her backdoor tightening around my dick is nearly enough to make me cum.

Patience. I need patience.

I drop to my knees between Heavyn's legs and grab onto her thick thighs. She flinches, but she doesn't pull away from me. She's done resisting. However wrong this is, she's fighting the same demons that I am. We share this lust. I can feel it. She pulses with her desire for me. I lick at her lower lips and suck the juices off Heavyn's thighs and pussy as she stifles moans by pressing her face into the mattress.

Her breathing gets heavier as her arousal increases and I flatten my tongue against her pussy and lap at her lips with slow strokes. When I reach her clit, I slide my tongue between her lower lips and move my tongue in slow, teasing circles that make it harder for Heavyn to stifle her moans.

I make her weak and I fucking love it. She cries out as I suck gently on her clit. Heavyn might deny me out loud but her body tells the truth about how she feels. Her pussy gets soaking fucking wet for me and it's impossible for me not to feel a surge of satisfaction. She wants me.

Her thighs tighten together as Heavyn gets close to cumming. She's so fucking sensitive. It's easy to observe her responses and know just how to tease her. As I rub her clit with my tongue, I press two fingers against her entrance. I know this is gonna drive her crazy. Heavyn responds instantly, her hips arching as her pussy desperately presses against my fingers.

I can't wait to feel her pussy wrapping around me, just not tonight. I ease her lips open and slide both fingers inside her at once. I don't slow down on licking her pussy as I spread her open with my fingers. Heavyn climaxes instantly and her pussy gushes like a waterfall into my mouth. She's so fucking sensitive.

Holy fuck. I go crazy licking her juices off her pussy lips and thighs, making her cum two more times before I'm done tasting her. I got her nice and relaxed with orgasms, so now I get my prize - Heavyn's tasty asshole.

This is it. The one action that will bond her to me forever

and force her to admit that we are perfectly made for each other. Our bodies have this fucked up magnetic pull that neither of us should bother resisting. What's the point? Life is short. My daughter loves her. She's having my baby...

I'm doing some crazy Rian shit again, but this time I know I won't regret it. I had a lot of time to think about the life I wanted behind bars. I didn't have any specifics, but I knew that I'd be able to tell immediately when I was happy. I spent so much time being fucking miserable that happiness became my only goal.

She's brought so much happiness to my life and she's only going to bring so much more into it.

How could I not fall in love with her?

Heavyn's hands fall away from her ass cheeks as she loses herself to the euphoria of climaxing. It's my turn to hold her butt up and spread her cheeks so I can access her backdoor.

My fixation with Heavyn's ass was immediate. It's my favorite part of a woman's body. Since I was a kid my dad used to slap the shit outta me for staring at our maid's ass. He especially hated it when the maids were Puerto Rican or Haitian. He didn't like that I had a predilection for women he considered "ghetto trash" when he was being polite.

I never cared to explain myself. My attraction felt fixed inside me like something I couldn't change. It wasn't like there was anything wrong with white girls. It's just that they were familiar — my sisters, my cousins, my mom. Black chicks and Hispanic chicks were different. They talked funny. They ate funny food. They made me want to know more about them.

And they teased me for being white which was funny as fuck since other girls wouldn't really be bold enough to mess with me that way. I didn't mind their bad tempers or their big nosy families either.

Chapter 19

Even with my lifelong pull towards black and Hispanic women, Heavyn is still different. She stimulates something beyond my fixation with cultural differences or my obsession with extremely large asses when I first met her.

She's smart and she's different from any other chick from my part of Boston. It's her education and the way she's fallen in love with my daughter. If she can knock down Tegan's walls so easily, this girl must be fucking special.

And right now, she's special to me. I exhale slowly, teasing her asshole with my warm breath as I prepare to spread her backdoor with my tongue, then my finger and then my cock. My shaft is so hard that my two largest piercings ache. I haven't been this hard in a long fucking time.

I run my tongue in a circle over Heavyn's backdoor. She stifles a moan as she shoves her face deeper into the mattress. I tease her ass with my tongue until I get her soaking wet. Her moans don't stop me from enjoying the taste and texture of her precious backdoor. I wouldn't give a fuck if her ass cheeks suffocated me. I'm in fucking heaven back here.

As my tongue hits a steady rhythm of swirling and licking at Heavyn's asshole, her thighs tighten as she gets closer to a climax. She protests a little more when I dip my tongue into her backdoor, but she loses herself in moaning once I lick her pussy and her asshole clean.

I spread her ass cheeks apart myself and give her long, purposeful licks from her clit to her backdoor until Heavyn can't take it anymore. She grips the sheets and makes a frustrated squeaking sound that she suppresses by sinking her teeth into her lower lip. It's not enough to hold back the power of Heavyn's moaning.

She cries out loudly as she cums. I keep sucking Heavyn's clit as she finishes in my mouth, gripping her thighs as I appreciate the absolute fucking beauty of me licking her ass and pussy to orgasm. I know she'll love my cock in her ass, even if it might hurt at first.

I'll just have to be gentle. I kiss the backs of Heavyn's thighs as she remains bent over the bed and completely spread for me. My cock jumps each time my eye catches her asshole. I want to bury my dick in there so bad that I ache with desire for Heavyn's backdoor.

I wish I had more self-control...

RISING to my full height behind Heavyn, my cock nearly bursts with desire for her. She's soaking wet and if I use extra lube and go slow, entering her ass should be nothing but pleasure for both of us. I position myself behind her and press my thumb against Heavyn's puckered hole.

She shudders as I finger her back door, already soaked with my spit and juices from her pussy that cover every inch of her flesh. I tap the head of my cock against her ass and Heavyn shudders again as goose flesh breaks out over every inch of her.

I press my cock against Heavyn's asshole and she whimpers, but her tightness doesn't give. I have to move slowly. Teasing her asshole with my fingers and lube, I finally rest the head of my cock against her ass and slide inside an inch. She moans as the head of my dick spreads her open.

It's just the head, but it's more than enough to hurt her. And pleasure her.

"Easy girl," I murmur. "Your gorgeous ass can take it. I'll be gentle. I promise."

My heart quickens as I fight every biological urge to

plunge my dick into Heavyn's tight backdoor. She is so fucking tight. My face reddens as I grip her hips for stability and enjoy how the lube dribbling around my cock from Heavyn's perfect ass makes entering her even more pleasurable.

"I want you," I growl. "I want to fuck your ass so bad..."

She cries out as I get more of my dick inside her up to the first barbell along the underside of my shaft.

"Rian... please..." Heavyn begs in anticipation of the pain she'll have to endure to get the first barbell on my cock in her tight ass.

I love how she takes my cock. Despite her protests and the way she wriggles beneath me, Heavyn was perfectly made for my dick. It's not just her pussy. Her ass has an incredible grip on my cock and even with an ocean's worth of lube, I can't plunge into her deeper without effort.

My fingers dig into Heavyn's curvaceous hips as I slide the first barbell and enough of my shaft to get her up to the second. She doesn't swear, but she shudders and makes an uncomfortable whimpering sound.

To ease her pain, I reach in front of her with one of my hands and massage Heavyn's clit. Her body relaxes noticeably as my thumbs move in slow circles around her swollen arousal. In her blissful state, it's easier for me to push the rest of my cock into her without too much resistance.

After several minutes, I move my thumb away from Heavyn's clit and appreciate the euphoric sensation of having my cock buried entirely in Heavyn's ass.

"Does that feel good, sunshine?"

"Rian..." she moans, but she can't form any other words aside from my name. Her body trembles as I move my hips slightly. I think I barely move enough to affect her, but then

Heavyn moans loudly and her body tightens so I can feel her pussy throb and her ass clamp down on my cock.

Holy fuck, she's cumming. I barely move my dick in her ass and Heavyn explodes in a magnificent orgasm. She looks fucking hot as she cums, so I move my hips more purposefully and watch Heavyn's body respond. She cums repeatedly as I move my hips, juices gushing from her pussy as I bury my dick in her ass with slow, deep strokes.

I love a slow deep ass fucking but this is even more than that. I'm making love to her ass, indulging in her explosive responses to me and intentionally holding back my own climax until I'm done pleasuring her. It's nearly impossible to hold back. She's so fucking hot, her ass is so fucking tight and tonight, I want to claim her.

I need to.

"You're mine..." I growl as I speed up fucking Heavyn's ass. Her orgasms are too intense. The desire to take her hard overwhelms my effort to control my instincts and make love to her slowly. I lean over as I fuck her ass, kissing her back at first and then her neck as my cock pumps into her.

"Your ass, your pussy, every fucking part of you is mine."

Heavyn moans in response and I finger her clit as she cums again from my cock in her ass. I hold back as long as possible, but my instincts take over. I need to cum and it needs to be with her. She's mine. The mother of my child.

THE ONE I'LL never let go. The sunshine to my darkness.

"I LOVE YOU," I growl into Heavyn's ear as I cum deep in her ass. I love how intimate it feels to say those words while spilling my seed in her ass. She shudders and then moans in a mixture of pain and pleasure. I kiss her shoulders as I slowly withdraw my dick from her ass. I hope I didn't hurt her although with the size of my cock and my piercings, I might have fucked her too hard towards the end.

I touch the large, shapely ass cheeks protruding from the bed and Heavyn emits another strangled whimper. Guilt surges in my chest. I love her, but did I go too far this time?

Should I ask if I've hurt her? There's no blood on my cock, but I still feel like I've gone too far. I want to see her face. I want to know that she's okay.

She's mine after all and that means she's mine to look after.

"I'll stay with you tonight," I say to her firmly. "I'll sneak out before Tegan wakes up but... I won't leave you alone."

"Yes, sir," Heavyn whimpers from the bed and my cock stiffens again...

20

Heavyn

Ever since Rian came in my ass, my life has been different. I know, that seems like a horrible and possibly stupid way to mark the change, but it really is the night everything changed between us. He said it again — that he loves me. I have a huge problem. I want to say it back. But I can't.

I want to say it, but I've never said those three words to a man before and it feels important that I'm sure he's the right one. I can't tell with Rian, but since that night, we've been getting closer.

Considering our sexual relationship ignited like a fire-cracker, getting to know each other has been slow and extremely cautious. He's more careful with his heart than his pierced dick.

I swear I haven't been able to walk straight since the night he took my ass. He was so much more aggressive than normal. So possessive that it scared me. It's just as scary as it is exciting to have a guy like Rian love you. His obsessive dominance gets me soaking wet but also scares the crap out of me.

Chapter 20

I know he's dangerous but... how dangerous? Dangerous enough that his dick made me walk funny for a week.

If Tegan notices the difference between us, she doesn't say anything. Her relationship with her father has improved significantly. Tegan hasn't really changed much but her father has. He doesn't stomp around the house scowling all the time.

For the past three weeks, he's been helping me and Tegan make dinner every night. He hasn't complained when she's asked to make Italian food and he promised her that he would allow us to make Puerto Rican food a couple times. He's not perfect about that yet and he still gets uncomfortable whenever Tegan mentions her Puerto Rican heritage. But he's still different.

HE'S SOFTER.

WHEN TEGAN GOES TO BED, he doesn't just slip into my bed for sex. He's more adventurous than I thought. One night, we slip into boots and wander around his garden at night with the fireflies out. Another night, we sit on the porch with mint tea and rock on the giant porch swing until I fall asleep on Rian's lap and he carries me upstairs.

We haven't stopped making love. Ever since the news that I was pregnant, Rian insists he sees signs of a baby bump, even if it's way too early. He doesn't care. The thought of a baby bump is enough to increase his sex drive. He wants to make love *all* the time. I'm not complaining because it's always so good... but I do get sore from taking his big dick and all those barbells all the time.

That being said, when he's not around, it's hard not to

daydream about him all day. It's hard not to return Rian's obsession. Without Tegan to focus my energy on all day, he would have me like an anxious high schooler, I swear.

I still can't tell him that I love him back. It doesn't seem to happen organically, so I come up with a plan to tell him on Friday night. Tegan plans on heading over to her aunt's house for a movie night with her cousins and a sleepover. We've both told her that I'm visiting family for the night — a small white lie Rian insisted on.

I didn't have a better alternative to the white lie anyway. It's not like we could explain our strange relationship to his daughter. Some stuff just ain't for kids.

Once Tegan leaves in Evie's white Volkswagen SUV, Rian enters the living room where I'm planning out Tegan's lessons with a big grin on his face.

"Heavyn? Would you put your work down?" He asks with a very suspicious tone. He sounds like he's plotting. My ass throbs involuntarily. Considering Rian's previous plans for me, his cocky smirk strikes me as extremely suspicious.

I hope he doesn't have anything crazy planned because I wanted to cook him dinner and then tell him... I share his feelings. I love you, Rian. It should be simple. I even practiced telling him in the mirror before.

Trying not to let my nerves get the best of me, I put my work down. My pussy throbs when my gaze meets Rian's. He seriously has no right to be that attractive. He's so fucking sexy that it hurts.

"You look like you're planning something."

"I've already planned it," Rian says. "Report to my bedroom in ten minutes."

"Rian, I have to get dinner ready. I can't report to your bedroom."

He gives me a disturbingly petulant scowl. He can't just

order me to his bedroom for sex because I'm his surrogate. I scowl right back at Rian Murray.

"What?" I snap, before he can say anything.

"I asked you to report to my bedroom in ten minutes. I didn't want an excuse," Rian says flatly.

He's the master of blurring the lines between boss and... surrogate. Or whatever the hell our relationship is. I've never been in a situation to ask "what are we", but with Rian, it seems appropriate to get some clarification.

"Are you ordering me to your bedroom as my boss?"

Rian's cheeks redden. "Yes. I find your disobedience frustrating."

How the hell did his mood switch up so quickly? I fold my arms and stand up, although I don't look as intimidating as I plan.

"I find your attitude frustrating. What the hell, Rian?"

"It's been weeks," he says, his voice dropping to an impatient murmur. "I told you I loved you weeks ago and you've said nothing. What about our future? Do we even have one?"

He *was* plotting something. But it was far worse than I could have predicted. Rian wants me gone. Or he thinks we don't have a future and this will all fall apart because I wouldn't share my feelings. My chest tightens.

"I want you upstairs in ten minutes," he commands when I don't answer his question. "We'll talk about our future then."

He leaves me in the living room with my work and his ten minute command. It's like he chooses the right amount of time to turn me into an anxious mess. He won't talk to me (I text him) until ten minutes passes. I didn't think he would. Rian is too stubborn for my begging to bend his will.

I've never really been inside Rian's bedroom before and I don't know what to expect. For all I know, he could drag me inside and keep me tied up in a freaky sex dungeon. That would be just up Rian's kinky alley. Hell, if he tied me up in a freaky sex dungeon, I'd probably have some fun myself.

This feels more serious. I knock on his bedroom door and he grunts instead of telling me to come in. Here we go again. Grumpy Rian's back...

I push the door open and he sits at the edge of his bed with his shirt billowing open. The walls to his bedroom are black and he has a gigantic four-poster bed with stained black wood carved with Celtic knots on the posters. It's a California King bed for sure. Huge. I glance at Rian and then a flicker of light catches my eye and I glance at the ceiling.

He has a mirror on the ceiling. Oh. My. God. I try not to react, but my pussy throbs and I notice the gentlest smirk crossing Rian's face. He quickly suppresses it when he catches me looking at his face.

"You're pregnant with my child," Rian says seriously, cutting straight to what's on his mind. "I've told you for weeks my feelings and... you don't share them. I want to send you away, but there's Tegan to worry about. She's attached to you. I might have overestimated my ability to handle your presence here."

It's really happening. My stomach sinks, but I don't want to show him any weakness. If I cry about this, I won't do it in front of Rian.

"You didn't," I respond with a tight, confident voice, which hopefully does a great job of hiding my feelings. "I'm fine. I can handle this."

"Right," Rian replies grumpily. "But I can't. I called Aiden and confessed. My brother agrees that we need space from each other. So instead of kicking you out... I'm going to Philly for two weeks to work. You can stay here."

"What?"

Chapter 20

I expected Rian to kick me out, but I didn't expect him to come up with an idea that was somehow even more stupid than that. Has he lost his mind? He can't go to Philadelphia. Tegan needs him here.

I need him here.

"I can't be around you and know that you don't have feelings for me. I keep taking it out on you, sunshine. I want to do sick and twisted things to you until you're bonded to me and only me. It's selfish."

It's not that selfish. Rian's twisted and kinky scenarios typically end with enough orgasms to knock me out for ten hours straight. I've never slept as well as I sleep in his house. Especially recently, since Rian's change, we've had great sex non-stop. Sure, I haven't expressed my feelings out loud but that doesn't mean he has to leave...

"I have feelings for you," I stammer out. I'm not good at this stuff. Rian doesn't understand how bad I've been hurt. He's fucking beautiful. He was probably born beautiful. He can't imagine the rejection I've faced. I didn't give up on losing my virginity forever and agree to become a live-in nanny for nothing.

I got burned so bad by the world, and by trying to find love, and I wanted nothing to do with love and romance. I didn't expect to lose my virginity to my boss. I didn't expect my boss to say he loved me.

"What feelings?" Rian asks impatiently, his blue eyes boring into mine. I hate that he looks angry.

"You know what feelings," I say as firmly as possible. "I don't see the point in saying it. You're my boss, Rian. After I have this baby, after you get tired of fucking the nanny... your love will fade away."

"Bullshit," Rian snarls. "That's bullshit and you know it. You have me by the fucking balls, sunshine. I hate not being in control. In two weeks, I'll be back. I'll be level-headed again. And I promise, I'll stop being such a cunt."

He takes my hand and at first, I think he's gonna hurt me out of anger or something. It's a silly, paranoid thought. Rian doesn't hurt me at all. He presses his lips to the top of my hand in an extremely soft kiss.

"It's just two weeks," Rian says. "Do you think you and Tegan can handle two weeks without me?"

"I can handle it," I say to Rian, even if I'm lying. I don't want to be away from him. I don't want him to go off on some stupid suicide mission because I'm slow to express myself. It's not worth it…

"But what about Tegan?" I ask him as if this last ditch effort to push against his stubbornness could ever stand a chance at working. Once Rian decided, he never changed his mind. I love his stubbornness as much as I hate it. He's a perfect contradiction, too perfect to ever be mine. Not forever.

"Tegan will be just fine with you," he said, his voice softening further. "You're the closest she's ever had to a mother. I don't want you to leave, Heavyn. But I don't want to make you stay either."

"I'll wait for you to come back," I say to Rian. "And I do love you. When you get back, we can talk more. We can figure this out."

Rian's body stiffens. I don't know what to make of his sudden stern change, but it feels like he's pulling away from me, which makes me panic. I don't want this to end us.

"I need to think, Heavyn. That's been my problem with you. Since you walked through my door with that sexy fucking ass, I haven't thought straight once."

. . .

Chapter 20

TEGAN REACTS SURPRISINGLY WELL to the news that her dad is headed out of town when she gets back in the morning. I try my best to make it sound like it will be a fun experience for her – like our very own sleepover. Tegan loves the idea. She's more secure in her relationship with her dad, which helps a lot. I know he doesn't want to leave her any more than she wants him to leave.

Rian packs his things while Tegan sits on his bed talking to him and helping him pick out clothes. I fuss around downstairs tidying up some of Tegan's things and deep-cleaning the hardwood floors. Rian leaves with a cordial goodbye. He's my boss again and I've got his daughter in this big old house all alone.

He texts me from the driveway.

Rian: You will be safe. I'll be back soon. Take care of my babies, sunshine.

HIS TEXT MESSAGE should make me feel hopeful, but I just feel put under the spotlight again. Should I have been more explicit? I have so much more to lose than he does. I just wish he could understand that. It's not that I don't care about him. I need to be sure before I say that I love him. Not just for me, but for Tegan and for the baby I'm carrying. I wasn't a fool in college and I'm not foolish with my heart. Rian is tempting but... maybe he's right. Maybe we need two weeks apart.

A LOT CAN HAPPEN in two weeks.

Heavyn

. . .

THE FIRST COUPLE days of Rian's absence, I spoil Tegan way more than I should. Rian leaves $45,000 in cash for me to use over the next two weeks for "living expenses". He demands that I spend all of it, which is completely ridiculous. He dragged a black Adidas duffel back filled with hundreds, fifties and twenties into my bedroom closet before leaving, so that's where I fund Tegan's frenzy of pizza, ice-cream and rented movies.

We barely get anything done for her schooling because of an Extended Edition *Lord of the Rings* movie marathon spurred by her cousin Patrick's obsession with the series. Despite enjoying the series, the movie marathon tires Tegan out from television and she shows an interest in her homeschooling without making a fuss.

By the time we get to the first weekend without her dad, I can tell Tegan misses him and that she has serious cabin fever. Rian's teen brother Odhran delivers all our supplies that we would otherwise get for ourselves and we rely on delivery services for everything else. Rian doesn't want us wandering far, but Tegan's moodiness by Friday evening worries me.

I try cheering her up by making her a special dinner – she's tired of pizza – but that doesn't work.

"I want to go for a walk," Tegan says. "My dad is paranoid. Uncle Aiden says I'm safe now. I believe him."

"I believe him too," I tell Tegan. "But your dad is my boss. He makes the rules."

"Do you see him anywhere?" Tegan complains. "Please, Heavyn... I need fresh air. This feels like..."

She sighs and says something I've never heard her say before.

"This feels like when that man had me under the stairs. I couldn't leave. I couldn't breathe fresh air. It sucked a lot."

I try not to overreact, although Tegan's pleas tug at my heartstrings. How could they not? This is the closest she's come to telling me about what happened to her – the traumatic events that keep her up at night. It feels cruel to put Rian's orders over her feelings.

"Hey, maybe we can text your Uncle Aiden about it and take a walk around the block. Would that be cool?"

Tegan nods and her shoulders relax visibly. "Thank you, Heavyn. I love you."

"I love you too, girlfriend."

I text Aiden that I'm taking Tegan around the block and courteously wait five minutes for him to reply before we begin getting ready. When Aiden doesn't reply after two minutes, I assume we're in the clear and tell Tegan to get ready. I admit that I don't wait very long in case he says no.

She puts on a pair of black leggings with a black hoodie and a pair of chunky hot pink Steve Madden sneakers. Her black hoodie is a gift from her cousin Patrick and has MURRAY on the back plus the number thirteen.

Tegan throws her hair up in a messy bun using my bedroom mirror while I struggle to get my arms through a Heather gray wool sweater. Once I get it on, I fix my hair up in a ponytail and slip into my sneakers – a pair of all-white Fila disruptors.

"Are you ready?" I ask Tegan, more excited than I thought about the chance at fresh air. Tegan nods excitedly and we hurry towards the door together.

"We'll only be gone ten minutes," Tegan says. "Daddy won't get mad at us if we're careful."

. . .

WE WALK DOWN the wooden porch stairs to the driveway together after I lock the front door and make sure we leave the house secure. Tegan throws her hands up and spins around, taking in the crisp, pine-scented air. It's early evening, so there's still a little bit of sun and the typical Massachusetts evening chill. I could almost use another sweater.

"Let's go this way!" Tegan says, pointing in the direction of some of the larger houses a quarter mile or so up the road from her dad's. I glance around to make sure we're safe and alone, which we are.

"Don't get too far ahead," I call to Tegan as I struggle to keep up with her. The girl is tiny and she walks fast as hell, but she waits for me to catch up. The brisk pep in Tegan's step makes me feel like I did the right thing. She looks more alive than she's looked in the past forty-eight hours and the big smile on her face warms my heart.

We're lost in our own little world when an off-white Dodge Caravan eases up behind us on the mostly isolated street and pulls up slowly as it gets near us. Tegan glances over her shoulder nervously.

"Ew, whoever drives a white van like that is a total creep," she says, walking a little faster. The van pulls over and stops. I glance over my shoulder and can't see anyone in the front seat. Weird. Nobody gets out of the car either. Maybe we should speed up.

"It's just a mom van," I tell Tegan. "Creepy white vans are the ones like what plumbers have."

The sound of the van's door sliding open gets my attention again. I glance over my shoulder for a second. A woman with black hair hops out of the passenger seat. I can't tell much about her except that she has pale skin and long black hair in a thick braid which she swishes over her shoulders.

Tegan and I walk for a few more steps.

"Who is that?" Tegan whispers.

"I don't know. Some woman. Let's just keep walking."

Tegan glances over her shoulder and her reaction to the woman scares me. She stops walking and turns all the way around.

"What are you doing here?" she yells at the woman, who now approaches us at full tilt. I get a bad feeling about her and a worse feeling about Tegan's reaction, but it's too late for me to act by the time I notice what's really off.

She grabs Tegan and as Tegan screams, the woman pulls Tegan against her and presses a taser into her stomach. I scream as Tegan screams, but I don't lose my shit and run away. Every instinct in my body tells me to defend Tegan. I act exactly like a mom would – I drag her away from the woman as she convulses in my arms and scream at her to get away.

The woman kicks my shins hard, but I don't let go of Tegan. I try to hold onto her and throw a punch at the woman's face, but I miss, nearly losing my balance. It's too hard to get a good hit in while holding onto Tegan and the black-haired woman knows she has an advantage.

I feel a sharp pain in my side, too sharp to be the taser, but I don't know. I scream Tegan's name and tell her to run, even if she's convulsing still and I don't think she's in control of herself. I just don't know what to do.

I don't want to let go of her, but she seems like she's coming to, and I want her to have a chance, so I let go of her. She groans and falls to her knees as I scream at her to run again.

"Heavyn!" she groans. "I can't…"

"Tegan, GO! Just try. You have to!"

I throw another punch at the woman's face and get her in

chest. I turn around to look at Tegan, hoping she gets another chance to escape, but she's still on the ground groaning. *No...*

I don't know what happens to her next, because I look away from the woman too long and then I feel a sharp pinch in my side like a needle sliding into my skin. That's probably exactly what it is because my world blurs almost immediately and all I remember is Tegan kneeling and powerless.

I don't know if she gets away.

21

Rian

Darragh, Callum and I meet up behind Callum's warehouse in South Boston, per Aiden's orders. When the boss commands a meeting, you show up and you look ready to work. We're all dressed in black and armed, our cars parked next to each other as we wait for Aiden.

We're sending a convoy to Philly, but I don't know what the fuck is going on, only that it's probably something to do with dad dying. Darragh knows, I can tell he's sitting on a secret, but Aiden clearly gave him orders to keep his fucking mouth shut.

My eldest brother doesn't make us wait long. He shows up in a black car that I don't recognize and when he steps out, Callum groans. "He looks pissed. We're fucked."

"Calm down," I tell Callum sharply. "Aiden always looks pissed. We already know we'll be gone for two weeks. It doesn't matter what he asks us to do."

"Speak for yourself," Darragh grumbles. "I'm having a baby. I don't want to miss the birth of my fucking child."

We shut up in Aiden's presence. He stuffs his hands in

pockets and gives us all scrutinizing glances as he approaches.

"Hey," Aiden says. "I don't want to ask any of you to leave the city for two weeks but... something important has come up."

Darragh's face reddens and he stares at the ground. Yeah, I can tell something is up. I just wish Aiden would get to the point.

"Do we have to kill someone?" Callum asks. "But you could've just sent Rian for that... So that can't be it..."

He's half talking to Aiden and half talking to himself. No. This is more than a simple hit. Darragh gives Aiden a pleading look that Aiden rolls his eyes at.

"Speak," Aiden says gruffly.

"My ex-girlfriend went to some Irish fucks in Philly and sold out a bunch of shit including some shit I'm not proud of and... they're forming a fucking army or some shit and they're coming after us."

"What ex-girlfriend?" Callum asks with a confused stare. "Did you end things with Kamari?"

"No, stupid," Darragh grunts. "Michelle."

"I thought you killed her," Callum replies bluntly, earning glares from my brothers.

I don't remember Michelle. Then again, I don't keep track of my brothers' fucks. Involving myself in their petty problems would be a complete waste of my time. I still don't know what Darragh means by "sold out a bunch of shit".

"He didn't kill her," Aiden says, drawing the conversation back in a reasonable direction. "But she thinks he tried so she's sold financial documents to the Kilpatrick family boss."

"Who the fuck are the Kilpatricks?" Callum asks. He's the second youngest, Odhran is the youngest, so Callum doesn't have the best grasp on the history of the Irish mob and the unhinged violence that broke out between the Irish mob families during the 80s and 90s.

Movies, television and documentaries fixed their eyes on the Italians while we shot each other, stabbed each other and dropped more bodies in the Charles River than the cops could keep track of. Fuck, we were the cops and in those glory days, as our father told it, and we ran out every disloyal Irish family from Boston.

Most fled to Brooklyn, begging refuge from our guns and knives from the Italian mob families in New York. Some went further west out to Chicago. Several families moved to Philadelphia and established themselves in the old mafia way in their new neighborhoods. I grew up knowing the disloyal families, names which drew extra attention in our part of Boston.

The Kilpatricks were one of those disloyal families. But what about Michelle's family?

I quickly explain the Kilpatrick situation to Callum, who nods with a glimmer of understanding behind his thick and possibly incredibly stupid skull. Callum thinks more about growing his biceps than his critical thinking. Still, he nods with a measure of understanding which exceeds my expectations.

"What about Michelle's family?" I ask once I'm done, directing my question to either Darragh or Aiden.

If I knew Darragh's ex-girlfriend, the one before Kamari, I don't remember her. Hm. Luckily, I don't have to worry about getting put in his situation. Lucia's too fucked in the head to be vengeful.

Darragh answers my question. "She's a Cronin. Her father and our dad were thick as thieves before Jerry died. But her dad's dead. There's no one to keep her in line now."

"Maybe you should have killed her," I suggest to Darragh.

My suggestion makes my brothers uncomfortable and Aiden grabs the reins of the conversation again.

"She's fucking with the wrong people," Aiden says. "I can't have any of you killing women. Michelle's brother wants her ass back here so he can personally assure she goes back to the old country. And I want the two Kilpatrick brothers dead."

"I knew this would be a hit," Callum says, flipping his Red Sox trucker hat around so his strawberry-blond hair sticks out the front messily. "What's the big deal, though? Why all the secrecy?"

"Leaving Michelle alive is an unpopular choice,"Aiden says. "The Doyle family holds her personally responsible for the incident with Seamus and they want her toe as proof that she's dead."

Aiden's referring to the incident at Darragh's birthday party where his ex-girlfriend Michelle screwed around on him with Seamus Doyle. Darragh handled the incident the best way he could but... that left a lot of pissed off Irish men who blamed his slutty girlfriend for the death of their family member.

"Fuck's sake," Darragh sputters, clearly uncomfortable with the position he's found himself in. I was right. It would have been much better for him to kill that girl.

Callum's face pales as he realizes what Aiden wants from us.

"You want us to cut her fucking toe off," Callum says, his face reddening with discomfort. Shooting someone is easy — maybe a little too easy. I don't share Callum's squeamishness around surgery (or torture, depending on your perspective), but I understand it. He's a clean killer.

"That's why you have Rian," Aiden says. "And he has you so he doesn't go too far and so that he doesn't go to jail. But you won't get caught. You have two weeks and they don't know we're coming. This should be easy."

"Easy for you," Callum says. "Are you sure it's worth it? I mean… Does Michelle's family know…"

Aiden's brow furrows. It doesn't matter how fair or patient a mob boss was before assuming the position. Leading a mob family means making choices that affect hundreds of people, if not more. The boss hates being questioned. He questions himself enough.

"I promised their daughter alive. I didn't promise she would return with all her toes intact. Two weeks. Don't let this escalate. If Michelle's family spreads word that we're weak, that we don't handle our business, we'll have more than blackmail to worry about."

AIDEN'S RIGHT. There could be a war. Power is fluid, like water. It shifts with the times and flows wherever it likes. Anyone could take advantage of divisions or displays of weakness from the Murray family. Aiden loathes excess violence, but sometimes, it's necessary.

"I CAN HANDLE THE SURGERY," I respond calmly. "But I don't need anyone to hold me back. I'm perfectly capable of controlling myself."

"Ensure that remains the case,"Aiden says stiffly. "I've got fifty grand for you fucks in my car. Get what you need and leave. I'll see you when it's done."

"Aiden, for what it's worth, I'm sorry for the trouble this has caused," Darragh says.

Aiden puts his hand on Darragh's shoulder sympathetically.

Rian

"We all make mistakes. We just have to make them right. Understood?"

AIDEN'S WORDS make me think of Heavyn. Is she my mistake? Am I doing what it takes to make it right? What would make it right? I fell for a woman who could never love me the same way. I probably deserve that punishment.

It's what Lucia went through with me. She tried everything to make me love her. She even gave me my daughter. I fell hard for Tegan. I loved her from the second I knew I was gonna have a kid. But nothing could have made me fall for Lucia.

She thought I was like my brothers, too obsessed with color to love her. It was never that. I've just always been strange. Lonely. Quiet. Dark.

I NEED a woman who draws me away from my solitary tendencies. My sunshine.

IF SHE'S A MISTAKE, she's a mistake I don't regret making.

"LET'S GO," I tell my brothers. "I don't want to waste any time. We'll need at least a week of watching them before we can strike."

They know I'm right. Aiden gives us the money and we all vote on heading down to Philly in my black Escalade. It's the subtlest car we own and there's plenty of room in the back for all our guns. Two weeks – Heavyn can handle two weeks with me away...

Chapter 21

22

Heavyn

I wake up with a sickening combination of a stomach ache and a headache. Tegan isn't with me. I reach out instinctively into the dark to attempt to figure out where I am and see if my hands will reach hers, but there's nothing but openness. We weren't gone for long — we just walked up the block. Rian promised we would be safe.

I don't even know what happened to her. My chest tightens in immediate panic. I did everything I could to give her a chance to run away. Maybe she got away from the black-haired woman. I groan and try to sit up, running my hands over the floor.

I'm lying on what feels and smells like an old shag carpet several decades old. It smells like smokers live here. My stomach lurches again as I inadvertently whiff more of the gross scents trapped in the ancient and dusty shag carpet fibers.

As I cough, I try to roll over and sit up. I have complete use of both my arms but when I try to jerk my leg, I realize that there's something wrapped around it. I scramble around a bit and feel around to get a sense for what's going on.

Chapter 22

Thick ropes bound around my right leg fasten me securely to what feels like the old radiator. I must be locked up in a bedroom. It's too dark for me to see and if there are any windows, they're covered up so no light comes in.

"Tegan," I call out into the darkness. My hands shake as I call her name out. I don't want her to be here with me, tied up in a dark room, but I want to know where she is. With my free hands I check my pockets for my cell phone and pat my hand all over the carpeted floor as far as I can reach in an effort to find my phone.

Nothing.

With no way out, no cellphone and nothing to do but wait for my captor to return, I replay my last moments of consciousness. There was nothing about the black-haired woman that roused my suspicions. But Tegan recognized her...

Was that woman Tegan's mother? Tegan didn't have any pictures with her mom and Rian didn't dwell on the subject when we were together. I don't have any better guesses, but I don't want to believe that the woman who tased Tegan and came after me could be her mother.

Maybe she was associated with the traumatic incident Tegan went through while her father was behind bars. Both options scare the shit out of me.

If Tegan didn't get away, she could be hurt.

I will never forgive myself if anything happens to her. Rian will probably kill me when he finds out. Hell, he'll probably kill me anyway for disobeying his orders. With Rian gone for another week, he may not even know we're missing. Will Aiden know? I don't want to rely on them to get out of here, but I'm powerless and tied to a radiator. Options aren't as plentiful as anxious thoughts about what the hell could happen to me. Or to my baby. I'm still pregnant.

The woman who kidnapped me may or may not have known. I don't want to expose myself, but I want to know if my baby's okay. And injection with a mystery chemical that knocks me out seems like it would possess some risk. I can't bear the thought, so I focus on escape and potential options for achieving that.

I scramble into the most comfortable seated position I can find, which involves pressing one side of my body against the radiator grates. Leaning against the radiator isn't that comfortable and the metal sends a chill through my arm. I'll get stiff quickly if I don't move every few minutes.

It's hard to stay in control of myself, but I have to do it. If not for me, for Tegan.

It doesn't matter who captured me. I need a way out and I need to get to her. I don't know where I am, if I'm even in Boston, or if Tegan got away. I've got nothing.

After hours alone in the dark, I hear footsteps. My body tightens against the radiator as one final terrifying thought enters my head. How could that little woman have moved me alone? She has to have had help. The door handle clatters as metal jostles against metal.

Now I know what direction the door is in. There's no light in that direction either. I can hear blood rushing past my ears and then I hear the door open with the slightest creak.

A soft voice whispers after the creaking, "Shit..."

It's Tegan.

There's still no light, so I can't see her, but I feel the cooler temperature from the hallway seeping into my room and hear her soft footsteps against the shag carpet, and her breathing.

"I had to wait for her to fall asleep," Tegan whispers. "I stole the key, but she has a boyfriend. He's asleep in the living room blocking the only way out."

I keep my hands outstretched until I feel a warm, gentle brush of Tegan's hand touching mine. She exhales with relief as her fingers interlock with mine. Her hands feel so small and fragile as they curve around mine, reminding me of how much danger we're both in.

"Who is that woman? Do you know her?"

She's on her knees next to me. I can hear her breathing now and feel her fear. Brave Tegan. She's terrified, but she still risked God-knows-what to find me. That girl is Rian's daughter through and through. I squeeze her hand. Rian's daughter. I love them both and I can't let Tegan be the only one facing her fears.

"Yes," Tegan whispers. "She's my mom. Lucia Esperanza Gomez. She doesn't want us to leave."

"She hurt you," I whisper. "Are you okay?"

I can feel her body shaking a little from where I'm holding her hands. I let go of her hand and use what leverage I have to pull Tegan's kneeling body against mine as I wait for her answer. Her head rests against my shoulder and my love for Tegan explodes in my chest. Is this what it feels like to be a mom? I know Tegan isn't mine, but the way I've bonded with her feels stronger than anything I've felt for one of my students.

She feels like my family.

"No," Tegan whispers back, holding me tightly with her nose pressed into my shoulder. "But I'll get better."

"Where have you been the past few hours? Did she hurt you more?"

Rian won't forgive anyone who hurts Tegan. His protectiveness over his daughter amplifies Rian's ruthlessness. Lost time and all of that. Surely Tegan's mom knows that. She experienced the worst of Murray ruthlessness.

"She's really mad," Tegan whispers. "She keeps saying that we're gonna be a family again and that daddy won't let us be a family."

Her grasp on me tightens, but Tegan's admission renders me speechless. Tegan is technically hers. I can't fault a woman for wanting to get her daughter back but... She hurt her. She tased Tegan. I could never imagine hurting Tegan like that and from what I've seen, the same holds true for Rian.

Something ain't all the way right with that lady.

"Okay," I whisper back, trying to sound calm and in control. "Can you get those ropes off my legs? Once you untie me, I can handle this."

Tegan pulls away from me and finally, my eyes adjust enough to the light that I can see her eyes. It's some suppressed human instinct to focus on eyes in the dark and Tegan's are wide with terror.

"I brought a knife," she whispers. "But I don't know if it's gonna work."

I didn't feel a knife on her when I hugged her but Tegan pats down the side of her leggings and sure enough, she emerges with a large kitchen knife. The blade is at least nine inches long but without serration, my ropes might not cut easily.

"Is there anyone keeping guard?" I ask Tegan as I carefully take the knife from her. This kid... She's resourceful, but I'm terrified to ask how she got away from her captors, unlocked my door and found a knife in the kitchen. She's never reminded me of Rian more.

"Yes," Tegan whispers. *Crap.* I'll find out more about that later, I guess.

Chapter 22

My hands are unsteady at first as I slip the sharp blade between the ropes and attempt to cut them at an uncomfortable angle. The house is so quiet that my efforts to slice through the ropes make me feel like we're making an ungodly amount of noise.

After a minute of sliding the knife along the ropes and pushing against the binds, I cut through. The loosening ropes allow blood to rush immediately to the calf and lower leg that had lost all feeling from the binds. Tingling takes over me and I nearly lose my grip of the knife as I finish slicing myself free.

The knife drops to the carpet as I cut myself free. I unravel myself from my uncomfortable position to rub the part of my leg where Lucia and her accomplice tied me up. I just need enough blood flowing down there so I can move properly.

"Are you okay?" Tegan whispers.

"I'll be a lot better if we can get out of here. Do you know a way out?"

23

Rian

Callum and I get rid of the Kilpatrick brothers' bodies while Darragh secures Michelle in the backseat of the Escalade. He thinks he needs to get her to a hospital, but Callum and I assure him she'll survive. I did basic EMT training after my first jail sentence at our father's request, and Callum has two of Michelle's toes on ice. Aiden wants us to have a spare and he's the boss, he doesn't have to give us a reason.

She has enough tramadol in her system to keep her unconscious until we get rid of the bodies and get her back to Boston where she belongs.

I drive because Callum did most of the heavy lifting getting the trash bags of Kilpatrick parts into the car. Philadelphia has a lot of great spots for this type of shit. Parts of the city smell so strongly like death and pollution that you could get away with tossing bodies in a dumpster.

We're a lot more careful than that, even if it takes way longer and pisses Callum off that he has to do most of the work. Hey, it ain't our fault he's a fucking giant. At 6'7" and 300 lbs of pure muscle, my brother is a fucking tank. Half of the brothers end up in the Delaware River near Penn Treaty park. The other half ends up in the Schuylkill River near the Montgomery Cemetery.

Callum smokes three cigarettes in a row at Montgomery Cemetery when we're done, replacing the foul scent in the Escalade from the dead bodies with a far worse smell. His clothes reek of tobacco and sweat even if Callum smoked outside, leaned up against a gigantic headstone with the last name MORRILL carved into it.

Cigarettes remind me of prison, but Callum can't get through nights like this without smokes.

"Think Darragh's still freaking out at the meeting point?" Callum asks as we return to the Escalade from his smoke spot. I keep pace with Callum, casting an eye on him to make sure his nerves haven't fucked him up. All my brothers except Odhran never took naturally to killing. If we didn't have rules about gender, I'm sure Evie would have been a better killer than any of them...

It's always been my job to keep them calm, or at least demonstrate calm for them. I put my hand on Callum's gigantic back. Nothing to worry about, big man.

"He's always freaking out," I say to Callum. "But we have nothing to worry about. We rule Boston. If Aiden wants people to stop fucking with us, maybe we need to expand our territory instead of fighting off invaders."

Callum grins and shakes his head. "You're fucked in the head, Rian. More killing? You really want more killing?"

"It's how power works, Callum. People respect a show of force."

"Sure shit," Callum says. "I just need a fucking break, man."

"We're in the mob, Callum. We don't get a break. We

205

keep the peace. We keep our people safe. We're too important to take a break."

Callum smirks. "You're not like Aiden or Darragh."

I glance at Callum suspiciously. We all share our similarities and differences, so I'm fascinated with how Callum is analyzing me now.

"What does that mean?" I say as we approach the Escalade door. I open my side just to hear Callum's response.

"You didn't let fucking the nanny change you," he says.

Fuck. How the hell does Callum know about that? When we get in the car and I start driving towards the meeting point, I want to ask him, but he puts a baseball game on the radio and I'd rather listen to the announcer than trace Aiden's rats.

Maybe I shouldn't underestimate him. Callum didn't find out on his own. He doesn't have the brains for it.

It's a painful drive back to the meeting point. Now that we're finished with our work, I want this all to end quickly. Spending this much time away from my daughter and Heavyn, who's still pregnant with my child, has been painful.

I hate being off the grid this long, but Aiden's right that it's safer for our families if we don't communicate while we work. I'd hate for Heavyn to see the inside of a prison cell for the shit I've done. The more secrets I keep from her about the mob life, the safer she will be. Some shit is just men's business in our line of work and there's nothing wrong with men being the ones to keep women safe.

In this time away from Heavyn and my feelings for her have only strengthened. If we can get this job over with quickly, I can get back to her. Back to Tegan. *I can go back to the quiet life that I want now.*

. . .

I WANTED to believe that I could take some space and get over her, but I want her to belong to my family even more. My love for her and the time away have allowed me to see my weaknesses. I love her so much that I want to control her. I want to force her to love me back.

But it's a trap. Forcing her to love me could never work with her. I've taken enough from her by force. She clearly wants this to feel like her choice. She wants to feel like this desire for me is genuinely hers.

I can't take every choice away from her, even if it scares the fuck out of me to give up the tiniest bit of control.

This will be my greatest test, won't it? I'll have to give Heavyn the choice to stay with me or to walk away. I'll have to expose myself to her rejection and accept the outcome. I'll have to do the right thing.

If she doesn't choose me, I'll let her walk away with our kid and all the money she needs to get on her feet. After all I've taken from her, I can't take that too.

That woman. She's made me so much less cruel. I've fallen in love with her and worse, I've fallen in love with the idea of us becoming a family. It's safe now. *And I could always keep her safe.*

We meet Darragh crouched behind a trash can at the meeting point, scowling and miserable. We aren't that late but Darragh lacks patience completely. He doesn't bother lecturing us about our lateness.

"It's fucking cold, you bastards. I fucking hate Philly."

He walks over to a 2012 white Chevy Cruze with two black racing stripes across the front. It's the family decoy car dad always kept at his place in Philly. Callum will drive the Escalade with Michelle in it back to our Fishtown lot and we'll get the fuck out of here. I'll get to see my daughter and Heavyn soon. I can't wait.

Darragh pops the back door on the car.

"Is she alive?" Callum whispers, as if whispering would make a difference to a dead woman.

Darragh grunts and glances at her, but I can tell looking at Michelle's body like this makes him squeamish. I don't share his revulsion and glance at the bandages around her feet. Blood hasn't soaked through them yet, which means we successfully achieved this as humanely as possible.

"Either that or she's bled out," Darragh grunts. "Fuck, she's a pain in the ass."

Michelle cheated on him before he met his wife, Kamari. Callum explained it all on the way into Philly. At Darragh's twenty-fourth birthday party, he caught Michelle fucking a cousin of ours or some shit like that. Darragh forced her to take an icy plunge in the Boston Harbor and never looked back.

I never liked Michelle, but I've never liked the way Irish girls looked at us like we were meal tickets. I preferred women who didn't give a fuck that I was a Murray. They just wanted... me.

"Let's get the fuck out of here," I grunt. "I have better shit to do than clean up your messes. I have a family to worry about."

"Fuck off, Rian. I've got a family too. And Aiden wouldn't leave his family the way he's asking me to leave mine."

"Maybe he would respect you more if you married her," Callum suggests stupidly. Darragh glares at him, but doesn't bother answering him. He clearly wants to marry this girl but weddings take time to plan – at least if you do them the traditional way.

"We've all got families then," I grumble. "Except Callum. So we'd better get the hell out of here."

"Aiden isn't fucking around," Callum says, nodding. "Can't hurt to hurry and stay on his good side."

He shuts the elevated back door to the Escalade.

"This is fucked up," Darragh snarls as he hops into the front seat of the Escalade.

"What's fucked up about it?" I ask as I start my engine and follow Callum driving in the Chevy Cruze down to Fishtown.

Once he drops off the car, another family member in Philly will pick it up and we'll all drive back to the city together.

"I'm starting to think you're right. I should have killed Michelle. She's not worth all this trouble," Darragh says bitterly, glancing back at her like he's thinking about it.

I understand my brother's situation, but it's not worth it. Killing without Aiden's permission isn't worth it and I've already pushed our older brother too much to risk involvement in another incident of disobedience.

"You'll get home to your girl soon," I reassure him. "You have nothing to worry about."

"I do want to marry her," Darragh says. "Soon."

I want to marry my girl soon too, but I don't mention it to my brother. I just nod and promise him that I'll get him to the city soon, but I understand his yearnings. It's exactly how I feel about Heavyn.

I ONLY FIND out there's something wrong when we get back to Boston. We follow Aiden's instructions and drive directly to my house once Callum drops off the car and gets back into the Escalade where he babysits Michelle's unconscious body in the backseat. Callum insists we play the Celtics playoff game recap on the radio as we drive into the city. None of us question Aiden's orders at first. I assume he commands me directly to my house out of consideration for me and the time I've spent away from my daughter. And Heavyn.

Surely he doesn't mean for us to unload Michelle or her severed toes in my basement with my daughter and her nanny sleeping upstairs. My father might issue a command like that, but Aiden wouldn't. It's just not his style. Darragh's tense the entire drive back to Boston. Even if it's Callum's job to look after Michelle, Darragh doesn't want her to die in our custody.

I don't blame him. Burying another body would be more trouble than it's worth and Michelle has too much importance as a bargaining chip right now.

As we draw closer, I wonder what he expects us to do about Michelle considering Tegan and my nanny will be home. By the time I park my car, I know there's a problem. Aiden doesn't operate like this. His black GMC Sierra isn't the only one parked outside my house. Conner Doyle's car flanks Aiden's and there are two other cars parked outside. I assume they belong to Michelle's brothers since we're meant to hand her over to them alive.

Aiden will handle the side of the family that wants her dead. I park the car and stare at the scene in front of me. Why are there so many cars here? I don't have my personal phone, so I can't contact Heavyn or Tegan. Maybe Aiden moved them to a hotel for the night.

I want to get rid of everyone outside my house as fast as possible, but this can't be good.

Even Darragh shifts uncomfortably in his seat, glancing back at Michelle still fast asleep in the backseat. He's piecing shit together too and it's not adding up.

"Did Aiden message you?"

"No," I answer flatly. I don't want to discuss this. I want to know where my daughter is. I burst out of the car and hurry to the front door. Aiden opens the door before I can unlock it from the outside. One look at his face and I know I'm fucked.

"Where's Tegan?" I ask anyway.

"Get in the house," Aiden growls. "I didn't want you losing your shit in Philly."

THAT'S NOT AN ANSWER. At least it's not the answer I want to hear.

CALLUM AND DARRAGH catch up to me, leaving Michelle in the backseat. Aiden scans our faces. We all nod, confirming that we followed his commands and nothing went wrong on the drive back. Aiden's shoulders release some tension, but the expression on his face still freaks me the fuck out.

Tegan's gone again.

"Callum, Darragh, take Michelle into the basement with her brothers. Bring her toes into the kitchen. Rian, we'll step into your office to talk."

Callum and Darragh exchange glances and both decide against questioning Aiden. They see exactly what I see on his face – the don't fuck with me expression he has when he has to take charge and make shit happen. He's also angry. *Very* angry. Callum and Darragh don't question Aiden's orders. He's as hot-headed as any Murray, so it's best not to get on his bad side.

Aiden leads the way to my office. My chest tightens as we close in on it. The house is empty. I don't hear Tegan or

Heavyn, and I find Aiden's silence too suspicious as he storms down the hallway.

I shut the door to my office behind us as I enter a few steps behind my eldest brother. Aiden makes a good boss. I have to be wary not to underestimate him. Maybe he's punishing me for messing with Heavyn. He has his woman, but our father wasn't above bouts of hypocrisy. If Aiden wants to punish me for an interracial dalliance, he would be well within his rights.

My cock aches at the thought of what punishment my brother could choose to impose on me. I suffered enough for my piercings. I'd rather avoid more physical pain. I scan my brother's face for clues, but he's capable of hiding his thoughts and intentions when he needs to. It's a good trait for a boss.

Aiden turns around to face me, leaning against my desk with a scowl. I stand firmly in the middle of my office, loathing how quiet my house sounds without my daughter and Heavyn in it. Where the fuck are they? I also want my phone back. I need to hear my daughter's voice. I don't dare to press Aiden, I just wait for him to speak.

He's quiet for a few more seconds, analyzing me carefully. He worries too much about me flying off the handle. My brother's scowl strikes fear into the heart of most, but right now, I just find it frustrating.

"How was Philly?" he asks, giving me permission to speak.

"Where is my child?"

Aiden runs his tongue over his lip slowly, delaying his answer.

Finally he starts to answer, and my stomach turns into knots as he speaks..

"Missing for a week along with your nanny," Aiden says

gruffly. "Heavyn messaged me... I gave her permission to take your daughter for a walk but I suspect they were taken shortly after that. I've had Conner searching all over Boston for them."

"And I presume you've found them?"

I can feel a slow angry burn heating up my chest. A week? Heavyn and my daughter have been gone for an entire week and my brother thought it would be best to keep this from me. Was getting Michelle back to Boston more important than my daughter's life?

My cheeks redden and I struggle to keep my cool.

"How can you really expect me to remain calm?" I answer my brother, my voice tightening. "Who took her? I thought we handled all the shit we needed to handle."

If another family took my daughter, we really are weak. It would be the end of the Murray family if another group of mobsters could repeatedly fuck with us like this or get a ransom out of us. I don't even know what other mobsters could want with my daughter. She's not the only kid in our family. Why is it always my baby girl?

Aiden scowls at me, waiting for far too many seconds before answering me. I can't lose my shit with Aiden. He's right that I can't afford to lose my shit in general. But I'm tired of going through this shit. I'm tired of Tegan going through this shit.

I'll kill whoever took her.

"I learned that much," Aiden says quietly. "That's why I brought you in here. You cannot kill the person who took Tegan under any circumstances. I need you to promise that."

I grin at my brother. Is he joking? I killed just about everyone associated with her first kidnapper. Nothing, not even my brother can stop me from doing what I must to get my daughter back and nothing can stop me from punishing her captor.

"I won't agree to that."

"You must," Aiden snarls.

"How the fuck can you ask me to do that?" I snap at him. I can feel the heat rising in my chest and my voice rising as I scowl at my brother and break every rule in our family by raising my voice at him. He's the boss. He makes the rules. If he tells me to drive to Ohio tonight, I get in my fucking car and do it.

But I'm a father too. And my protective instincts about my daughter override every order my brother could possibly give. He can't ask me to just "let it go" that someone else violated my daughter's safety. She's been through enough. Too much.

It's not just her. Heavyn's carrying my child. She might not be my blood, but that woman is mine...

"Trust me," Aiden responds calmly. He doesn't take offense to my anger. His face falls with a mixture of guilt and sadness. "Please, trust me Rian. Make this promise and we leave now to find them. Just you and me."

"Aiden... How can I spare someone who hurt her?"

"Just promise," he says firmly.

Our eyes lock. We have such a long history together, Aiden and I. Our bond was always different from the one I had with my other brothers. He's the only one who I believe loves Tegan as much as I do. And right now, I have to believe that he would only ask me this if he had a good reason.

And what would Heavyn want? She would tell me to do whatever my brother asked and to put Tegan first. She wouldn't want me to be selfish or prideful, or the egotistical bastard I was when I climbed through her window and demanded her obedience. Heavyn would want me to be a better man.

"I promise," I tell Aiden. "But if it comes down to saving Tegan's life, all bets are off."

"Good enough," Aiden grunts.

THEN HE REVEALS my daughter and Heavyn's kidnapper.

"LUCIA HAS them and from what I've found out, they've left Boston. She's living with a Puerto Rican fella and they just moved. It'll be a while until I find out the exact address but we know what city they're in. We can do our own search while we wait for confirmation."

"How soon can we leave?" I ask, before finding out where the fuck we're going.

"We have a general direction, some possible contacts... We can leave now," Aiden says. "My niece is gone and I promised her I'd never let that happen again. It doesn't matter if it's her own mother. We gotta get her back."

24

Heavyn

"There's only one way out," Tegan whispers. "But her boyfriend is asleep there. We could try to knock him out or something if he wakes up."

While I appreciate Tegan's efforts to strategize our way out of here, she shouldn't have to be in this position. She's just a kid and I don't care if her dad is in the mob, she should be having fun and learning how to be her own person, not knocking guys out.

"If he wakes up," I whisper. "I'll handle him. I just need you to be quiet and if anything happens to me, you just run."

"I won't leave you," Tegan says.

"You have to. You're smaller and faster. Once you get back to your dad, he can come find me. Please, Tegan. If you see a chance, you take it. Promise."

She hesitates as I bounce against that familiar Murray stubbornness. But then she gives me a reason for relief.

"Okay," she says. "But I don't even know what state we're in. I tried to find out but..."

"It's fine," I whisper. "You just run and you go to the

police station or something. Find a cop, find anyone who can help."

I'm sure cops are the last people a mobster wants their daughter to end up with, but I don't know who else could help Tegan get from wherever the hell we are back to her dad. I can't do the mob thing, but I can do the responsible thing.

I can finally move my leg enough to get to my feet. I take Tegan's hand and with our eyes adjusted to the dark room, it's slightly easier for me to see. Tegan reassures me that there's a bit more light in the hallway.

Running my hands over the walls, I feel old, peeling wallpaper. It's hard not to make any sound as I walk. Since I'm carrying more weight than Tegan, my steps sound so much louder in the quiet house. I'm terrified of waking someone up.

The door opens with a slight creak and a bead of sweat falls down my cheek from my hairline.

Tegan's right about the hallway having more light than my room. There's a dim night light at the end of the hall which doesn't make seeing our way easy, but at least we have the tiny orb of light to guide us towards something.

"This way," Tegan whispers as she squeezes my hand and pulls me toward the night light. As we get closer, I see that it's plugged into the wall in front of a closed door which must lead us closer to our exit. We have no weapons, no cell phones...

"Do you have a key?" I whisper to Tegan. I don't even know if we need one, but it seems unlikely that Lucia didn't lock up.

"Yeah," Tegan whispers. "For the front door. I stole it."

I purse my lips and fight back my disapproval of theft. Considering her circumstances, she probably didn't have a choice, but some of Tegan's adaptations to her situation concern me deeply. She reaches her other hand into the pocket of her hoodie where I'm guessing she's keeping the key.

Once we get to the door at the end of the hall, she gives me a terrified look, like she's searching my face for guidance and calm. That little girl puts so much trust in me that it scares the ever-living crap out of me.

Tonight, I can't let fear win. She's my student, my precious girl. I love her so damn much that even if I didn't love Rian too, I don't know if I could ever stop caring about Tegan. I can't afford to be too terrified to do this. It's the first time in my life that I've had to put myself out there all the way to protect someone, and it's the scariest thing I've ever had to do.

I can't believe I thought sharing my feelings with Rian was so terrifying when this is much worse and I could die without ever telling him the truth. *My feelings for him are so much more complicated than I love you.*

If I get out of here alive, I won't screw that up again. I don't like my chances. My ankle still hurts from where I was tied up and I know that if it comes down to running for my life, I won't be capable of running very much. I haven't even seen the man between us and the door yet. He could be a giant. He could be armed to the teeth.

I might have to sacrifice myself to get Tegan out of here alive.

As long as Tegan escapes with her life, I'll be okay with that choice. Getting out of here wouldn't mean a damn thing to me if I lost her. I love that little girl so much. I love Rian too and I love him too much to go home to him without his baby girl.

If I don't make it out of here, if I cost him the big family he wanted, I want to at least save his daughter and hope he forgives me for the unforgivable — putting Tegan in danger again. I thought I was doing the right thing, but that doesn't make it hurt any less.

"I've got the door," I whisper to her. "Get behind me in case he's awake. And remember your promise."

"Okay," Tegan whispers, her voice trembling a little as her grip on my hand tightens. "I'm ready."

As I attempt to push the door open, with Tegan standing behind me to avoid any potential danger, I instantly know that I'm fucked. I mistake the resistance for the door jamming, but once I push hard, I realize there's someone standing on the other side of the door. Someone very much awake.

But it isn't Lucia's boyfriend, it's her. Tegan's mother resists the door pushing open at first, but doesn't stop me from pushing the living room door all the way open and stepping into the dimly lit room. There are two small lamps with warm orange bulbs in the corner of the room barely offering any light but offering enough to blind me temporarily after spending so much time in pitch blackness.

She steps between me, Tegan and the door with one arm crossed over another arm that holds a large, sharp machete.

Her black eyes glimmer as she sees me and smiles. In the dim light, she looks like a demon although I know realistically she's just a very unwell woman. I'm not trying to be an armchair psychologist or anything...but I watched the woman use a taser on her own daughter. That shit can't be normal. Tegan stays behind me, but she doesn't stop gripping my hand.

I can see the door clearly behind Lucia and behind an L-shaped couch that Tegan would have to jump over to reach the door quickly. Lucia's boyfriend lies fast asleep on the L-shaped couch, but we can't count on him staying asleep.

"Where are you going with my daughter?" Lucia asks me calmly, the machete dangling purposefully in front of her body. She wants to scare me, which makes me want to act tougher. Without that weapon, that little thing knows I could take her ass.

But she doesn't just have the machete. The bitch has back up – a boyfriend sleeping on the couch behind her who could awaken at any minute – and I have to do everything in my power to keep Tegan safe. That means distracting her and giving my smart cookie a chance to get out of here.

"I don't know where I am," I reply calmly. "So I don't know where I'm going. I'm Tegan's nanny. I know you're her mom and I know you probably have a good reason for doing this, but you have to let us go."

Right, Heavyn. Because reasoning with crazy people always works out so great. I swallow slowly, steadying my own nerves and running my finger in a slow, soothing circle on Tegan's palm. She needs to know that I've got her and I won't let that woman hurt her if I have the chance.

"I am her mother," Lucia snaps at me. "But I doubt you're just the nanny. I know Rian. He can't live without a woman. But he's not yours. He doesn't belong to anybody."

She sounds more defensive over Rian than she does her own daughter. I don't like the look in her eye or the way she sways that machete as she talks. I keep going back to the way Tegan shrieked as her own mother pressed a taser into her stomach. This woman isn't right in the head and I can't worry about what might have made her this way.

"You're right," I say softly, carefully considering Lucia, trying to assess her the way Rian would. "I'm not just Rian's employee. I'm Tegan's friend. I love her and I understand that you're her mother, but she lives with Rian for a reason. He loves her too."

Chapter 24

Lucia's tough expression cracks for a second.

She stares at me intensely and for the first time since looking at Lucia, I can see Tegan in her. The little girl takes after her father for most of his features, including his eye color. But the way Lucia's brows pinch together and the way her nose wrinkles are pure Tegan.

"Rian doesn't love anyone but himself," Lucia says. "Now, let go of my child."

She's wrong about him. Rian loves Tegan. Rian loves me. Rian is so full of love for other people that he hides with grumpy comments and his quiet, unassuming personality. But his love runs deeper than Lucia thinks and unlike her, Rian would never intentionally hurt his daughter.

Tegan's grip on my hand tightens. It doesn't matter what this woman does to me, I can't willingly give Tegan up to her. We're still close to the door. I glance quickly at the door over Lucia's shoulders, hoping she doesn't notice it.

If I wake her boyfriend up and have both of their attention, I could create enough of a distraction for Tegan to get out. I'll worry about myself later. I won't be able to live with myself if I don't get Tegan out of this. I just wish I could talk to her and give her a big hug, tell her exactly what to do and guarantee Tegan's safety.

"Tegan wants to live with her dad, Lucia. I understand this might be upsetting, but she's been through—"

"Ay, what the fuck is wrong with you, broad?" Lucia interrupts impatiently, her voice rising loudly. Her boyfriend's foot moves and then he coughs a little, one of his eyes flickering open as Lucia waits for an answer to a question I assumed was rhetorical.

She has a machete and the upperhand — plus she has backup. I'm an out of shape nanny who spent her entire life with her nose in a book. If it wasn't a romance novel, it was

one of my textbooks. I'm not equipped for an armed Puerto Rican woman or mobster drama.

"Lucia," I answer calmly, hoping using her name will humanize me to her. "There's nothing wrong with me."

But I have to come up with a distraction. I have to trigger something in this woman so all hell breaks loose and there's just enough of a distraction that Tegan can reach the door. I squeeze Tegan's hand gently and point my gaze in the direction of the door just long enough that I hope she'll notice.

There's only one bolt and a deadbolt. If she locked the deadbolt and left the key somewhere else, we're screwed but... we'll just have to take that chance that it's unlocked.

"But I was lying to you," I say out of nowhere, catching Lucia's attention. Her boyfriend yawns loudly and sits up, barely acknowledging us as he leans forward and presses his forehead into his hands. He mutters a couple words in Spanish, which makes me think he's Puerto Rican like Lucia, or at least Hispanic.

"What was the lie?" Lucia asks, pretending like the question bores her when I notice her grip on the machete tightening. Her boyfriend gets off the couch and walks towards us. He doesn't look at me or Tegan, just Lucia. She's his boss, maybe not literally, but it's clear he doesn't have a clue what's going on.

"I'm more than Rian's nanny. I'm pregnant with his child. If you let Tegan go, you can keep me here and do whatever you want to me, hold me for ransom or whatever you want. I just need you to open that door and let her out."

Lucia's boyfriend shrugs and makes a face that suggests he thinks I have a good idea. The ransom probably appeals to him more than holding us here for Lucia's unprofitable personal reasons.

"I told you, ignorant ass bitch," Lucia says with a tightening voice. "I want my daughter. She's mine and I won't have a bunch of fucking racists holding on to her. I don't believe you're pregnant with Rian's kid."

I let go of Tegan's hand. It's not that she doesn't need me anymore, or that I don't need her. I just want her to be ready. Lucia isn't great at hiding her emotions. When I mention that I'm pregnant, she becomes visibly upset even if she's claiming that she doesn't believe me. We're still living on the prayer that the door behind her isn't deadbolted.

Her boyfriend puts his arm over Lucia's shoulders and whispers in Spanish. I know and teach Spanish to Tegan, so we both understand exactly what he says. I can't betray that I know what they're saying, but it's nearly impossible to contain my pleasure. The door isn't deadbolted, and Lucia's boyfriend doesn't seem like the brightest bulb when he asks her if he should do anything about it.

If Tegan sprints and can outrun both of them, she'll make it. Lucia doesn't appear to have faith in Tegan's Spanish skills, but surely she heard it too and after our weeks together, she can understand enough to get the message. We just need an opportunity.

I'm this close to getting Lucia to do something crazy. I can feel it. Maybe telling her about my pregnancy was risky, but I have limited options to rile her up and I can't put Tegan in more danger. Lucia already injected me with a mysterious chemical to knock me out. The longer I stay without doing something, the worse for me and my baby. I technically don't even know if my baby's okay.

I should have listened to his orders. If I hadn't taken Tegan out, this never would have happened. I swear I'll carry the guilt forever, especially if something worse happens to Tegan. I don't know how I'll cope if I lose the baby.

"Rian isn't the same person," I say to Lucia gently. Tegan

takes a step to my left, giving her a better vantage point to sprint to the door. Lucia and her boyfriend are both fixated on me. "He's not a racist. He loves his daughter and he loves me. We are in love and we're starting a family."

"Shut the fuck up!" Lucia hisses. "He would never do that. He would never abandon Tegan and risk death for a... for a... oh fuck it."

She raises the machete and lunges for me. Her boyfriend grabs her arm, stopping her from slicing my arm clean off. I scream and stumble backwards. My ass lands against a table and I yell again, "Tegan, RUN!"

I don't focus on what Tegan does next. I dive forward to football tackle Lucia. Her boyfriend yanks the machete out of her hand, throwing her off balance enough that when I lunge forward, I take Lucia to the ground instantly. I hear the jiggling front door, the sound of the handle, and then her boyfriend's loud, heavy footsteps. He's a big guy and you can tell just from the way he walks.

I don't know if Tegan's outside or still fumbling with the handle. She has to be outside by now... I lose my sense of what's going on, but I can only hope that I just missed the sound of the door.

"TEGAN!" I yell again as Lucia gains control of herself and hits me in the face with a hard punch. "Tegan, get out of here!"

LUCIA PUSHES hard and then knees me right in the groin. Sharp pain spreads through me, but I can't let this tiny bitch take me down. Her boyfriend must be running after Tegan and I have to pray my girl can outrun him. It's my job to handle Lucia.

I'm no fighter, but I won't back down from one if it comes to it. I ball my hand up in a big fist and use my size to my advantage against Lucia as I hit her in the chest, knocking the wind out of her.

I glance up at the front door. Tegan's gone. But so is Lucia's boyfriend, making Tegan's fate uncertain. We still don't know where we are or how to get in touch with her dad. Still, if Tegan can get to the authorities, she doesn't have to worry about all of that. I don't have long to assess the situation before Lucia throws another punch, hitting me hard in the cheek.

I grab her collar and slam her back against the ground. Lucia cries out and my human instinct feels guilty as fuck for hurting her. She scratches at my face and another instinct takes over.

Survival.

25

Rian

Aiden sits in the passenger seat with an unloaded sawed off shotgun on his lap. He has the chamber open and three shells rolling around his palm. We've been driving along the highway to Providence for twenty or so minutes. Providence has wicked Puerto Ricans and it's just far enough from the city that an impulsive wackjob like Lucia would think it's the safest place in the world to run and hide with our daughter.

Plus, we have good information. Our family networks extend all over the East Coast. Lucia should know better than anyone how hard it can be to hide from the Murray family. I just want to see Tegan. I've been driving 90 mph the entire way and I'd go 100 mph if Aiden would let me. It's over 30 miles over the speed limit, but I can handle it. I'm in complete control of everything except the slower sedans on the highway. He doesn't need to freak out.

"It doesn't matter how quickly we get to the city if we don't know where to look," Aiden growls. "We can run a grid search, but that will take hours. We need to tap our connections. Our cousin has seven different corner store owners and bar owners reporting to him and they know exactly who to look for. We just need a minute for the information to filter my way."

"Do you really think Lucia will bother with a bodega or a bar when she has our kid captive? Fuck, Aiden. How the fuck did this happen?"

I white-knuckle grip the steering wheel of my Escalade, which smells like Lysol spray from the shitty last minute clean-up job we did after Michelle. Aiden successfully avoided a war and Michelle will be up and walking around soon – across the Atlantic. It's better for everyone, especially Darragh.

If I'd known Lucia would go this far, kidnapping our daughter and Heavyn, I might not have fought so hard for my father to spare her life. It was bad enough that I couldn't love Lucia back, and that I wanted our daughter but nothing to do with her. I thought I didn't have to crush her completely but... maybe I was wrong.

"You can't blame yourself," Aiden says. "I gave them permission to leave. I was under the impression that Lucia had given up on Tegan entirely. She ignored all my offers to see her right after I got her back from the kidnapping."

It's so fucking hard to hear that shit. Lucia had one chance after another to be with our kid and she always gave it up. How dare she act like she's the only one with rights to Tegan now? It pisses me off that she would do this.

"I'm gonna kill her..."

I know I shouldn't say that shit to Aiden, but it just comes out of me, the impulse to kill. Most of my recent dark urges have been purely sexual and acted upon with Heavyn. This is the first time since I killed my father that the dark urges have turned towards murder.

I feel like an addict with violence sometimes. Other times,

it feels like this shit keeps coming up and it doesn't matter what the fuck I do, my fate is totally out of my hands. I was born a Murray, so I'll have to kill as long as I live to protect the people I love.

I can already envision my knife slicing through Lucia's neck... You hurt my daughter, you die. That's the way I want to live from now on. I don't want Tegan going through any more hurt.

"You promised that you wouldn't do that," Aiden says gruffly, snapping me out of my murderous fantasy. "So you won't. I'll handle Lucia."

"What if Tegan's dead?"

Aiden's phone buzzes aggressively and he reaches into the pocket of his jeans to grab it, wriggling ridiculously in the seat to get the phone trapped against his leg. He answers it in time with his usual brusque voice. I've criticized Aiden in the past for being too soft-hearted, but his voice now sounds anything but soft.

He doesn't say much, just a gruff answer and then he blurts out an address. I don't need to be a genius to know that's where he wants me to go.

"Thank you. Hold onto her, we'll be there soon."

He hangs up as I enter 17th Lexington Street into the GPS. We're ten minutes away.

"They've got Tegan," Aiden says, sounding visibly relieved. "She's in Providence like we thought and she seems to have escaped from somewhere. She said a man with a machete was chasing after her but Mike McLean has her at his pub downtown."

I don't know who the fuck Mike McLean is, but we have enough McLean cousins to tire out a genealogist, so he must be one of those Rhode Island cousins. I thought they mostly kept out of mob business, but this stuff is Aiden's problem. I keep to myself too much to worry about keeping the extended family united.

Fuck, I've got to worry about keeping my immediate family together.

"I can make it in five minutes if you let me drive how I want?"

Aiden purses his lips. I wait for his orders. I hope he senses my urgency, my desperation to get to Tegan.

Aiden nods and holds onto the door in anticipation of me driving like a fucking crazy person.

"Do it," he says. "I don't want Tegan alone for much longer."

"Did he mention anything about Heavyn?" I ask as my foot grinds into the accelerator. We just have to get lucky.

"No," Aiden says softly. "Nothing about her."

AIDEN'S white as a sheet when I park on the sidewalk outside of 17th Lexington. He puts his ammo in his pocket and conceals his sawed off shotgun in a shearling lined denim jacket. I have a small pistol in my suit jacket, but I keep it there for now. I don't want to use a gun in front of my daughter.

I just want to hold her and then I want to find Heavyn...

Aiden talks to the store owner, but I don't have a fucking second. I interrupt and ask where Tegan is and then I push in the door to the break room for his employees and there she is. She's sitting on a chair, leaned forward over a table and my heart does a fucking backflip when I see her.

I freeze in the doorway. She's okay. Thank fucking God, she's okay.

"Tegan…"

She glances up at me and I worry that she'll reject me again. I've failed her. I've allowed her to fall into dangerous circumstances again when I promised myself I'd never allow that to happen again. But Tegan smiles. She hops out of her seat and she sprints towards me.

We run for each other, arms outstretched, and I hold my baby girl tightly, clutching her to my chest. Tegan's arms wrap around me and I remember the first time I held her, how I promised myself that I'd do anything to keep her safe. I remember finding out I would have to go to jail and leave her behind, and how much it hurt.

For so many years, I grew apart from my daughter and I nearly lost her forever. I hug her so tightly that I can feel her breathing.

"I love you, baby," I murmur. "You're okay. Daddy's here… You're okay."

"Dad…" she whispers back, pressing her nose to my neck. "I knew you would find me. I love you so much."

Aiden's voice in the other room sounds like a soft murmur. I'm glad I get to have this moment with Tegan alone. After several minutes, I pull away from her and examine her for injury.

"I escaped five days ago," she says. "Heavyn's still with them. I keep trying to find the cops or someone to help me but… he's hunting me. He has people on the streets and they're watching me. I can't trust anyone who isn't Irish."

I can't tell if Tegan's being completely truthful or if this is the trauma she's been through influencing her thinking. She's pretty far from any police officers or police stations, but how has she survived on the streets for three days?

I scowl and my worry about Tegan's state heightens. I'll need Aiden to sort this out. I take Tegan's hand and thank the store owner for keeping her safe. Aiden gives the man a hefty sum of cash and we head outside with Tegan, getting her safely into the car before we regroup behind tinted windows.

Aiden sits with Tegan in the back seats right behind the driver's seat so he can get her story out of her. I'm driving because I don't know if I can take this shit right now. If I have to hear one word about Lucia grabbing hold of my kid and hurting her, I don't know if I can keep my promise.

Right now, I'm thinking *fuck this promise* because these people still have Heavyn Wagner with them. As easy as it would be to blame her for everything that happened and to blame her for taking Tegan outside, I know Heavyn would have never done anything deliberately that could hurt my daughter.

While Tegan talks, it's my job to take the Escalade in a large loop around Providence. Until she can give us more specifics about who took her and the man coming after her, there's no point in us leaving the city or in us sticking around somewhere anyone could ambush us. I take the slow, old colonial roads around Providence while I listen to her speak.

Aiden knows just how to calm her down, which I'm grateful for. Once he gets Tegan calm and certain of her safety, she tells us what she knows and remembers. She starts with her mother pressing a taser into her stomach and then staying locked up in a room somewhere. She tells the whole story without crying until she gets to the part where Heavyn helped her escape.

Tegan buries her face in her hands and sobs despite Aiden's efforts to calm her down.

"We have to go back for her," Tegan says. "I tried... But I can't remember where it is and... I'm hungry..."

The shop owner must have given her a little to eat, but I

imagine it wasn't enough. Since we aren't exactly any closer to finding Heavyn and I've just driven a couple miles out, Aiden asks me to go through the nearest McDonald's drive-thru so Tegan can get something to eat quickly. I don't indulge in fast food often, so I don't know what to order from the blindingly colorful menu. I just get what Aiden gets – a bacon double cheeseburger with fries. Tegan gets a spicy chicken sandwich, no fries, and a diet coke.

The food helps her talk more. She tells us more about the man with a machete, who has apparently been hunting her for the past few days.

"I've had to steal to stay alive," Tegan says proudly. "But I've been sleeping in the library. I'm so small, they don't even notice. It's genius but… I can't find the house. I ran away too quickly and it was dark."

I don't know if I should be concerned for my daughter or proud of the lessons I've taught her. I suppose I've spent too much time locked up to take credit for her being a survivor. And I suppose the credit belongs to Heavyn too for letting her go.

"It can't be far from where we found you," Aiden says, which is a good point. "Anything you remember could help us, Tegan… Just tell me everything you remember. Any detail."

"I remember that Heavyn's pregnant," Tegan says, taking a loud sip of her diet coke. Aiden clears his throat, or perhaps just buys himself time so he doesn't have to tackle this question.

Fuck.

"He isn't even denying it," Tegan says. "Ew."

I glance at Aiden quickly in the rearview mirror. He seems to have gained some control over himself.

Chapter 25

"When did the subject of pregnancy arise? Does Lucia know about this?"

"Heavyn told everyone so there'd be a big distraction and I could get away."

Tegan's voice gets heavy again and she lets out a loud, sad sigh straight from her heart. I never expected her to bond with Heavyn so strongly. I thought this could all be simple, but I've made it more complicated. I just wanted a family. I wanted closeness after so much time alone...

"How did Lucia react?" I ask my daughter, although I know her answer to the question might not be an answer that I like. It doesn't matter. I need to know the truth.

"She got mad," Tegan says. "I don't know what happened."

Aiden clears his throat, so I back off. "Don't worry, Tegan. We'll get her back. I just need you to stay put in the car and listen to everything I say, okay?"

"Yes, Uncle Aiden."

"Rian, bring the car back to where we found her. We'll start a grid search from the shop and since she'll be in the car, she can jog her memory without worrying for her life."

"Yes, boss," I grunt, turning back in the direction where we found my daughter. I'm only a few minutes out, but they're painful minutes and I swear every face I see could be Heavyn. Tegan presses her face to the window with Aiden crouched near her in the backseat, scanning the streets himself.

"Rian," he growls. I glance over my shoulder briefly to answer him, but it's a mistake taking my eyes off the road. I look back in front of me and there's a giant ball of something careening into the street. I swerve and slam on the brakes as hard as possible, but I'm going too fast to have complete control.

. . .

Rian

Oh fuck, we're gonna crash.

26

Heavyn

here's a car. I didn't see it until it was too late. Five days of torture, I finally escape, and this is how it ends – I get hit by a car. I fall hard on my face trying to jump out of the way, but the car swerves at the last minute and slams into a parked red Ford Fusion. There's another car behind them, but I can move just enough to roll out of the way.

I lose consciousness as I slam into the side of the gigantic tires on a Ford F-150 parallel parked on the side of the road. I'm lying on my back with the Rhode Island sun searing through the clouds to blind me. My mouth is so dry and I'm in so much pain that I just let the sleep take me.

I don't even care that I'm in the middle of the road. I just want to... be free. So I fall unconscious.

THUD.
    Thud.
    Thud.

. . .

THERE'S A HEARTBEAT. And warmth. They both wake me up. The warmth spreads from my throbbing ear across my cheek-and down the length of my neck. The heartbeat is slow, steady and comforting. I'm barely awake yet, but I know I'm safe. I can feel the warmth cradling me and I want to yield to it so badly. An unwilling groan escapes my lips, forcing me awake.

I'm in so much pain, but I want to move towards the heartbeat. I want to move towards life.

"I've got you, Heavyn."

I would recognize that voice anywhere. I don't know how I could ever mistake it for another man's voice or confuse him for any other. Rian Murray. My chest heaves with a mixture of relief and fear. There's relief, because if Rian Murray has me, I made it. I escaped on my own and I've made it to his arms – safety. I'm afraid because I'm only here because I screwed up.

I can't guarantee Rian's sympathy for what happened to me when I disobeyed his orders and put his daughter in danger. I don't even know what happened to Tegan. I can only hope she ran away, but everything I heard from Lucia over the past three days before I could escape again suggests that Tegan might still be in Providence.

She's the first name I say when I wake up.

"Tegan… Tegan…"

I feel a pair of soft lips against my forehead. The warmth spreads through me immediately and my eyes flutter open. I hear the sound of a trunk opening, which doesn't give me hope. I stop my arms hanging limp and quickly throw them over Rian's shoulders so he doesn't stuff me in a trunk somewhere.

I glance over my shoulders and nearly hit my head on the

open Escalade trunk door that Aiden Murray holds open. Tegan crouches back there with a smile on her face.

"I gotta talk to the guy we hit," Aiden says. "I'll give him enough cash to scrap the car if we can just get the hell outta here."

Aiden struts off to find the owner of the red Ford Fusion, who hopefully isn't very far off. His heartbeat keeps me steady, but as I gain consciousness, more panic sets in.

Just because Rian's here doesn't mean we're completely safe.

"Can you handle yourself?" Rian asks as he gently lowers me into the back of the Escalade. I nod, even if I don't know. My body is sore and I just jumped into traffic, barely escaping with my life.

Rian's car functions, but the fender is fucked up from him slamming into the parked car.

"Did you see him?" I choke out as I try to swing my legs into the back of the Escalade. Tegan scrambles over to me and wraps her arms around me from behind. I close my eyes and hold onto her arms, feeling relieved and as she drapes her body over mine.

"See who?" Rian asks gruffly.

"AIEEE!" Tegan screams, flinging her arms away from me as she scrambles away from me and towards the front of the car.

"Daddy, watch out!" Tegan screeches as she puts distance between herself and Rian's would-be assailant.

The machete swings down at Rian's head before I can scream. I leap off the back of the Escalade and run to the front of the car as Rian dodges the blow from Lucia's boyfriend. Aiden's across the street talking to the Ford Fusion owner and he doesn't realize we have a problem until Tegan screams.

Rian has to have a gun in here if he doesn't have one on his person. I just have to hope he can dodge Lucia's boyfriend until I find one. I don't have to wait. I glance over my shoulder and see Aiden leveling a gun at his hip across the street.

"Tegan, get down!" I yell at her before I slam my body to the ground parallel to the Escalade, whose tail sticks out in the middle of the road. Aiden shoots twice. I can hear sirens in the distance and convince myself that they're closing in on us.

I throw my hands over my head and stay on the ground. I don't know if there will be more gunshots.

"Tegan, stay down!" I yell at her, but I don't get any response. I hope she's okay. A man slams on his horn and swerves around the Escalade. The street is moderately active. I can't imagine we'll get out of this without all of us going to jail. Except Tegan.

She'll probably go back to her mother. The thought makes me sick to my stomach.

I hear a loud grunting sound and then a voice that sounds like Rian speaking in Celtic.

"Rian, you promised," Aiden growls.

"I lied," Rian says. I hear three gunshots in quick succession. There's a funny smell and then after that, the distinct smell of blood.

"Tegan, don't open your eyes!" Aiden growls. "Whatever you do, don't open your eyes."

"I'm not sorry," Rian says. "This is what Lucia needs to learn that she can't fuck with me. If this doesn't warn her to stay away, I don't know what will."

"We have to leave him here," Aiden growls. "You stupid motherfucking fuck. Get in the car and get us out of here."

I can hear Aiden's angry footsteps drawing close to me.

Chapter 26

He crouches to my level and his face softens slightly. I slowly draw myself out of my tense, sheltered position and roll into a seated position. Aiden stretches his hand out to help me up.

"We don't have time, Heavyn. I need you to get in the car and look after Tegan. Can you do that for me?"

I nod and take Aiden's hand, rising to my feet. I don't want to look over in the direction of the gunshots, but I don't have to. Blood spills into the pavement, running in a river around my feet. I hear Rian start the car and Aiden opens the back door for me, guiding me inside. He closes the trunk and points to Tegan, still sheltered in the trunk.

Somehow, I have the instinct for what to do. I put my hand on her back and whisper to her gently.

"Keep your eyes closed, honey. I'm right here."

Aiden jumps into the passenger seat of the car and Rian speeds away. I glance out the back window and there's a body on the ground next to the red Ford Fusion.

Rian killed him. I can feel myself wanting to slip into unconsciousness again, but with my hand on Tegan's back, I can feel her heartbeat. Hers is different from Rian's. She's small and fluttery. Her heartbeat reminds me of how young she is and how much more life she has ahead of her.

Tegan's heartbeat reminds me that I have to be strong for her.

AIDEN SPENDS the rest of the car ride on the phone. Once we're three miles out of the city, he allows Tegan to sit up in the car. She's a bit pale, but she seems otherwise fine. Apparently, they bought her fast food because she eventually continues munching on her chicken sandwich.

I'm hungry, but I can't bring myself to eat. Rian and

Aiden have been too focused on our escape from Providence (I read the highway signs on the way out of the city) to ask how I got free from Lucia and her boyfriend. I don't know how much I want to tell them. I just know that I have to find out about the baby.

If I lost the baby, I don't know how Rian will ever forgive me. I don't know if he'll forgive me period. It's a very quiet car ride back to Boston and not just because of Rian's 100 mph speeds making it impossible to move without succumbing to intense nausea.

It feels like I'm driving to my death, which is painfully ironic since I did everything in my power to get back to Rian. I don't know what I expected. Not to witness a murder.

I CAN SAFELY SAY, I didn't expect that.

27

Rian

Aiden doesn't punish me for the murder since I didn't kill Tegan's mother, just her boyfriend. I haven't heard from Lucia and I haven't heard from the police either. The cops and the media blame the death on a local gang and Aiden assures me that our connections down there stretch far enough to keep my ass out of trouble.

We get word of all that only a couple hours after we get back to Boston. It feels weird to go back to my normal life after the shit we've been through, but I don't know what the fuck else to do. I take Tegan and Heavyn inside the house. Camilla bounds over to Tegan who squeals her name and runs over to her cat again.

She throws her arms around Camilla and I sense she'll be alright once she gets clean. After Tegan cuddles and kisses Camilla for a while, I instruct my daughter to take a shower and get clean for dinner. She pulls away from Camilla who follows her upstairs, most likely to return to sleeping curled up on Tegan's bed somewhere.

I offer to order pizza, like ordering pizza for your family can make up for them witnessing you killing someone.

I couldn't help myself. Tegan wanders upstairs and I wish I could command Heavyn the same way, but I can't. I can just appreciate that we're alone and that Tegan is too worn out to protest my orders for once.

Once we're alone, Heavyn gets close to me, close enough that she can look me in the eye, but not so close that I mistake her intentions as romantic. She looks both puzzled and angry.

"What happened, Rian?"

"You heard what happened. Maybe you saw it. Did that man touch Tegan? He had her for days in that house and I know some of these fucks are–"

"He didn't do that," she interrupts, clearly hoping to assuage my worries. It's not enough.

"My daughter needs to know I'll do anything to protect her."

"But she doesn't need to fear you," Heavyn says. She's close enough that I get a proper look at her for the first time. She has bruises all over the left side of her face, a partially healed burst lip and her arms are scratched with belt marks like she fought off beatings.

"Heavyn..." I murmur, incapable of stopping myself. I touch her cheek gently. She flinches, but then leans into the warmth of my palm. I don't want her to pull away. "Are you afraid of me? Because that's not my intention. I want you both to feel safe."

"I suppose I'll always feel a little of both with you – terrified and safe."

"That's a contradiction."

"You're a contradiction," she says, staring back at me straight on. I love when she looks at me. There's something deeply powerful and arousing about getting her attention. I become fixated on earning her attention when I'm around her in the most primal way.

"Yes," I whisper, running my thumb idly over her lower lip, swirling around the cut, red part of her fleshy lower lip. "But I would kill and die for you. For both of you."

She swallows slowly and shakes her head a little.

"Aren't you going to kick me out for being completely disobedient and causing all of this?" she asks. Is that what's been on her mind?

I confessed with my entire heart that I loved Heavyn. The entire time she's been gone, I haven't stopped worrying about her. It's not just because she's my surrogate. With or without the child in her womb, I would want her. I wanted her the second I saw her. Disobedience...

When you love a strong woman, you get disobedience because strong women don't always listen to you. They fight back. They stand up for themselves. Strong women raise strong daughters and that's why Tegan survived this. I don't blame Heavyn for what happened to my daughter. I appreciate her for keeping Tegan alive. For putting her first.

I can't hide the emotion in my voice. "Do you really expect me to punish you after what you've gone through?"

She gives me a wide-eyed look. Her large brown eyes captivate me completely. They're so dark and deep that I can lose myself in her eyes, especially the way they're set in her round face. I rest my hand against her sepia skin. She's so fucking beautiful. And she's mine. She will always be mine after tonight.

I refuse to let Heavyn go. I can't imagine going through with it.

"I didn't listen to you."

"You're not my slave, Heavyn. I don't expect perfect obedience to my commands... except in the bedroom."

That quickly brings a gentle smirk to her face. I feel good that I've assuaged some of her worry, but that only lasts a second before the sad expression returns. I run my thumb along her jawline and my cock throbs unwillingly in my pants. Touching her brings me irresistible amounts of pleasure. I can't help it. I run my thumb over her lip, hoping to bring her smile back, but she tucks her lips inside nervously.

"What's wrong?" I murmur.

"I just feel like I screwed up and I don't know if the baby made it. I know you're happy to see me, but I feel like I ruined everything and I've been too insecure at all the wrong times."

"You didn't screw anything up. If you did, I'll fix it for you. I'll fix everything until it's alright."

I run my thumb over her lip again, appreciating the fullness of Heavyn's perfect lips. The first kiss we exchange sends a shiver of desire straight through me. I touch her face as I tease her lips open and slip my tongue into her mouth. We probably don't have long until Tegan comes downstairs…

I kiss Heavyn as long as I think I can get away with. When I pull away from her, my cock throbs with urgency again. I want her so badly.

"We need to order pizza," Heavyn says. "Tegan will be hungry."

It's hard not to be smitten with a woman who loves my daughter this much. I never wanted Tegan to grow up without a mom, but I didn't see the point in rushing to fill the role once everything happened with Lucia.

Heavyn loves Tegan all on her own. She loves Tegan the way a mother should and that makes me want her even more.

"You nearly got hit by a car," I whisper, wanting to kiss her and make love to her against all reason since we're still standing in the kitchen. "And you're still worried about Tegan."

The slightest smile returns to Heavyn's face again. I feel closer to her than I've ever felt before but that closeness still comes with complicated feelings about our future. I can't let tonight end without laying everything on the table.

"She's my girl," Heavyn replies. "She's our girl."

"Yes," I whisper back. "She is."

My feelings for Heavyn rise in my chest urgently. Getting her back and kissing her like this only makes it that much more real that she nearly slipped out of my grasp. I can't let her go. If she lost the baby, we'll work through the pain and we'll try again. I don't want the surrogacy pact to be the reason I lose her.

She's worth so much more than that...

"I love you, sunshine. The thought of letting you go when this is all over fucks with my head. I'd rather go back to prison than wake up in this house without you. Tegan already knows about us and she's smitten with you."

"Then don't let me go," Heavyn says. "I'm sorry I took so long to get here, Rian. I've never been in love like this before and it scares me to put myself out there after keeping to myself for so long. But I want to be with you and I don't want to lose Tegan."

My hands move from her cheek to her hands. I want to lock my fingers with hers and pull her close to me for as long as we can stand here intertwined. As I hold her hand and pull Heavyn's body against mine, she reminds me why we can't actually stand like this forever.

"Pizza," Heavyn whispers. "Don't forget the pizza."

I order a large cheese pizza for the three of us to split. Tegan shows up downstairs freshly showered in her pajamas before the pizza arrives. Heavyn offers to braid her hair while she waits with us at the kitchen bar. Tegan sleepily agrees to have her hair braided and I pour myself a glass of Glenfiddich as Heavyn and Tegan wander off to get the hair braiding supplies.

I've done my share of braiding Tegan's hair, but Heavyn has an unusual talent for braiding that fascinates me completely. She splits Tegan's hair into several parts and then begins her work. She braids my daughter's hair up quickly and by the time she's done, we don't have to wait very long for pizza.

I grab the pizza from the door and sit next to Tegan who brightens up immediately at the delicious greasy smell of a hot pizza. Both Tegan and Heavyn are tired. I can tell because Heavyn barely eats, which is definitely out of character for her. I suggest that she clean up once she's done and offer to put Tegan to bed.

Tegan perks up from her slice of pizza.

"So Heavyn's allowed to stay?" Tegan asks.

I glance at Heavyn who smiles and nods. "I think I'm gonna stay."

ONCE HEAVYN'S upstairs washing the nightmare she's been through off her, I eat pizza with Tegan and try to talk to her. I don't talk about what she heard or God forbid, what she saw. I ought to consult with Aiden first on how to handle that. He's more experienced than I am with mafia family matters.

All I know how to do is look after Tegan, no matter the cost. Once she's done eating, Tegan grows very sober, which concerns me, since I thought she was gaining a bit more energy. I suppose she spent so many days on the streets that she needs some sleep.

Chapter 27

"Want me to carry you up to bed?"

"No," Tegan says, shaking her head. "I just don't want Heavyn to ever leave us. She says she's pregnant, dad. Mom got pregnant and that ruined your relationship."

"That's not true. Your mother and I ruined our relationship all on our own. I wasn't ready for the type of shit I was messing with and she had her own demons to fight. I'm here now and I love you and I won't abandon you or Heavyn or anyone else."

I can't resist throwing my arms around her and giving my daughter a big, tight hug. I don't hug her enough and I don't feel like I've hugged her enough today. It still sorta hurts my heart to put my arms around her and feel how fucking tiny and helpless she is.

"I know you won't abandon me, dad. I love you."

"I love you too, kid."

Tegan pulls away from me and gives me a very serious look. "And do you love Heavyn? Because, you'd better."

I smile at her and nod. "Yeah, I do. Problem is, sunshine, I hired her. That means if we're gonna be together, I have to untangle the mess I've made."

"What mess?" Tegan asks.

"That's grown up stuff. Think you can sleep tonight? I can read you a story if you want."

"I'm too old for stories," Tegan says. "But you can tuck me in. I'm not too old for that yet."

Too old? I don't believe that for a second. Tegan will always be my baby girl. I take her hand and walk her upstairs. It's not terribly late but like I suspected, she's exhausted. Her bedroom smells like her and she has all her possessions organized nicely with the music box from Uncle Aiden still displayed prominently. Camilla sleeps on the pile of laundry spilling out of Tegan's hamper. Tegan tries to call her over to bed but Camilla just opens a sleepy eye for a few seconds before shutting it again and returning to her deep slumber.

Tegan climbs into bed and I kiss her forehead before pulling the covers over her and telling her one last time how much I love her...

I WALK over to Heavyn's room with no need for secrecy. I still feel a rush of emotion and a racing heartbeat as I approach her bedroom door as if I'm doing something terribly wrong. We're no longer a secret. I knock on her door gently and my cock stiffens when I hear Heavyn's perfect voice command me to enter.

"Come in!"

She sounds like she's singing whenever she talks. I love her lilting voice, her accent and most importantly, her bluntness. I push the door open to see Heavyn standing there in a towel. That makes the situation with my dick that much worse. She looks great, but I have to control my urge to make love to her – for now.

"We should get married," I blurt out. "I'll buy you the ring you want – a yellow stone like Citrine or yellow tourmaline set with diamonds in yellow gold would look great with all your yellow dresses. We'll get married somewhere private and quiet, just you, me and Tegan. I don't want the Irish making a bloody fuss over us. I... For once in my fucking life, am talking too much."

Heavyn clutches the white towel against her dark skin.

"Somewhere private and quiet, like where?"

"Are you saying yes?"

"I'm pregnant, Rian. Hopefully. You're my kid's dad, I love you, I love Tegan... I already live here. At this point, we might as well stop pretending. I need to stop pretending that I want to be anywhere else."

"Finally," I answer with a sigh. Heavyn looks incredible in that towel. She has her hair tossed up in a sexy messy bun and the towel makes her curves look that much more delicious.

"Do you want me to get down on one knee?"

Heavyn shrugs. "What's the point? We're already getting married. Plus, I'm naked in a towel, so it's not exactly a viral moment."

"I can think of a lot more things I can do on my knees," I say to Heavyn, closing in on her and grabbing her hips before dropping to my knees.

Proposing is the second happiest a man can make a woman when he gets on his knees. I grab Heavyn's towel and pull it away from her forcefully so she can't resist me and keep herself covered up. I want to appreciate every fucking inch of this woman's body right now. There's no part of Heavyn that can escape me. My fingers sink into the curvy flesh of her stomach and I instinctively kiss her protruding tummy, getting incredibly hard as I imagine my kid growing inside her.

"Tomorrow, we check on the baby," I murmur, kissing her stomach again. "But I know God will look out for us, sunshine. We're meant to have this baby. I know we're meant to be a family."

I kiss the top of Heavyn's mound and nearly cum in my pants as she slides her fingers through my hair. The lightest touch from Heavyn is enough to nearly make me lose my fucking mind. Her fingers feel incredible as they part my strands and I want nothing more than to spread her lower lips apart and press my tongue between her legs.

"You smell fresh," I murmur, grasping her hips more

tightly so I can hold her closer and appreciate more of her curves. Her hands slide back through my hair and my cock jerks in my pants again. I spread Heavyn's lower lips with my fingers, exposing her tender clit. I cup her ass cheeks with one hand as I use another to hold her open. My tongue eases over her clit in a slow smooth stroke that makes Heavyn moan. The sound of her moans drives me fucking wild.

I can't restrain myself and I don't want to bother. My tongue moves instinctively over Heavyn's pussy lips, teasing her most sensitive parts and returning to her clit every time her moan gets so loud that I think she'll cum. I pull away from the last second each time Heaven gets close, teasing her gently.

When I'm ready for her to cum, I plunge my tongue deep between her folds and wait for Heavyn's juices to erupt all over me. I hold her up on my shoulders as I lick her clit and suck her dribbling essence off her thighs. She tastes so fucking good.

I pull away from her, still on my knee, gazing up at her. *My surrogate. My wife.*

"I want you now," I growl. "But I know you must be tired after what you've gone through... so let's cuddle tonight. In my bed."

"You're allowing me to sleep in your room? I've barely been in there."

"I think that's where you belong now. So come... Let's cuddle in my bed until you forget everything bad in the world."

She takes my hand and I promise myself that I will never let Heavyn go.

28

Heavyn

The Due Date

We have to induce labor medically at exactly thirty-nine weeks. I can barely walk at that point and my feet always feel swollen. Tegan helps a lot and she's so excited about the baby that it's even scaring her dad. Rian paces around the doctor's waiting room impatiently. He doesn't agree with this, but Aiden insists we have a family doctor as my obstetrician.

He makes a good point. Not everyone in his family or in the world of the Irish mob approves of interracial relationships. The more privacy we have, the safer we are. Considering everything we've been through, I choose the safer option: inducing labor early so my trusted doctor can go to Michigan on an elk hunting trip with his brother afterwards.

"I don't understand the point of this," Rian grumbles. "What could be so risky about giving birth with a midwife in the privacy of our home?"

"There could be complications, Rian," I explain to him

with an impatient grunt. Considering I'm the one about to go through this, I don't see why he's so fussy.

"I understand that," Rian says, attempting to gain some control of his patience. "I just wish they would hurry up. I don't want you in any pain."

I purse my lips. Rian has a daughter, so I know he's well aware that he can't stop the pain I'm about to experience. Luckily, our doctor shows up and everything happens quickly. Nurses and the doctor talk to me, they inject me with a bunch of stuff and then I experience motherhood.

There's no way to describe it to someone who hasn't gone through it, but I'm in labor for eight hours. Rian was so nervous beforehand that I wasn't sure how he would handle the process, but he made me feel better. He made me feel like everything would be okay and he was the first person to hold our baby — our precious little girl.

I never wanted to know our baby's gender and Rian felt the same. Tegan pleaded with us to find out, but we waited, and our little baby girl was the best surprise I could have ever hoped for.

Before they take her away to clean her, Rian brings our baby girl to me and I hold her for the first time. She has dark, cinnamon skin, a shock of black hair, but her eyes are closed. Her little lungs shudder as she takes her first breaths and I don't ever want to let go of her — not for a second.

"Her skin is very dark," Rian says, a first comment which draws a look of immediate frustration from me.

"Is that a problem?"

"No," Rian murmurs. "It's like yours. Pretty. Tegan was so pale, it was hard to believe she was half-Puerto Rican. I can tell that she's ours…"

He kisses the top of my head, and it feels real that we're a family. The nurses and hospital staff clean our daughter up and bring her back to my hospital room. We can go home after a night of observation. Even if I'm exhausted, I don't want to miss a second of our daughter's life. I feed her, I hug her and I think about what we're going to call her.

Rian brings her name up like he can read my mind.

"We should name her something Irish."

I give Rian another funny look. "How about an African American name?"

Rian suppresses a strangely huffy sound. He quickly recovers and puts his hand on my back.

"Like what?"

"Like Ciara," I tell him. "I always wanted to name my kid after either Ciara or Beyoncé, but I think Beyoncé would be too obvious."

"You know Ciara is an Irish name, right? We just pronounce it differently."

Crap. He's actually right.

"We aren't agreeing on Ciara, are we?" I ask him, gazing down at our baby girl. She doesn't look like a Ciara or a Beyoncé now that I look at her.

"She doesn't look like a Ciara," Rian agrees, using the more Irish pronunciation as he mirrors my thoughts about our baby girl. I know technically we don't have to choose her name right away, but I can't imagine going to bed without giving her a name.

"I think she should have one Irish name and one African American name."

"Hm," Rian murmurs, kissing my forehead. "I don't know any African American names."

"You know my name," I point out to him. "Plus we have all night..."

"Wouldn't you rather sleep?" Rian asks. I shake my head. I don't want to fall asleep until our little girl has a name.

Heavyn

. . .

WE SPEND all night discussing baby names and all the hopes we have for our daughter's future. In the morning, we leave the hospital with our baby girl: Ava Iyana Murray. The first few days of her at home are a complete blur. I hardly sleep, she needs food all the time, and I feel guilty for how little time I've spent with Tegan.

Settling into a routine with Ava gets easier over time and as she reaches those first baby milestones, we get closer and closer to another important day for our family – our wedding day. The only Murray who knows about the wedding is Aiden because Rian can't leave Boston without telling the boss. Rian wants absolute privacy, which I completely respect. After everything with Lucia and her boyfriend, I don't want any surprise guests showing up at our wedding.

Tegan starts school a couple months before our wedding, so we plan everything so that we fly out during her spring break for the private destination wedding. Rian still has too many trust issues to send Tegan to public school, so she goes to a private day school in Boston. Her first few weeks at school, a new friend of hers convinces her to try out for the school's soccer team. She's never played before, but she becomes instantly obsessed and Rian goes all out getting her gear and practicing with her in the backyard every day after school.

I've never seen him smile this much. It's like he's finally put the darkness from prison behind him. I know he's done some bad things but when I see how much he loves Tegan, Ava, and me, it's hard for me to see him as the villain. If he's the bad guy, he's my bad guy, and I'll go to the ends of the earth for him the same way he would for me.

I know Rian still has enemies and that because of his

family and his business, he'll have to keep the darker parts of him alive. It feels good to be the peace he comes home to. It feels good to be his safe place to smile and laugh with his daughter. I didn't think it would, but it feels good to be a step-mom to Tegan and a mother to Ava. I think I agreed to Rian's proposition not because I was afraid of him, or because I was messed up or something. I just wanted a family.

I wanted... *this*.

Once Tegan's out of school for spring break, I prepare Ava for her first flight. She won't remember her first trip to Northern Ireland, but I will *never* forget my first trip out of the country. Rian springs for us all to fly first class so I'll be more comfortable with the baby. When we get to our luxurious castle, I hardly want to rest for the wedding and I definitely don't want to spend the night away from Rian, but Tegan insists we sleep in separate rooms like she's the boss.

"I don't want your wedding cursed," Tegan says. "Haven't we had enough bad stuff happen to our family?"

Kid has a point. I put Ava to bed and Tegan promises she'll help with her on the wedding day. Tegan's bond with Ava is incredible. Every online parenting blog I read while pregnant warned that step-siblings can sometimes become cruel and jealous, but Tegan has been the opposite. She promises to check on Ava in the middle of the night and to change her diaper on the morning of our wedding.

I ache for Rian all night before we get married. The tradition of not seeing the groom before the wedding is complete agony. I miss him. I can hardly sleep without him in my bed. When I wake up in the morning, Tegan waits at my door with Ava in hand. She already changed Ava's diaper which means I just have to feed her. Tegan brings me water and some oatmeal for breakfast as I feed her sister.

"I'll get the wedding dress," Tegan says excitedly. "It's downstairs. It's *perfect*."

I hope it still fits. Finding the perfect dress for my curves was a challenge. Most places don't cater to plus-sized women with large hips, a large butt and gigantic boobs. If you don't have a certain shape, it's hard to find cute dresses. With Tegan's help, I finally found *the one*. I feel like a real princess. I've always loved dresses, but there's nothing like the glamor of a wedding dress.

I almost wish I could dress up like this every day. Tegan brings the dress upstairs and I eye it nervously. Rian will love it, I tell myself, and the nerves go away. Tegan holds Ava and plays with her as I slip into the dress. The tulle skirt flows around me like a ballgown. The short sleeves are modest and cute so my arms don't feel uncomfortable and the scoop neck makes my boobs look great.

Once I'm dressed, Tegan reads a text from her dad and tells me that he's already at the wedding site – the beautiful Dunluce Castle. It's a typical cloudy day in Northern Ireland, but the sun through the clouds makes everything look spooky and beautiful. It's the perfect wedding day for a couple that fell in love living in a black Victorian mansion.

Tegan rides in the front of the limo with Ava on her lap. They both wear sage green, a color which brings out Tegan's eyes and Ava's cinnamon-brown skin color.

When I see Rian for the first time, my emotional reaction is almost hysterical. My dress feels suddenly warm and I'm nervous about exchanging vows with him, even if I love him and even if I don't ever want to leave him. I tell myself this will be the moment everything breaks apart again, but the closer I get to Rian, the more I realize that nothing bad is going to happen.

We're just finally doing this. We're finally getting married.

Chapter 28

Tegan follows me down the aisle holding Ava who is remarkably calm throughout the private ceremony. Rian is shy and red in the face as he says his vows but he never takes his eyes off me and as our officiant speaks he mouths, "You're beautiful."

It's enough to make me melt. I don't even need this dress to feel like a princess, really. I have Rian and he makes me feel like a princess every day.

Our wedding kiss makes me weak at the knees. Rian grabs both of my cheeks and pulls me to him fiercely like he doesn't care who's watching. Tegan makes a grossed out noise, but he doesn't seem to care. He kisses me with tongue and everything until I have to step back to stop myself from moaning or doing something else embarrassing. Rian is too good of a kisser.

We have a wedding cake, a fancy lunch, and then we spend two days in Belfast before visiting Dublin for another two days. Ava handles traveling well, and Tegan loves shopping in every city we visit. Rian doesn't hesitate to spend money on both of us and we travel back to Boston with two gigantic suitcases each.

The love doesn't wear off after the wedding. That's what most cynical people think about happy endings – that a wedding isn't a real one because it's just where the trouble starts. That doesn't happen with me and Rian when we get back. Tegan returns to school, Rian returns to work at the casino, and he comes home every night for dinner. Without tutoring Tegan, I want to get another job, but I'm not ready to leave Ava.

Rian doesn't seem ready to leave me at all. He comes home one night in the early summer right before Tegan's school lets out for the year with a brilliant idea. I'm in bed reading a new vampire romance novel by my favorite author as Rian undresses from a late night at the casino. It's a damn treat to watch him slowly take his clothes off.

"You don't have to get a job," Rian says. "You could just have another baby. That would be a full time job."

"Ava's only nine months old. Is having another baby right now a good idea?"

Rian smirks. "It depends on your perspective, I suppose. I'd very much like to have a baby with you right now."

"I think you mean you're horny."

Rian unbuttons his white shirt, exposing a very swollen red chest with fresh black ink. He's definitely horny, since that's Rian's permanent state of mind, but I don't want to let the fresh tattoo go without bringing it up.

"Horny?" Rian mutters. "That's how you describe a little boy. I want my wife."

He takes his shirt off completely.

"Is that a new tattoo?"

"Yes," he says. I squint so I can see it better. As Rian comes into view, I see it up close. It's a Celtic knot inter-twined with the word "Ava". He got our daughter's name tattooed on his chest. "It's a surprise for you."

"Did it hurt?"

"Yes. And it took several hours in my office when I should have been working but... it's my promise to you both that I will never let anyone hurt you again. We're lucky Ava made it and I want to get lucky again."

Rian takes his pants off, dropping them to the ground and exposing a gigantic bulge in his boxers. Damn, his dick is big. It's the type of big dick that forces you to acknowledge its impressive size no matter how many times you've seen it.

"I can't be unemployed having babies forever."

I fidget with my engagement ring. It's yellow gold with an 8mm citrine stone surrounded by a halo of diamonds. It's beautiful, exactly what I dreamed of, and almost too good to be true. I love kids and I always have, but I thought I'd end up a single teacher, not mama and teacher to my own kids.

"Why not? Do you think you'll be bored? Ava has cousins."

"Why would you do all that for me, Rian? I can't imagine your dream life is having a woman living off you."

Rian scowls. "Don't be ridiculous. Whatever money you spend belongs to both of us. You care for my daughters, you clean my house, do my laundry, remember my doctor's appointments, cook my food and tell me when I'm being a grouchy asshole. Not to mention I *love* you. I want to take care of our family. I want to make our family bigger..."

Rian climbs into bed next to me. His body is still just as toned as it was when he first got out of prison. He's put on more muscle since I was first pregnant with Ava since he has access to better food than what he got in prison, but he's still so damn hot that my instincts drive me not to fight against his desire to knock me up.

I would be crazy to say no to him. I shut my romance novel and set it on the nightstand. Rian has my attention as I feel his weight on the mattress. Reading can wait... He slides his body over mine and I wrap my arms around him as Rian pushes the sheets off me so he can get between my legs.

"This is the sexiest thing I've ever seen you in," he murmurs, pushing my t-shirt up over my underwear and stomach. I push his hands away from me and drag the t-shirt back down.

"I'm wearing a gigantic t-shirt that smells like the baby," I tell him.

"Yes," Rian says. "And don't you dare push my hand away again when I'm appreciating the body that gave me a child..."

"You don't have to be so dramatic about it," I protest as

Rian's hand returns beneath my shirt. He doesn't care that I'm always a little gross since I've had Ava. Rian doesn't give a crap. He reaches behind me to unhook my bra and gets it done with a quick pinch.

He kisses my neck and all my resistance to Rian's baby idea drains out of my system. Neck kisses make me think having another baby with a mobster is a *very* good idea. I spread my legs around Rian and hook my ankles around him so I can keep his body close and appreciate his sexy ass muscles.

Once he moves his head away from my neck, I lure his lips over to mine so I can kiss him properly. He smells so strongly like cologne and his sweat. Since having Ava, the smell of Rian's sweat has been like an aphrodisiac to me. His scent instantly makes me want to have sex. As our lips meet, I grab Rian's face, appreciating his stubble, his soft skin and his strong, masculine jawline.

"Have I changed your mind?" he whispers between kisses as I whimper for him needily. Rian pushes my shirt over my head and takes it off along with my bra. He can tell from the way I kissed him that I've changed my mind, but I nod anyway. He slides my panties off as I grip his firm ass cheeks and enjoy the curve of his muscular ass.

"Take those off for me," Rian murmurs as he slips his fingers between my lower lips. "I can't wait to feel your tight pussy wrapped around my dick."

I don't hesitate to take his boxer briefs off. Rian's dick smacks my mound as it slips out of his underwear. The warmth from his shaft spreads through me before he enters me as Rian's dick rests against my entrance.

"You smell so good," I whisper, running my fingers through his brown hair and pulling him close to me. "I want to feel you inside me."

Rian pushes his finger inside me first, teasing me open and preparing me for his dick. As his finger teases me, I moan and hold him close to me, covering his body with kisses as he fingers me slowly. It doesn't take long for me to cum all over Rian's fingers. He pulls out of me and rests his bare cock directly against my entrance as he pushes his fingers into his mouth and licks my juices off himself.

"I've waited all day to taste you," he growls. "You're worth it."

Rian eases his cock inside me, taking his time to get the barbells from his Jacob's ladder piercing inside me. I run my fingers over his lower back muscles and let the pleasure over-whelm me as Rian enters me. *My husband.* I gasp as he buries the final inches of his cock between my legs. Rian's large size makes the slightest movement between my legs euphoric. He kisses me slowly as he makes love to me with slow strokes. It doesn't take long for me to cum from the friction of Rian's barbells rubbing my inner walls as he thrusts into me.

Rian isn't ready to cum until he's made me cum three more times. He rubs my clit as he fucks me slowly and kisses me each time he makes me cum. When he's ready to finish, Rian kisses me and sucks on my lower lip, easing his hips forward as he empties his seed inside me. He presses his weight into me as he releases and I tighten my thighs grasp on Rian's torso.

"I don't want to pull out," he growls, pushing hair out of my face and kissing me as a sleepy smile crawls across his face. I don't mind. I want him here as long as possible.

"Then don't," I whisper. "Stay in bed with me, Rian. Stay with me all night."

"That's the plan..." Rian murmurs.

· · ·

BUT THEN HIS PHONE VIBRATES. I sigh and release my grasp on Rian's torso. My thighs spread open and Rian groans as he pulls out of me. There's only one person who could be calling this late at night. The boss – Aiden.

Rian gets out of bed and gets on his phone. He doesn't bother hiding his phone calls from me unless absolutely necessary.

"What's going on?"

He grunts and gives a few one word answers before hanging up and tossing his phone on the bed. He looks so good naked that I almost forget he's about to give me bad news. Rian slides his fingers through his hair with frustration and sighs.

"Sunshine, I need to go. I should be back in an hour or two, but duty calls."

"What's going on?"

Rian responds like he's saying the most normal thing in the world.

"Callum needs to get married and Aiden wants me to kidnap his wife," Rian says, putting on his clothes that we left strewn all over the bed and the floor.

"Kidnap his wife?" I ask, pulling the blankets over me and trying to decide whether I should worry about Rian engaging in yet another crime. It's been months since Aiden has asked him for anything, especially not something this serious.

Rian seems unperturbed.

"Well, she's not his wife yet," Rian says. "But after tonight, she will be. Don't concern yourself, sunshine. I'll be home soon."

THE END

Chapter 28

Callum & Zariyah's story, *Mafia Possession,* Book #4, will be
released on July 31st 2023

Click here to order the book.
bit.ly/bostonirishmafia4

Click here to receive text message updates when the next
Jamila Jasper book releases:
bit.ly/textjamila

About Jamila Jasper

The hotter and darker the romance, the better.

That's the Jamila Jasper promise.

If you enjoy sizzling multicultural romance stories that dare to *go there* you'll enjoy any Jamila Jasper title you pick up.

Open-minded readers who appreciate **shamelessly sexy romance novels** featuring black women of all shapes and sizes paired with smokin' hot white men are welcome.

Sign up for her e-mail list here to receive one of these **FREE hot stories,** exclusive offers and an update of Jamila's publication schedule: bit.ly/jamilajasperromance

Get text message updates on new books: https://slkt. io/gxzM

Dark Mafia Romance
Preview #1

Sample these chapters from my Amalfi Coast Brotherhood Italian mafia romance series while you wait for the next mafia romance series.

If you enjoy dark & twisted mafia romance stories, you can binge the entire completed series on your eReader.

Enjoy the free chapters.

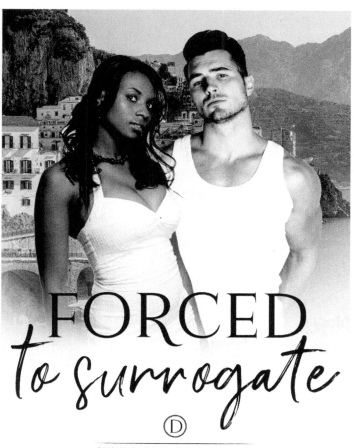

FORCED
to surrogate

Ⓓ

BWWM DARK MAFIA ROMANCE

the amalfi coast mafia brotherhood #1

JAMILA JASPER

Description

The last thing Jodi remembered was a shot of tequila.
Next thing she knows,
Italian sociopath Van Doukas has her chained in his basement...
And he's claiming she agreed to become the mother of his child.

There's a detailed contract and everything... with her signature.
Jodi will do whatever it takes to get away from him...
But she doesn't count on the 6'7" Italian Stallion being skilled with his tongue and excellent in bed.

Series Titles

Forced To Surrogate
Forced To Marry
Forced To Submit

Content Awareness

dark bwwm mafia romance

This is a mafia romance story with dark themes including potentially triggering content, frank discussions and language surrounding bedroom scenes and race. All characters in this story are 18+. Sensitive readers, be cautioned about some of the material in this dark but extremely hot romance novel. The character in this story is *forced by circumstance* into her situation.

Enjoy the steamy romance story...

1. Produce A Pure Italian Heir
Van Doukas

There aren't enough cigarettes in the world for meetings with my father. The boss. Tonight, I meet with him to discuss something 'very important'. He calls everything 'very important', but tonight, I know exactly what he wants from me.

He wants me to kill again, this time for my foolish sister, who can't seem to keep herself out of trouble. Everyone in the family heard about what happened to Ana by now. That idiot Jew was foolish enough to put his hands on her with witnesses and expect nothing to happen? That's not how the Doukas family works, which he'll soon learn.

You mess with the Doukas family, we retaliate. If the Jew had any wits about him, he would disappear from the Amalfi Coast and head for the mountains or Sicily, or somewhere we don't have ears. He could go to Albania like Matteo. Maybe then we wouldn't find him. But fuck, I don't want to carry out another hit. Why can't that lazy fuck Enzo do it? Or better yet, Eddie. I carried out my first hit when I was two years younger than him. We spoil the new generation and wonder why our family falls apart.

None of this would be my responsibility if Matteo would get over himself and come down off his fucking mountain.

I stop my motorcycle and approach my father's front door. The all white old European style mansion sits on an excessive and opulent lot on the coast, right above the cliffs with a long path to the beach, a 'fuck you' to the tax collectors and the government who want to stop us from doing business.

Most of my siblings still live here, but I prefer keeping myself far away from papa and his... associates.

I can hear the party from the entrance. Seriously? On a fucking Tuesday afternoon? I assumed he called this meeting because he was working for once. He's intertwined in a different business based on the noise filtering outside. Please, Lord, let me not walk in on my father having sex with a model... *again*.

I open the front door to our old family home without knocking and immediately regret it when a completely naked foreign woman runs giggling toward the door, too high and drunk to feel self-conscious, exposing her completely nude body to a stranger. At least I didn't find her twisted in bed with papa, although this isn't much better.

"Oh! Good afternoon, sir!" she teases me in crude Italian, spinning around to show off her assets. *Whore. Foreigner. Her tricks possess little interest to me.* My brothers Lorenzo and Matteo would sway more easily.

"Where's my father?"

She giggles and spins around again. Fucking hell, I wish the ground would swallow me up. My father's prostitutes do not interest me.

"Your papa?" she says, standing to face me with her legs slightly apart, daring me to ogle more of her body. I have no interest in whores and I want her to answer my fucking question.

Before I can answer, another one of my father's toys saunters into the foyer, naked. This one is young—she looks eighteen just about—far too young for my father. I grimace and keep my gaze firmly fixed away from the nude females. Just because the men in my family are bastards doesn't mean I have to follow suit.

If we don't conduct ourselves with respect, how can we expect the respect of the Amalfi Coast?

"Yes. My father. Sal," I grunt, failing to hide the irritation in my voice.

The woman ignores my irritated tone with her response.

"Oh, he's in the back with Boyka. I can take you there after we take you to bed upstairs."

How much is he paying these women? We're still struggling to get Jalousie off the ground and he spends all his money on Slavic hookers.

"Not interested. I have a meeting with him."

"Are you sure?"

I don't dignify them with a response. I walk past the girls, keeping my eyes away from their bodies. Where the hell is my father? I pass the long hallway with the family portraits and follow the loud music and the louder giggling from near the pool. The familiar sound of pool jets betrays papa's location.

He's in the fucking hot tub again, I know it. He spends all fucking day in the hot tub, dishing out orders and expecting work to happen without him lifting a fucking finger. It's a fucking miracle anything gets done around here.

My father chuckles loudly, and I brace myself before approaching him. He's the boss and you don't question the boss, even if he's your father and even if he cares more about partying and women than our family — than our future.

When I enter the back patio, the pungent smell of tobacco

and marijuana surrounds me. Judging by the bottles of vodka on the ground, the piles of cigarette butts and the other piles of detritus, they've been at this fucking party since last night.

Fuck. I put the cigarette tucked behind my ear into my mouth and approach my father's outdoor speakers, unplugging them and stopping the little dance party happening around his hot tub. Three women, each wearing next to nothing with their tits out belly dance for him while he chuckles loudly, his fat stomach causing waves in the hot tub. When the music stops, they stop too and look up at me indignantly.

They don't have to ask who I am. The ones who don't know Van Doukas can tell that I'm related to Sal. I have my father's eyes, but thankfully, I don't have his overweight body or his bald head. The girls make booing sounds at me, but I brush them off.

"I'm here for our meeting," I say sternly to papa.

He chuckles and nods. "Yes. The meeting. I almost forgot."

Almost? He doesn't look like he's fucking prepared for a meeting.

Papa dismisses the girls, except for one — Boyka. She slides into the hot tub next to him, twirling his thick plumes of chest hair around her fingers and sliding his freshly cut cigar between his lips. Nauseating. Papa coughs after a puff and taps the cigar over the edge of the hot tub.

"You're early."

"I'm twenty minutes late."

"Oh?"

"Papa, you said it was important. Shouldn't we conduct this business alone?"

None of the girls are dumb enough to rat on Salvatore

Doukas, but unlike my father, I don't see the sense in taking risks.

Boyka's hand moves down my father's chest and I don't want to imagine what sorry shriveled part of him she touches next. I just want my orders so I can get the fuck out of this bachelor pad.

"I'm getting old, Van," he says. "I'm getting old."

He didn't call me down here to bitch about his old age. I furiously puff on my cigarette, waiting for him to get to the fucking point. Papa grunts as Boyka touches something... sensitive. Cristo...

Watching my father grunt through a hand job might be the only thing worse than watching him stick it to a woman.

"Do you mind postponing your fucking hand job until later?"

Boyka's hand rises guiltily from the water and I choke down bile. She really was touching the old fuck. I shouldn't swear at him or set him off. Papa might seem old, but he can have me killed. Any of my brothers would do it if he gave the command. Tread carefully, Van.

"Maybe I should leave," Boyka says, giving me a flirty glance as she plays with her tiny pink nipples.

"Yes," I snap. "Please get the fuck out of here."

Papa scowls. "Be respectful, Van. Boyka is a very dear—"

"I said please."

Papa smirks. "Boyka, return in thirty minutes. If we're not done..."

"We'll be done," I interrupt, glowering at my father. I don't have all afternoon for his games when I have the club to attend to.

Boyka reluctantly leaves.

"Are the women in this house allergic to fucking clothes?"

"None of them are allergic to fucking anything."

I'm not doing this with the old man today.

"Why did you call me here?"

I start another cigarette. I keep swearing I won't touch another, then I spend five minutes around papa and change my mind.

He leans back in the hot tub, displacing several pints of water over the edge.

"I'm tired, Van," he groans, leaning back and rubbing his forehead.

"From working?"

My father doesn't pick up on the sarcasm. He hardly leaves his fucking hot tub anymore, and he hasn't done anything even remotely resembling working at either of the nightclubs, restaurants, apartment complexes or construction sites around town.

If it wasn't for me and Enzo, he wouldn't have the fucking time to boink Boyka or whatever the fuck he does with all these young Slavic women.

I still have to tread carefully around him. He's still my father, my boss, and I must obey him.

"Yes," he says, coughing. "From working. I need someone to take my place and lead the family soon. I want to retire, Van. You and I both know I need a break."

He spends every fucking day on vacation while his sons and nephews run his businesses. Vacation? We're the ones who need a fucking vacation.

"Perhaps you should contact Matteo about that."

My older brother spent his entire life preparing to be the boss. It's not my fault he fucked off, leaving his worthless children with us, I might add. I'm already halfway through my fucking cigarette and he hasn't closed in on the point.

Papa scoffs. "Matteo hasn't left Albania in four years. He

left his children, his business, his fucking money, and he's not coming back. Give up on him."

"You're the one who trained him for the role. Send Enzo after him. Better yet, send his fucking son."

I don't want to go into the mountains to bring my jackass older brother back and I don't want to have this conversation with my father.

"Why don't you go to Albania?"

"Every time I'm in the same room as Matteo, he tries to kill me," I remind papa. I love Matteo, but he isn't exactly easy to get along with.

I'm surprised a woman tolerated him long enough to allow him to give her Eddie.

"Fair. But I need a replacement, Van. I don't want to be the boss anymore. I can't take the stress much longer."

Stress? What stress? Does my father seriously think sitting in his fucking hot tub banging whores counts as a job?

"Have you considered the role?" He asks before I can spew something disrespectful in my father's direction.

"Why would I want to be the boss of this fucking family? It's filled with degenerates, fuck-ups, people who need more violence to be kept in line. I kill enough as it is. You don't want me to be the boss and nobody in this fucking family wants me as the boss."

"People respect you, Van."

"People fear me. There's a difference."

Papa nods. "Exactly. Personally, I think you would make a good boss."

"I disagree."

But I don't completely. Yes, the job would be horrific and I'd have even more blood on my hands than I do now by the end. I could bring honor back to our family, clean the streets of our scum, stop the Jews from fucking with our shit... but I can't. Not with Matteo gone. Even in the fucking Albanian countryside, he would find out what I did and Matteo would kill me.

"No," Papa replies calmly. "You don't. But I agree with your assessment that you're not quite ready."

"I never said that. I said I didn't want the job."

Nobody smart wants my father's job. He spent twenty years walking around with a target on his back before he built up enough trust, enough loyalty, enough captains in the streets of Italy to ensure his safety. I don't want to lose my freedom.

"You didn't have to say anything. I know my son."

"Hm."

Arguing with my father is entirely senseless.

"You need an heir, Van."

"What?"

"I will give you the leadership of this family without the ritual, without the sacrifice and without the financial investment required. All I want is an heir."

"Why don't I go up to fucking Albania, then? Because I can't produce a child out of thin air."

Papa chuckles. "Don't you have women? If you want a woman... I filled this house with them. I have very young ones too. Eighteen. Nineteen. They make good mothers."

"I am not interested in fucking teenagers."

"Then find a whore like that old Greek Pagonis fuck. I don't care how you get the heir. You can prove how serious you are by giving me a child. I'll be generous. I'll give you a year."

"I don't want this role," I snap. "So the likelihood I'll produce an heir is slim."

Papa laughs, which only infuriates me further. There's nothing funny about bringing a child into the world.

"You can't lie to me, Van. You were always the most ambitious child. Maybe it's because you were smack in the middle and we didn't pay any attention to you. Who fucking knows?"

My father spent little time raising any of us, except for Enzo, and look how that fucking turned out.

"Thank you for the psychoanalysis."

Every time I visit my father, my desire for alcohol increases exponentially, along with my cravings for nicotine. He brings the worst out of everyone, especially me.

"No problem," he says, again ignoring my sarcasm.

"What happens if I don't produce an heir? Eh? You still need someone to take your place."

"I make this offer to Lorenzo if you don't produce what I want."

"What?" I would have at least expected him to mention one of our cousins, one of the very obedient captains from the northern coast, or even fucking Eddie, Matteo's 18-year-old son, would be better than my irresponsible fuck of a brother. That old fuck really knows me well because he just said the only thing that could get me to reconsider his stupid fucking offer.

"You heard me."

"Lorenzo would ruin this family. For fun."

"I know. And it would become your responsibility to save it. You would have to act as the boss to save Lorenzo from himself. You might as well earn the position."

Fuck this old man...

"I don't want a family life, papa. I don't want the fucking wife or the fucking family. I want this life. It's what I'm good at. Business. Killing. More killing. That's who you taught me to be."

I'm not a man who can picture himself kicking around a football with my children or taking them to the beach. I'm not built for seducing women for more than a night and dealing with the danger of introducing them to my life or worse, hiding it the way papa did with our mother.

He can pretend it's not his fault what happened to her, but we all know the truth. No woman deserves our life. I can't afford to react. He loves when he can draw a reaction out of me.

Papa continues, as if my reaction is irrelevant. "Part of this life means having a family. I can't expect my other children to carry on my bloodline."

"Matteo has a son. You have a fucking bloodline. Why don't you make him the fucking boss?"

"Eddie? Eddie will not survive long the way he lives."

"That's a way to talk about your grandson, eh?"

"Have another cigarette, Van."

I'm already on my fucking third. But I'm not in a position to turn down his offer, considering the shit he wants me to deal with right now. An heir? I thought he wanted me to kill someone. Producing an heir in a year... It's just fucking impossible. I stick the cigarette in my mouth and light it.

"You can't let the family fall apart. We aren't the only people who would suffer. What would happen to our people, good Italian people, when the only people around they can get money from are the fucking Jews, who hate our guts?" He says.

I can't let his guilt trip work on me.

"I want an heir."

"Hm."

"Consider what you would sacrifice by turning down my

offer, Van. It's not just about the family. It's power. You act like you're a fucking saint, but you are my son. You enjoy power. You're just too much of a stuck up cunt to let yourself enjoy it."

"Thanks papa."

"You're welcome. Now, onto the matter of the Jew."

Fuck. I hoped my father would only piss me off one way today, but if we're discussing the matter of the Jew, I won't leave here tonight without an assignment. Someone else could easily do this job, but he wants me to kill. Because I'm good at it.

"I suppose none of my other brothers have the free time to do this?"

"I don't care. I need you to do it. The cunt offended this family."

"Perhaps we waste too much time retaliating for every offense. Ana told you to drop it."

I'm taking a risk just questioning his order, but he's pissed me off so much that I stopped caring.

"Decision making isn't women's work. It's our work. The man signed his own death warrant. I want it done soon. Call me when you finish the job."

"Hm."

"If you don't like the way I run this family, Van, you know what to do. I want to retire. Make an old man happy."

Drugs and whores are the only things that make my father happy.

"An heir," I scoff. "You want me to have a fucking bastard child to continue your bloodline? A bastard won't have any loyalty to his family. Children have a mother and a father, a mother they spend all their time with. If I fuck some poor woman, you won't have an heir. You'll have a problem on your hands."

"Then get creative. If you need to get the baby and kill the mother, do what you must."

What's happening to this family? When did we lose our way and talking about murdering women for our own ends? Papa... This life changed him. It was slow, but it changed him completely. Too bad there's no getting out.

"Thank you for the advice."

"You're welcome. Now get Boyka back in here and get the fuck out. I need relief."

"Good evening, papa."

I drop my cigarette on the ground without bothering to step on it. Maybe my father's right — it's time for him to retire. But how the fuck will I get an heir? I need help.

There's one person I can call on for assistance in these matters. I don't like involving the Greeks in Italian business, but... they're our cousins. She answers after a few rings and it sounds like she's at a nightclub. She has an inordinate amount of time for parties...

"Ciao?"

I can barely hear her over the sound of the music.

"Miss Pagonis. It's Van."

She giggles. "Duh. What's happening? You finally have work for me?"

"How soon can you come back to Italy?"

2. Single AF On The Amalfi Coast
Jodi Rose

I'm the last single woman in my family.

Three months in Italy, and I haven't had so much as a kiss, but my younger cousin Raven gets married to her college boyfriend and he looks like a dream. I drop a congratulatory comment on her photo, but my heart sinks.

You ugly, Jodi. Get used to it and stop chasing all these men out of your league. Settle with Kyle. He's the best you can do. Maybe mama was right. I'm not the marrying kind, anyway. I spent all my dating years focused on school and look at where that got me...

"Edo!"

The bartender gives me a sympathetic look. Ugh. Edo is so hot. Too bad all the hot guys are gay, especially in Italy, apparently.

"What happened?"

"Look at this."

I show him my phone and Edo cracks a smile. "Beautiful! Is she your sister?"

"No, my cousin. She's getting married and here I am... single... again."

And I'm running away from my problems with a one-way ticket to Italy. When my family finds out I'm not coming back, they're going to lose their minds. Everyone already thinks I'm crazy for leaving Kyle...

"Fuck your ex, Jodi. Seriously, fuck him," Edo says with all the passion of a best friend, even if we barely know each other.

I have major regrets about getting drunk my first night here and spilling all the drama about my ex-boyfriend to a bartender, but at least it made us fast friends. Although I'm not sure if Edo just likes the fact that Americans tip, unlike our Italian friends. He always has a way of scamming some extra euros out of me. At least he's a damn good listener.

I groan and dramatically lean against the bar as I make a proclamation that I wholeheartedly believe.

"I'm never going to get with another guy again. This is it. I'm dying alone."

I've read the statistics. Or at least I've read what women on Lipstick Alley say about the statistics. I'm a thick, well-educated black woman who is tired of the dusties and has real ass standards — according to the internet, I'm dying alone.

Edo grins and shakes his head. Since he learned I was American, he's done everything in my power to take me under his wing since I got here. I just hate getting too far out of my comfort zone, so I've ditched all his invitations to visit the local clubs in favor of spending my nights drinking cocktails alone and checking social media. I'm in Italy. I should have daily adventures and bread. I can't forget the delicious ass bread.

"You will not die alone," Edo says. "At least not without trying... my latest cocktail creation."

Edo does a dramatic dance before revealing some clear

beverage that looks like some horrible mix of vodka, vermouth and orange juice.

Good. I want to get completely fucked up.

"That looks… clear."

"You'll love it, I promise."

"Will drinking really make the pain go away?" I muse, twirling the glass around so the little orange peel swirls inside it. Kyle. Why do you always miss the ones who fuck you up the most?

Hopefully, this drink will get my ain't shit ex off my mind, but let's be real. What I really need is a summer romance. Ha. Like that's going to happen in a country where half the people think I'm a prostitute because of my skin color.

"Yes. It will. Absolutely." Edo replies with a wink.

"Cheers." I swirl the drink around despite Edo's repeated claims I ruin his creations by doing that. I pour it down my throat and taste a pleasant citrus flavor before a powerful vodka burn. It takes everything in my power to get the rest of the drink down my throat. Whew! That was a damn burn.

"What the hell did you put in that?"

Edo winks, but offers no response. Tricky ass Italian.

"My shift ends in ten," he says. "I'll take you out tonight to Jalousie. No getting out of it this time to watch *Empire* in your apartment."

How the fuck does this skinny ass white boy know me so well already? I shake my head, prepared to reject his offer to take me to the club, but Edo won't let it go. He wriggles his brows suggestively.

He loves regaling me with stories about all the shenanigans that go down at the Amalfi Coast nightclubs. I'm not really a nightclub girl. Small bars like this one fit me better, but didn't I come to Italy to have fun? Meet someone? I should put in some effort.

The only men who give me any attention are the creeps on the beach who say so much nasty shit to me in Italian that I'm glad I don't understand.

Maybe I'll meet better men at the club, especially a club with a fancy ass French name like this one. Jalousie. Wait... Edo's mentioned Jalousie to me before in the past.

"Ain't that the club with the mafia shootout you told me about?"

I don't believe half the shit that comes out of Edo's mouth, but he loves regaling me with stories about the real Italian mafia, which he claims is apparently far worse than any mafia in Long Island or Staten Island. How could anyone who lives in one of the most beautiful parts of the world hurt and kill other people? I think he likes telling tall tales to impress tourists.

I get people on Staten Island killing each other, but the Amalfi Coast? Hell fucking no. The sea is perfectly blue, the air smells fresh constantly, and it's plain peaceful out here. Italians have a rich culture, amazing food, better wine and the guys here are hot.

Not every guy, but when you walk down the streets here, you definitely encounter more than a few hotties. They all dress like supermodels, too. I've never seen so many regular ass people sporting Gucci and Fendi.

"Yes," Edo says. "But you're here for 9 more months, right? Have a fling. Don't tell him your real name... and disappear. You can find a hot and incredibly rich man to spoil you during your trip."

"Wait... is this a gay club or my type of club?"

Edo chuckles. "The guys are hot. I didn't say they were gay. You haven't earned your way into going to a gay club with me yet."

"Wow, Edo. I thought we had something going here."

Edo shrugs. "My private life is my private life. That's how it is in Italy. Your private life, on the other hand, is my playground. I'll introduce you to people. I know people who frequent Jalousie."

"Hot guys?"

"Eh…"

"Hot straight guys?" I correct myself before he answers. I don't want Edo tricking me into going out for nothing.

"Not exactly… I have a girl friend in town who goes all the time — Cassia Pagonis."

He says the name like I'm supposed to know who the fuck that is.

"Who the fuck is that?"

Edo chuckles. "A very fun girl with very hot brothers."

I perk up a little until Edo tells me they're all married. Great.

"Great. They're married…"

Before Edo can reassure me (again) more customers wander into the bar and Edo scurries to the other end of the bar to take orders.

I gaze into my phone again, looking at pictures from Raven's wedding. My cousin looks gorgeous, but I can't help a twisted pang of envy. I know it's wrong but… will that ever happen for me?

My homegirls from college keep sending me articles about the sorry state of marriage for black women. Alyssa says that we need to divest completely from marriage and just have fun.

My idea of fun isn't keeping a collection of all "my dicks" in a private folder on my phone. I want the real fucking thing! Even if the world loves reminding me that 'the real thing' only happens for white women or black women with the lightest dusting of melanin… I want to believe in love.

I scroll past Raven's pictures and my feed is all babies, new puppies, new jobs, new houses, new apartments, new husbands... new everything. Before Italy, I was just doing the same old shit. I wanted to shake things up. I don't know why my life hasn't transformed entirely. I'm in the prettiest place on earth — the Amalfi Coast.

Edo's shift ends, and he calls my name from the other end of the bar, beckoning me over to the cash register.

"Any tip for me today?"

"I saw you slip that five euro note out of my wallet. I think we're good."

Edo shrugs. "Sorry, this job doesn't pay well."

"I get it. I'll pay for our drinks tonight. Happy?"

"Incredibly."

I shouldn't be offering to pay for anyone's drinks, honestly, but I tell myself that I'll worry about all the damn money I'm spending once I get back to America. I have nine months of freedom and then I can worry about these damn bills and loans and everything else.

Edo drags me off my stool, and we step outside into the cobblestone street. I'll never get over how beautifully blue everything is here. The streets smell like the ocean, pastries, wine and cigarettes, of course. People sell jewelry and fruits on the streets and the Italian accents are... gorgeous. My Italian's still crap, despite Edo's best efforts to teach me a few phrases.

At least I don't have to hear all the street harassment thrown my way, which is plentiful. Edo replies defensively to a grey-haired man who calls something lewd in my direction and grabs me tighter. "Fuck these guys," he says. "You aren't that fat."

I swear, I'll never get used to how fucking blunt they are. But I appreciate Edo doing his best to defend me. We can hear the music from Jalousie echoing down the street before we get close.

"Isn't it early for the club?"

"Why are you so fucking American?" Edo asks, linking arms with me. "Relax."

"EDOARDO!" A shrill voice with a strange accent calls from across the street. I know Italian accents by now, at least how people from the Coast sound when speaking English, and this girl sounds different.

"That's Cass," Edo says to me, a smile breaking out across his handsome face. "Chin up. She'll love you."

Edo waves to the girl across the street and she struts over to us, sticking her hand out to stop the cars making their way down the cobblestone streets. They don't even honk as she passes.

The first thing I notice about her is how striking she is. She's tall, with curly dark brown hair pinned up out of her face and flowing down her back. She's wearing crazy high heels, like all the European girls do, a short leather skirt and a tight black leather crop top.

With her dark red lipstick, she looks like a film noir femme fatale... and she stares like one.

"Edo... is this your American friend?"

She turns to me and smiles. Shit, her accent might be strong, but her English is perfect. Cass's hair falls over her shoulders, her curls carrying a soft eucalyptus scent.

"Jodi Rose," I say, happy to have some female company around here, not like there's anything wrong with Edo. "Nice to meet you."

She takes my hand, three silver Cartier bracelets sliding down her wrist. Wow. Her bracelets aren't the only expensive item of clothing she has.

"Cass Pagonis. I'm sure Edo has told you all sorts of horrible stories about me."

"I did not!"

Edo definitely did. But Cass doesn't seem like a crazy party girl. She rolls her eyes and brushes him off.

"I'm here on the Coast working for my cousin's family," Cass says. "I'm from Thessaloniki. My idiot brothers want me back next week, unfortunately. But I could use a night out before I go."

Edo claps his hands. "Yay! Party time. Too bad Jalousie only caters to the most chauvinistic mafia pigs you can imagine."

"I thought you said they were hotties?!"

"They are," Edo says. "But they might be assholes."

Now he tells me. Edo would have said anything to get me out of my damn apartment. I hope I don't regret it.

"Watch it," Cass cautions, an impish smile on her face. "Those chauvinistic mafia pigs are my cousins and brothers."

Edo shrugs. "Fine. Fine. But I need dick too. Gay rights."

Cass swats his shoulder.

"Edo, why don't you let me take her for the night? There's no one at Jalousie for you, and you can go meet up with Klaus or... that other one."

Edo suddenly straightens his back and reminds both of us that just because he's gay doesn't mean he's given up on old world chivalry.

"I can't send Jodi off with a stranger," he says.

I appreciate the sentiment, but I don't know if Edo would do much damage against... any man who weighed more than his slight 108 lb frame.

"I'm fine," I tell him. "Seriously."

"I'm armed anyway," Cass says. I think she's joking, but neither of them laughs. Is she serious? She doesn't look armed, and she looks more like a model than someone who knows how to use a weapon.

I could use a female friend in my life over here. I've got plenty of female friends back home, but they all want to talk about Kyle and my "healing journey". They don't want to hear that I'm still lost after all these months.

Edo shrugs. "If you insist."

"I insist," I tell him. "You've done enough taking care of me. Plus, I'll get to know my new friend... Cass."

"Exactly," Cass says. "Jodi... I think we can become wonderful friends. We can swap stories about Edo."

"There are no stories about Edo," he chimes in. "Because Edo is an incredible friend and a better bartender."

"Shoo," Cass says. "I can handle things from here."

Edo doesn't quite walk off, but he checks his phone and begins texting furiously to plan his next move.

"It's the last time they have DJ Fat Camel playing here. We'll dance, drink and later, I'll take you home, yes?"

"That sounds good to me."

"Well, you have my number if Cass abandons you on the top of a Ferris wheel," Edo says as he swipes four times quickly across his screen and then shoves his phone into his pocket.

Cass rolls her eyes. "I have done nothing of the sort. Get out of here, you big drama queen."

"Ciao!"

Cass and I say "Ciao!"

Edo walks down the cobblestone streets and lights a cigarette before disappearing around the corner. Cass breathes a sigh of relief and turns to me.

"I just think you're perfect," she says.

Weird comment to make, but I mumble a gracious thank you, assuming something got lost in translation.

"Do you have friends with you?" Cass asks, taking out a hand mirror and fixing her bright red lipstick.

"No. I'm here solo tripping. Had a quarter life crisis and... here I am."

"Do you like Italy?" she asks genuinely. Her eyes are so intense.

"It's beautiful."

"Not as pretty as Greece," Cass says. "But I agree. Shall we go in?"

"We should head to the back of the line," I say, my stomach knotting as I see the line stretched around the block. I hope we can even get into the club.

Cass grins, unperturbed by the growing line outside Jalousie.

"My cousin owns the place. Come on, we go in through the back."

Before I can protest, she takes my hand and we walk around a back alley that smells like trash, vomit and again — cigarettes. Cass drags me over to a door and surveys me once before touching the handle.

"Very proper outfit. Excellent. Let's go. Ready to dance?"

I nod, even if I'm nervous. Sure, I'm trying to have an adventure tonight, but I just met this chick. How do I know she isn't crazy? Well, she has Edo's backing, so at least she'll be a good time. Edo definitely knows how to have fun if his clubbing stories are even 55% true.

Cass punches in a six-digit code and the back door to the club opens. I can smell the club before I hear the music and Cass drags me in through the back before I can second guess myself. What am I really doing? I don't know this chick at all and I agreed to go clubbing with her? Is Edo's word really enough?

Once we're in the back door, a man appears. He's tall,

with dark brown slicked back hair, tattoos all over his arms and grey eyes. He has broad shoulders, but is otherwise lean and very muscular. He's handsome, but it's too bad he smokes. I can smell the cigarettes from a distance.

"Cass? What the fuck are you doing here?" he asks, seeming genuinely upset.

"Shut the fuck up, Enzo," Cass snaps, her expression changing suddenly into a disapproving scowl. "I have business here."

The man smirks. He's around Cass' height, but he looks... greasy.

"Is that her?"

"Mind your fucking business."

Cass pushes him hard so we can get past him. The grey-eyed man's eyes land on me and he runs his hand over his jawline before snickering.

"He's going to kill you."

"Shut up," Cass snarls. Enzo laughs and raises his hands in defeat.

"Enjoy your night," he says to me in a sing-song voice. For the first time, I feel real hesitation. But Cass grabs my hand and drags me inside of the club.

Cass drags me all the way to the tables and chairs surrounding the dance floor, chatting excitedly and peppering me with questions about America. I struggle to understand her accent at first, but then I get into the rhythm of her voice and it's easier for us to communicate.

I have to listen in so hard that I barely scan the room we enter. At least the nightclub has a nice interior, and it doesn't seem like any ghetto shit might pop off. Another Edo exaggeration, it seems. I relax as Cass sets me up at a small, two-person table.

"I'll get you a drink. Wait here. If anyone comes to talk to you, tell them you are with Cass Pagonis. That will shut them up."

Before I can protest, or offer to come with her, Cass disappears. Shit. I guess I have to wait here. I already have five texts from Edo about the hotties he met at the club a few doors over. Damn, he moves quick. I've been here for weeks already and I still haven't met a heterosexual male who hasn't been an incredibly old and excessively horny man offering for me to be his 'African prostitute' — offers I have obviously declined.

Cass returns quickly, before I have any time to worry with two shots, each one with some blue flavoring at the bottom.

"Okay, Jodi. This is to a long and beautiful friendship between us, starting with one crazy night, yeah?"

I nod. "Hell yeah. I've never done anything like this before."

I blurt out the last part nervously, but Cass has a way of soothing me. She just smiles and nods. "Don't be scared! I'm a good Greek girl. Now come on... we'll take the shots together."

She counts us down.

"1... 2... 3..."

I take the shot — and it's the last thing I remember about that night.

Click here to keep reading:
https://bit.ly/amalficoast1

Extremely Important Links

ALL BOOKS BY JAMILA JASPER
https://linktr.ee/JamilaJasper
SIGN UP FOR EMAIL UPDATES
Bit.ly/jamilajasperromance
SOCIAL MEDIA LINKS
https://www.jamilajasperromance.com/
GET MERCH
https://www.redbubble.com/people/jamilajasper/shop
GET FREEBIE (VIA TEXT)
https://slkt.io/qMk8
READ SERIAL (NEW CHAPTERS WEEKLY)
www.patreon.com/jamilajasper

JAMILA JASPER

Diverse Romance For Black Women

More Jamila Jasper Romance

Thank You Kindly

Thank you to all my readers, new and old for your support with this new year.

I look forward to making 2022 an INCREDIBLE year for interracial romance novels. I want to thank you all for joining along on the journey.

Thank you to my most supportive readers:

Cortney, Yolanda S., MonaGirl, Dianna, Mary, Nysha, Fayola, Ty, Shyra, Andi-Mariee, Keisha, Jennett, Fredericka, Candece, Lydia, Sabrina, JM, Jackie, Mo, Ashaunte, Tolu, Lori, Dionne, ZLB, Nicol, Elbert, Jesi, Brenda, Desiree, LaShan, Only1ToniD, Debbie, Tiffanie, Shawnte, Lisema, Christine, Trinity, Monica, Juliette, Letetia, Margaret, Dash, Maxine, Sheron, Javonda, Pearl, Kiana, Shyan, Jacklyn, Amy, Julia, Colleen, Natasha, Yvonne, Brittany, June, Ashleigh, Nene, Nene, Deborah, Nikki, DeShaunda, Latoya, Shelite, Arlene, Judith, Mary, Shanida, Rachel,Damzel, Ahnjala, Kenya, Momo, BJ, Akeshia, Melissa, Tiffany, Sherbear, Nini, Curtresa, Regina, Ashley, Mia, Sydney, Sharon, Charlotte, Assiatu, Regina, Romanda, Catherine, Gaynor, BF, Tasha, Henri, Sara, skkent, Rosalyn, Danielle, Deborah, Kirsten, Ana, Taylor, Charlene Louanna, Michelle, Tamika, Lauren, RoHyde, Natasha, Shekynah, Cassie, Dreama, Nick, Gennifer,

Rayna, Jaleda, Kimvodkna, Jatonn, Anoushka, Audrey, Valeria, Courtney, Donna, Jenetha, Ayana, Kristy, FreyaJo, Grace, Kisha, Stephanie E., Amber, Denice, Marty, LaKisha, Latoya, Natasha, Monifa, Alisa, Daveena, Desiree, Gerry, Kimberly, Stephanie M., Tarah, Yolanda, Kristy, Gary, Janet, Kathy, Phyllis, Susan

Join the Patreon Community.
www.patreon.com/jamilajasper

Patreon

12+ SEASONS OF BWWM ROMANCE SERIAL CHAPTERS

🔥 NEW RELEASE 🔥
Powerless: Dark Bully BWWM Romance

Read the ongoing story **POWERLESS** and **ALL** the previous releases for a small monthly cost.

Patreon

Instantly access all six seasons of *Unfuckable* (Ben & Libby's story) with 375 chapters.

For a small monthly fee, you get exclusive access to my all this & my recently completed serial Despicable (275 chapters)

www.patreon.com/jamilajasper

Patreon has more than the ongoing serial and previous serial releases...

⚡ INSTANT ACCESS ⚡

- NEW merchandise tiers with <u>t-shirts, totes, mugs,</u> stickers and MORE!
- <u>FREE paperback</u> with all new tiers
- <u>FREE short story audiobooks</u> and audiobook samples when they're ready
- #FirstDraftLeaks of Prologues and first chapters **weeks** before I hit publish
- Behind the scenes notes
- Polls and story contribution
- Comments & LIVELY community discussion with likeminded interracial romance readers.

LEARN MORE ABOUT SUPPORTING A DIVERSE ROMANCE AUTHOR
www.patreon.com/jamilajasper

Printed in Great Britain
by Amazon

23511111R00182